Fenicus Flint & the Dragons of Berathor

C.W.J. HENDERSON

FIRST KNIGHT PRESS

CASTLETON NEW YORK

Library of Congress Control Number: 2012933929

Copyright © 2012 C W J Henderson

Published by First Knight Press

ISBN: 0615584500
ISBN-13: 978-0615584508

DEDICATION

For my twin sons, Alexander and Tristan, who inspire me
to better myself every day. For my wife Nicole who is my
most vigilant defender, supporter, and voice of reason. To
them I dedicate this work.

ACKNOWLEDGMENTS

I would like to thank all those who both supported and assisted me over the years editing, revising, and preparing this novel for the eyes of the world: Jen, Lindsay, Dan, Colleen, Katy, Karen, Kristen, Noelle, Sean, and Mary Ann. And special thanks to Alison Hosier for her amazing art work that graces the cover. Her dedication and enthusiasm to this project helped pull it all together.

1

Fenicus Flint raced across the sky, a golden flash slicing through the air. The cool spring wind aloft whistled past his flattened ears. His leathery wings flapped vigorously, pushing him harder and faster toward his opponent. With subtle flicks of his long tail, the adolescent dragon swerved left and right around plumes of searing steam that rose from thermal vents along the valley floor. As his speed increased, so did the wind resistance. Fenicus tucked his arms and legs in tight to his torso to make his body more aerodynamic. In his periphery, the rolling grasslands of Berathor Valley and the surrounding peaks of the Tatra Mountains registered as nothing more than a brown and green blur.

Don't lose your cool, Fenicus warned himself. The last thing he wanted to do was bail out too soon. If he did he'd be considered a coward, and that was a shame no dragon could bear. He needed to forget everything else and keep his mind focused solely on his adversary racing toward him. Yet in the back of his mind, a chorus of cowardly voices begged him to turn tail and flee. Fenicus clenched his jaw in opposition to them and braced himself for the impending collision. But as he came upon Darius, who cut across the heavens toward him in an aerial version of chicken, a geyser erupted at the point of impact. Both dragons swiftly altered their flight paths, banking hard to avoid the dangerous steam burst. Their momentum carried them far away from each other in just a few moments. They pulled up and turned back in preparation for another pass—two jousting knights amidst a stalemate.

When Fenicus came about, he saw Darius swing around, angrily crack his tail like a whip, and roar in frustration. Fenicus could only shake his head in response. *Will this ever end?* Growing weary of Darius's endless attempts at vengeance, he screamed, "You're kidding, right? Can't you just drop it?"

"Drop it? Oh, you've got some nerve, Flint." Turning his head sharply to the side, Darius pointed to what remained of his right ear. Unlike the one that graced the other side of his head, this ear was drastically shorter in length. More so, the flesh was badly maimed; each scale appeared to be melted into the next like a plate of golden armor, protecting the wound. His fingers crunched closed in a tight fist. "Alright, coward," he growled, "when you can make this scar go away, I'll drop it."

Even though Fenicus knew all too well from previous

attempts that Darius's anger would not be quelled by words, he made one last attempt at solving their quarrel peacefully. "C'mon, Darius. It was an accident. How many times do I have to say I'm sor—"

"No apology will ever be enough!" Darius cut Fenicus off, his voice hissing across the sky.

Fenicus paused for a moment. "It was so long ago. What more do you want from me?"

"I want you to bleed! That, and nothing else, will end this." Darius made a horizontal slashing gesture with his arm. "You've got to suffer just like me."

Fenicus nodded with resentment. He hated hearing those words. He was tired of them, but he was far more tired of Darius. Fenicus then realized what he had to do; he had to take a fall. It was the only thing, he decided, that would bring an end to this insanity. Conjuring up his nerve, Fenicus urged Darius to action, "If you want revenge, scumspine, then come and get it!"

Rearing back like antelope about to charge, the two adolescent dragons roared across the blue expanse, two projectiles on a collision course. Fenicus watched Darius rocket toward him. He braced himself for impact. Within a few wing flaps of contact, Fenicus heard the deep guttural moan of his family's homestead horn. *Oh no! My Hatching Day celebration,* he remembered as he saw Darius bearing down on him. *I don't have time for this. He waited this long to get his revenge, what's one more day?* Without a moment to spare, Fenicus ducked beneath Darius's flight path and soared off into the distance. As he flew off into the late morning air, he breathed a sigh of relief and called out to

Darius, "Another time, old friend. Another time."

*   *   *

Crossing the threshold of his family's mountainside lair, Fenicus stood in the main chamber, which served as a central hub for the series of small caverns that made up their home. Like most dragon warrens in Berathor, the Flints' home was a testament to frugality and simplicity. There were mounds of dried grass and brush that acted as beds and lounging areas. The walls of each cavern were relatively bare; the only visible markings were ancient Dragonian runes that detailed such things as family lineage, fundamental proverbs, and how to reach the Golden Vale. While some sunlight filtered into the warren through the small airflow cutouts in the outer wall, most of the illumination came from candles that sat in alcoves along the inner walls.

While nothing seemed out of place, it wasn't what Fenicus expected to find upon his arrival. There were no signs of Hatching Day congratulations. Though the main celebration would take place in the gathering square in the middle of Berathor Valley at sunset, it was the excitement of the impending celebration and the attention to detail that made young dragons feel special on their special day. It was the one unmistakable time during the year where a dragon warren came to life with vibrant, colorful decorations, where parents fretted over making sure everything was just right, and where family and friends milled about wishing the lucky dragon early congratulations. The Flint warren was as quiet as the grazing plain at midnight.

Fenicus's heart sank. *They forgot! After all these years,*

they forgot! With great effort he fought back the tears welling up in his eyes, refusing to succumb to the swaying tide of his emotions. Then he wondered if he had made a mistake. Fenicus perused the main chamber for any sign of impending preparations.

The faint sound of footsteps coming from his left interrupted Fenicus's assessment of the situation. His mother approached. Mariel's golden head emerged from the hallway. With each day that passed, Fenicus began to notice more and more of the differences between female and male dragons, along with those differences that separated children from adults. Yet it was the females that he noticed much more. Unlike his younger sister Ariel, his mother wore the marks of a mature female. As the females grew from childhood into adulthood, the pale, softer flesh that ran along their undersides would take on a reddish-pink hue while the males remained unchanged. With the onset of years, the change in color would slowly spread from under the chin to the tip of the tail. Mariel's body had nearly completed the transformation. Fenicus's mother stood as a model of femininity for him. Yet, as soothing as her presence was, it did little to allay his sadness.

"Oh, Fenny! You're home." Mariel beamed a wide smile at Fenicus, which melted away the moment her eyes fell upon her son's sad face and slumped frame. "Are you okay?" Mariel prodded gently.

Realizing that his body language betrayed him, Fenicus raised his head up high and straightened his posture. Then he wiped his eyes, pretending the dampness lingering there was no more than weariness.

"Just tired, Ma," he said through a forced, weak grin. "I had another run-in with Darius."

She shook her head. "I can't believe he's willing to throw away your friendship over such an honest mistake. You know I don't condone violence, but I think you might be better off giving him what he wants and get it over with."

Fenicus cast his mother a sideways glance. She was the last dragon that he expected to make such a suggestion. Yet, her conclusion was the very same one he had come to recently. It was the same answer his father, his sister, even his best friends, who stood torn between their two closest companions, had suggested. No one wanted to see this feud go on any longer than necessary, least of all Fenicus.

"Well, I tried to do that, Ma, but then you called me home."

"So, why didn't you finish it first? You've never come home that fast."

"Because I..." he stopped short of admitting the truth. He didn't want his mother to know that he headed home under the false assumption that it was to prepare for his Hatching Day celebration. It hurt too much for him to put it into words. As long as he didn't say it, he could control his emotions. Fenicus frantically tried to think of another reason for coming home. "I...I thought you needed me for something."

Mariel smiled wide. "Actually, I called you because you ran off without your molting draught this morning. By the time I realized you'd left, it'd cooled off and turned rock hard. You know what happens if you don't get enough minerals when you're shed—"

"I know, Ma," he interrupted before she could finish the lecture. "I know."

Fenicus knew all too well the dangers of not obeying the laws of nature. His Aunt Lillian had met an untimely end as a result of ignoring the subtle hints that she was drawing near the time of molting. Preoccupied by the small egg that grew in her womb, she had misread the signals her body sent to her. By the time she had realized what was happening, it was too late. Her death and that of her unborn dragonling had left Fenicus's poor Uncle Balthazar alone in the world.

While his deceased aunt had the ability to melt down gold ore for herself with a breath of fire, Fenicus, like all dragons his age, was unable to breathe a single spark. Though it wasn't necessary for the gold ore to be melted down to serve their needs, centuries of experience told them that when liquefied, it was not only easier to eat, but gentler on their digestion. But since his body was still some twenty years away from reaching maturity, no fire would purse his lips any time soon.

Mariel continued, "Your sister flew out of here right after you this morning, so I couldn't send her out to track you down."

Ariel was always a bit lazy, so her early-morning call-to-action surprised him. "Where'd she fly off to?"

"Something about exploring caves with Sorgi. And you know how much she likes him."

"Yeah, yeah, yeah...that's all she ever talks about!" Fenicus hated how much his sister carried on about their teacher. It was non-stop. Sorgi this, Sorgi that. His sister's annoying little voice bounced around inside his head like a crazed chipmunk. "Doesn't she have anything better to do?"

"I guess not," Mariel giggled. She turned and walked down the hallway toward the workroom where food preparation took place. The deafening sound of rushing air and brilliant flashes of light filled the hallway leading to the storeroom. A wave of intense heat generated by Mariel's fire breath rolled toward Fenicus, quickly raising the temperature of the main chamber.

Moments later, Mariel reemerged with a large bowl, its contents glowing red hot. She placed it on the floor beside Fenicus. The sweltering steam coming off of it made him pant. Small air bubbles rose through the pool of molten gold to the surface, making a *glub* sound as they burst. The aroma that escaped each bubble made Fenicus's mouth water. Unfortunately, he knew that the aroma didn't match the flavor. He hated the putrid, metallic taste gold left in his mouth. Its flavor, however, was nothing compared to the sensation of his mother looming over him, waiting for him to drink it. Rather than getting into an argument with her, he picked up the bowl with both hands and slurped it down.

"Thank you," Mariel said as she took the empty bowl from Fenicus. She leaned down and planted a kiss on the top of his head.

Fenicus squirmed away from her touch. "Ma! Must you?"

"Oh, don't be such a hatchling," Mariel teased him before returning to the workroom.

Still upset and unsure what to do with himself, Fenicus made for the entryway tunnel, intent on going off to his special hiding place to sulk. Just before he reached the opening of the passageway, he heard his mother's voice call out to him. "Fenny?"

He rolled his eyes. "Yeah, Ma?"

She emerged once again from the workroom area. "Be sure to stop by your uncle's while you're out. He stopped by this morning after you'd left. He had something he wanted to give you."

"Oh, great!" he snapped at her. "What 'historically significant artifact' is he hoping to pawn off on me now?" Fenicus lowered his voice to a deep tenor in imitation of his Uncle Balthazar, reciting the stock phrase he utilized when doling out gifts to his nephew. "Ma," Fenicus whined, "all he ever gives me is junk that he finally realizes he has no room for. He's a hoarder."

His mother cornered him with her eyes. "You know how much he values his time with you. He's just trying to be a good uncle. I know most of his gifts aren't very exciting."

"Exciting? Ma—"

She held out her hand in a silencing gesture. Her tone turned firm. "He's trying to impart some of his knowledge on you. Can you just try to keep an open mind? He's my only brother, and he doesn't have anyone else. If it's something you don't like, pretend to be interested and throw it in your room when you get home. And try not to lose it this time."

Fenicus felt ashamed of himself. He swallowed hard. "I'll do my best, Ma. I promise." Without another word, he left the warren and was off to the home of his Uncle

Balthazar.

*   *   *

Having made his way down the entryway passage of his uncle's warren, Fenicus peered inside. Rays of sunlight filtered through an open airshaft along the eastern wall of the great room. The light bounced and bent around flecks of dust that floated about in search of somewhere to settle. Piles of massive books lay scattered across the floor and upon the bookshelves that lined the northern and southern walls. Uncle Balthazar was nowhere in sight. Fenicus stepped inside. A soft rush of air through the passage sent loose papers floating to the floor.

Further within the warren, Fenicus heard a quiet murmur of activity. *He must be working in the den.* With great care, Fenicus made his way through the maze of books. Though he tried to be careful, his tail brushed against a towering, precariously stacked pillar of dense, leathery volumes. They began to tip and sway violently. Fenicus wheeled around to catch the teetering stack only to have the lot topple over onto him. A thick cloud of dust encircled the young dragon when he fell on his back, and he grunted as the topmost book landed upon him; its binding struck him cruelly in the solar plexus, causing him to suck in a lungful of dust. A wild coughing fit ensued. When the painful spasms in his chest subsided, he righted himself, gathered up his tail in his hands, and gingerly resumed his stroll through his uncle's literary minefield.

Having reached the back of the room, Fenicus entered a smaller chamber to the left—his uncle's study. He peered within to find his uncle squatting on the floor with his back to him at the opposite end of the room. A single flickering candle provided the only illumination.

Fenicus grunted aloud, announcing his presence.

Balthazar glanced over his shoulder. "I expected you sooner." He rose from the floor and walked to another unkempt set of shelves covered with piles of paper, empty inkwells, tattered ledgers, and assorted trinkets. "I have something for you that I have been holding onto for quite some time." He began to rifle through the hodgepodge of items there. "I found it on an excavation of Weylark's old cavern some months ago."

Fenicus, meanwhile, stood nearby with a grimace on his face. *What rusty relic is he gonna give me now?* To his surprise, Balthazar's flurry of activity ceased with the uncovering of something Fenicus didn't expect. His eyes locked on a luminous golden amulet. As Balthazar approached his nephew, the golden chain of the amulet twisted and spun it in glittering circles. Wisps of candlelight reflected off its surface, dancing like excited pixies upon the walls of the study.

Balthazar held out his hand, presenting the gift to his nephew. Fenicus reached out for the intriguing artifact and his uncle lowered it into his eager hands. Examining it closely, the amulet appeared to be fashioned from leaf-thin fibers and sheets of pure gold compressed together by a skilled smith. Though expertly crafted, it showed signs of wear in spots where minor scratches or dents had attempted to spoil its beauty.

Fenicus then noticed a raised border around the outside of the amulet, encircling a similarly raised figure on each side. One of the figures he immediately recognized as the silhouette of a dragon. The other figure, however, was unlike any creature Fenicus had ever seen. Its size matched that of the dragon emblem, yet its limbs were much more proportional in size to its torso. It had a small round head that sat affixed to a stumpy neck.

"Do you know what sort of creature that is, Fenicus?"

Fenicus's trance broke from the amulet. He shrugged his shoulders. "No! I've never seen anything like it before. What is it?"

"I'll show you." Balthazar smiled. "Follow me."

Turning away from Fenicus, Balthazar moved toward another passageway obscured by a brown curtain. Fenicus followed closely behind. The short tunnel opened up into a massive, dome-shaped inner chamber. A series of lit alcoves, situated at measured intervals along the wall, illuminated the cavern. Yet, these alcoves contained no candles, only yellow flames that seemed to float in the air without the aid of wick or wax. A long, narrow pathway carved from the cavern floor extended into the center of the room where it expanded into a circular platform. Fenicus followed his uncle as he moved along the walkway toward the center of the cavern. Along the way, Fenicus glanced at the sand-like substance that filled the surrounding sections of the floor.

With both of them having reached the circular platform, Balthazar craned his neck to look upon his nephew. "Do you remember your lessons about the alliance between ourselves and mankind?"

"Yes," Fenicus responded confidently.

"Do you know what that is?" Balthazar inquired as he pointed to the sand.

Fenicus stared at the seemingly unremarkable substance that surrounded the two of them. He carefully slid his hand into the sand, scooped up a portion of it, and then let it fall through his fingers. Unimpressed, Fenicus looked to his uncle. "Sand?"

Balthazar let out a warm chuckle. "Not just sand. It is an extremely rare substance called Seer Sand."

Fenicus leaned down and inspected it up close. He hoped he might see something happen, but nothing noteworthy occurred. He shrugged. "I don't get it."

"Of course you don't," Balthazar interjected, "because you can't do this." Balthazar breathed in a lungful of air and then exhaled it in a sweeping motion around the chamber, forcing out a blast of fire that engulfed the sand with a sizzle. A cloud of foul smelling smoke billowed upward, blinding Fenicus momentarily. He reeled back, covering his snout with his hand. Moments later, the smoke drifted away to reveal a clear, gelatinous liquid that had taken the sand's place.

"Cool!" Fenicus exclaimed. Again he tried to touch the substance, but this time his uncle slapped the back of his inquisitive hand, causing Fenicus to pull it away. "Ow! What was that for?"

"If you want to keep your fingers, I would think twice about doing that again."

Fenicus's eyes flashed wide. He pulled back several steps from the edge of the platform and looked to his uncle, rubbing his hand. "I see."

Balthazar laughed at his nephew's reaction. "It's okay. Come close, get a better look."

Hoping his uncle wouldn't ask him to do something truly dangerous, Fenicus took a few careful steps forward. Standing beside Balthazar, he looked once more into the liquid. Small arcs of energy pulsed through it like bolts of lightning bouncing from cloud to cloud. The collective energies created a warm glow that grew upward from the floor, illuminating both of their faces. The floating flames that encircled the room began to fade in intensity. Each spark within the liquid generated a subsequent ripple that made the whole thing appear as though some creature lurked beneath the surface. Fenicus forgot all about the danger. His tail flicked in anticipation of what would happen next.

Balthazar's voice broke the silence, bringing his nephew's eyes to him. "The war between us and mankind raged for centuries with no end in sight. Though both sides had suffered massive casualties and were growing weary of the bloodshed, they continued to fight hoping that one side would eventually vanquish the other. Both sides were equally confident that they would claim victory." Balthazar's eyes locked on the shimmering liquid where an image had begun to form.

Fenicus followed his uncle's gaze. "Whooooa," he whispered. The image of a creature adorned in fine clothes and linen ascending a craggy, snow-covered mountainside appeared in the molten Seer Sand. Fenicus pointed to the strange creature and asked his uncle, "What's that?"

Balthazar smiled knowingly and proclaimed, "That is a

human. A man."

Fenicus, riveted by his newfound knowledge, refocused on the images. Though soiled by his difficult climb, this man possessed an air of nobility that seemed to transcend his worn appearance. Fenicus heard his uncle speak again.

"Though most of the leaders of mankind were consumed by greed and power, Alan Broman was different. He was a strong, honorable king whose only care in the world was the safety of his people. Even though he never cast so much as a stone at our kind, we attacked his kingdom time and again."

"Why would we do that?" Fenicus asked, shocked by his uncle's assertion.

"Well," Balthazar paused, biting his lip, "being a time of war, we did not know which humans were threats and which ones were not.   And since they attacked us indiscriminately, we repaid them in kind." Balthazar shook his head. "It was not our proudest moment.

"Anyway," Balthazar waved his hand through the air as if brushing away the previous topic, "Broman did everything he could to ease the suffering of his people, but it was never enough. So, he sought out Weylark, the last king of our species, carrying nothing but a banner of peace."

As Balthazar spoke the words, the human king pulled a strip of white cloth from his pocket and waved it about in the air as he drew near the mouth of a cavern. Thick, white smoke billowed from the opening. Before he could enter the lair, Weylark emerged and reared up in front of Broman, towering over him. Opening his massive jaws, Weylark prepared to incinerate the human in a burst of firebreath, but something stopped the dragon king.

"Showing his courage, Broman did not cower in Weylark's shadow. Instead, he stood his ground, waving his flag and pleading with Weylark to spare his life in the interest of peace. Able to sense that the man's intentions were honest, he offered Broman one chance to explain the reason for his intrusion. Luckily for Broman, Weylark found his proposal promising."

The images within the liquid changed to show the inside of the dragon's lair. Broman sat cross-legged before a rolling fire. Across from him, Weylark lay curled up with only his head and neck sticking out. The two appeared to talk animatedly about their plights. Though their conversation was inaudible, their gestures conveyed the passion each felt for their respective races and their desire to protect them.

Balthazar continued, "After six days, they managed to forge a pact that they believed would ring in a new era of peace for both races; an era free from war and suffering. They promised each other that they would present the treaty to their people and fight voraciously for it, even though they knew it might be met with great resistance. Nevertheless, they knew that it had to end this way. No other solution made sense. So, before they departed, Broman and Weylark each took with them a symbol of their peace accord."

Looking into the liquid, Fenicus watched as both Weylark and Broman exchanged glittering golden trinkets around their necks before saying their goodbyes and parting ways. He immediately realized that the amulet he wore around his neck on a long golden chain was identical to Broman and Weylark's. His eyes broke from the Seer Sand one final time to settle on the amulet his uncle entrusted to him. He now understood what the second figure on his trinket represented—a human. Fenicus gazed in astonishment upon the amazing gift. He clutched it in his hands and marveled at what it symbolized. It was truly remarkable.

In a flash, the light that flooded from the floor receded, and Fenicus and Balthazar stood there blinking their eyes as the floating flames in the alcoves returned to full strength. The Seer Sand had already returned to its previous granular form. Fenicus impulsively moved his hand toward it, but remembered the corrective slap from before. He shot Balthazar a questioning glance that was returned with a nod. Fenicus swiped his hand through the sand. It was cool to the touch.

"This amulet is all that remains of the truce between mankind and us." Balthazar paused for a moment, rubbing his chin. "Legend has it that the amulets were magical, but I have yet to unlock its power." A helpless grimace overcame Balthazar's face. "I was hoping that you might help me uncover its secrets."

"Of course I will, Uncle! Of course!" Fenicus could not hide the excitement and pride that overwhelmed him upon learning the nature of his new prized possession. It was like a fever racing through his body. *A magical amulet!* It caused him to smile so wide his face nearly split in two. Any sense of disappointment over the rest of his family forgetting his Hatching Day now seemed a mere triviality.

Balthazar shuffled his nephew back out to the great room and the warren's entryway passage. "Well, off you go.

You've got a busy day ahead of you."

Before Fenicus stepped into the passageway, he turned back to his uncle to pose a question, "Uncle, whatever happened to the other amulet? You said there were two."

"That is an excellent question. To be honest, I am not sure." For a moment he stood there shaking his head. "Knowing humanity's lust for gold, it most likely became part of someone's treasure trove. Humans have no sense of history. They may have even melted it down into its base metals. Either way, it is likely lost forever."

"Unbelievable," Fenicus replied, appalled by humanity's apparent foolishness.

"Indeed." Balthazar urged his nephew into the passageway with a gentle nudge. "All right, off you go!"

Before losing sight of his nephew, Balthazar called out to Fenicus, "Happy Hatching Day!"

With a pleasant, thankful grin, Fenicus exited the warren and took off into the late morning sky.

2

Sorgi stood in a small circle of young dragons as he explained to them how the cavern was formed. He pointed to long stalactites that hung from the ceiling and stalagmites that stood along the dank floor. Some of the dragons, Ariel Flint in particular, listened attentively as he described the process by which these icicle-like formations grew.

"As water finds its way down through the cracks and fissures of the mountain, it picks up all sorts of mineral deposits like limestone and calcium. And when that water finally trickles through the ceiling of a chamber such as this, it moves along in small droplets toward the lowest point."

A couple of Sorgi's less interested students, Narix and Remus, began to yawn loudly near the rear of the group. Sorgi paused for a moment to glare in their direction. The two lazy dragons straightened their slouched necks, pretending to pay attention. The moment Sorgi turned back to resume his lesson, they too continued their disinterested ways.

"Where was I? Oh, yes! The droplets then begin to evaporate, leaving those mineral deposits behind. Ah, look over there!" Sorgi turned to lead the group toward a particularly prominent pair of stalactites and stalagmites that had grown together to form a column deeper within the cavern. With his back turned, Narix and Remus slunk away from the rest of the class and slid into an unlit adjacent cavern.

"As more water seeps through the rock," Sorgi continued, "the calcium deposits continue to collect, growing in length and width to form stalactites; these are often..."

Narix and Remus covered their mouths to muffle their laughter. They listened as Sorgi's voice trailed off into the distance.

"Do you remember how to get out of here?" Remus whispered to his partner through the darkness. He reached into a small sack slung around his shoulder and withdrew a wooden stake, covered in leather and dipped in oil. Remus then continued fumbling through his bag, making quite a racket in the process.

"I think so," Narix replied weakly. His long claws scratched at the scales of his right ear. "We only took one or two turns and then it was a straight shot back to the valley." Through the darkness, he tried to see what Remus was doing that was making so much noise. He could not. "What are you doing? Someone's going to hear you."

"I can't find my tinderbox or flint to light the torch. Did you bring yours?"

Narix reached for his sack. It was gone. "Damn it! I must've left it back there."

"Great! Now what're we gonna do?" Remus whined.

"Give me that!" Narix yanked the sack from his hands. "It's got to be in here." He tousled around through its contents to no avail. Narix slammed his tail against the ground with a crack, frustrated by their situation. "I can't believe this!" Narix tossed the sack back to Remus. It smacked him square in the snout and hung there from its carrying strap. "Now what?"

"What are you blaming me for?" Remus hissed an angry reply and yanked the sack from off his face. He threw it back over his shoulder. "This was all your idea."

"Mine?"

Remus shook his head, frustrated. His eyes grew wide and he snapped his fingers. "Maybe we can catch up with the group. We'll just tell them we got lost or something."

Though Narix hated the idea, he knew it was their best and only option without torchlight to guide their way. "Fine. I just hope we can find them."

Narix turned to make his way out of the chamber when he felt a sudden tug on his tail. "What's that?" the young dragon screeched.

"I've got your tail," Remus answered. "If I can't see where I'm going, I'm not letting you get away from me. I designate you leader."

"Oh great, so I get to walk into walls and fall into

chasms. Thanks," he snorted.

"Just think of it this way. If you do fall in a hole, I've got you."

"Yeah, right! More like I'm going to cushion your fall."

The two dragons went off in search of their classmates and teacher. They tried to go in the same direction that they last saw everyone heading, but with no light to guide them the going was tough. The ground was very slippery. Both dragons had to walk gingerly to ensure a safe footing. With every couple of steps they took, one would suddenly slip, sending both of them crashing to the ground. As they made their way through the caves, they kept calling out to their classmates, hoping that sooner or later someone would hear them. They seemed to wander for hours without any luck. Frustrated and fearful that they might be seriously lost, they stopped to rest.

"Maybe we ought to just sit still and wait," Remus pondered. "Who knows how lost we might get if we keep going."

Narix didn't want to hear any of his reluctant companion's musings. "We've gone this far. We can't stop now. Anyway, I could swear I heard something right before we stopped."

"What did you hear?" Remus asked, a doubtful tone accenting his words. "Or more likely, what do you *think* you heard?"

"I don't know, but it sounded like voices."

"Could you make out any words?"

"No. It sounded really muffled, ya' know, like someone was trying to be quiet." Narix's voice fell into a harsh, hissing whisper. "Maybe someone's screwing with us, trying to teach us a lesson."

"I don't think so," Remus countered, shaking his head. "Where did you hear the noise coming from?"

Narix tried his best to ascertain the location from which he heard the sound. "C'mon, it's this way." He led the way with his hands extended before him, groping for a wall to follow. "Eww!"

"What?"

"I just put my hands in something."

"Quit screwing around," Remus hissed. He cuffed Narix in the back of the head with his hand.

At that moment, Narix spotted what looked like flickering torchlight coming from another cavern off to their right. "Did you see that?"

"Yeah," Remus confirmed.

"Let's go!"

Moving in the direction that the light came from, they heard faint murmurs and unintelligible voices echoing through the cavern. They stood still in the darkness for a moment and listened.

"It must be them," Narix insisted. "They're messing with us."

"Why don't we teach *them* a lesson?" Remus cracked his knuckles, grinning deviously.

"Let's!" Narix wasted no time in whipping up a daring plot to scare the rest of their classmates and teacher. Having solidified their plan, they pressed themselves up against the moss-covered wall and began to shimmy their way in the direction of the voices. Fifteen paces later, Narix came up to a narrow tunnel leading away from the chamber they were in. Craning his neck, he peered around the corner, exposing as little of his face as possible. His head finally maneuvered far enough across the opening of the tunnel to where he could see something. To his surprise, this tunnel was not completely dark. In fact, he briefly caught a glimpse of a shadow stretching across the wall.

Turning back, Narix sneered at Remus. "It's them all right. I just saw a shadow."

"How could you see a shadow in the dark?" Remus scoffed. A cuffed hand struck him across the side of the head. He winced, grabbing hold of his cheekbone.

"You twit! The tunnel's lit. They must be looking for us. C'mon. Time to scare 'em good."

"Yeah!"

The two continued down the tunnel in the same fashion that had brought them there. The tunnel walls began to bend sharply as they moved along its length. Approaching the bend, they slowed up to ready themselves for the game. Two large shadows danced across the wall toward them as they prepared to jump their prey.

* * *

Ariel Flint carefully assisted Sorgi in removing some of the soft glowing moss from the cavern wall. Taking a long, flat, metal tool in her right hand, she pressed it against the wall, slid it behind the blanket of growth, and worked it up and down and back and forth to free the roots. Sorgi invited the other members of their class to assist her in dislodging the cluster of growth. Each of them worked diligently until the moss came free in one long sheet. He showed them how to carefully lay it down on the floor and then use a long slender blade from their tool kits to cut it into strips. Ariel was the first to get to work trimming free a length of moss.

"Be careful not to crush the moss as you separate it," their teacher warned them, holding a torch high above their heads as they performed the duties he described. "Try to gently unhook the roots. They should come apart without exerting too much force."

A few others joined in to assist Ariel. While they worked to accomplish their goal, one of the smaller members of their class, a boy dragon by the name of Julius, approached Sorgi. Being so small in stature, he approached his teacher unnoticed. He reached up and waved at his teacher saying, "Excuse me," over and over, but Sorgi did not notice him amidst the activity of his other students. The diminutive dragon breathed out an exasperated sigh.

"Good work, everyone," Sorgi applauded his class. As he looked around the chamber at his diligent students, Sorgi noticed that Narix and Remus were missing from the group. *Great! Where'd they go now?* He felt a bit panicked, fearing the worst may have befallen them. But that emotion lasted only a brief moment. He remembered all too clearly just how much trouble those two had caused in class. Sorgi decided that he would not interrupt this lesson to deal with them like he had so many times before. He shrugged off their absence and continued with his lesson.

"Now, the best way to preserve the moss until we get it back to Berathor is to roll it up like parchment and slide it into these fur-lined sacks." Sorgi handed out five of the sacks to his students. Keeping one for himself, he did as he always did when teaching a new skill—he modeled it for his students. Like participants in a game of Double Dragon, each of his students who helped to trim the moss into strips mimicked Sorgi's every move. First, he folded the moss over itself at the very end. Then he rolled it up gently, without applying too much pressure, until it looked similar to a coiled-up snake. Finally, he lifted the roll with his right hand and slid it into the sack. Some of the students tried to pick up the roll of moss in one hand but then dropped it, not yet as big or as strong as their teacher. So they worked together to load up each roll into the sacks.

Without warning, Julius flew right up in front of Sorgi's face, throwing him off balance for a moment. He grabbed at his chest to make sure his heart was still beating after such a scare. Julius did not seem to notice his poor teacher's state of shock. He simply hovered in place, hands clasped together.

"Sorgi," Julius's mouse-like voice eked forth. "Why are we collecting the moss?"

"You mean I forgot to tell you?" Sorgi felt a hint of embarrassment. The soft flesh along his underside turned green for a moment. "Thank you," he said in a calm, soothing tone to little Julius. He reached out and patted his student on the head like a small pet. A wide grin pursed Julius's lips before he fluttered off to join the others on the ground.

"Does anyone know why we're collecting the moss?" he asked aloud to his students. They all cast uncertain looks at one another. A few of the older students, Ariel included, raised their tails pensively.

Clink, the oldest student in the class, thrust the tip of his tail high and confident into the air, *oohing* and *ahhing* to get Sorgi's attention.

Sorgi never liked calling on Clink when he made such loud attempts to garner his attention. In recognizing how hesitant everyone else was in responding to his inquiry, Sorgi had no choice but to call on his impatient student. "Clink?"

Clink puffed up his chest. "The moss is used to insulate the walls of our hatching chambers." His voice was loud and unwavering.

"That's correct, Clink," Sorgi responded with a dry, unemotional tone.

Herrod mumbled, "He stole my answer," and snapped his fingers in frustration.

Gabby shook her head.

Ariel, however, seemed to be the most upset at missing the chance to impress Sorgi. She put her head in her hands.

"But," Sorgi's voice boomed out. Everyone's attention centered back on him. "What else do we use the moss for?"

If his students appeared confused and unsure of themselves before, their faces now held a simple, dumbfounded grimace. Well, all but one. While everyone else visibly struggled to come up with an alternate use for the moss, Ariel's face lit up. Her tail shot into the air with a jolt. Her wings flared open, smacking Clink in the face and knocking him back a few paces.

Sorgi fought to stifle his laughter. He gladly pointed to her. "Yes, Ariel?"

"We use the moss juice to light the valley at night."

Sorgi snorted approvingly, followed by the rest of the class. It was no surprise that she knew the answer since Farimus, her and Fenicus's father, worked to maintain the lighting. At night it was his job to move throughout the village and pour a small amount of the incandescent moss juice into the lanterns that hung about on lampposts, providing the soft blue glow that illuminated the grounds.

The unexpected return of Narix and Remus cut short Sorgi's lesson. The two missing students lumbered awkwardly into the chamber. All eyes snapped to them.

Barely able to contain his anger, Sorgi stalked heavily in their direction, ready to give them a thorough verbal lashing. The throng of students parted to let him through. When the light from his torch fell upon Narix and Remus, an odd, metallic glimmer caught his eye. He hadn't the faintest idea of what it was, but a bad feeling began to brew in the pit of his stomach. Taking one more wary step closer, he realized that the glimmer he saw was in fact a series of iron bands that were secured around both of their ankles, wrists, and neck. And attached to each of those bands was a taut chain that disappeared into the darkness.

"What's going on? Where've you been?" Sorgi shouted. He wasn't about to be fooled by another one of their pranks. Yet, the two troublesome students were uncharacteristically quiet and unmoving. They just stood there slouching as if they were half-asleep.

A brilliant burst of light flared forth from the darkness, illuminating the entire cavern in a warm, red glow. Sorgi flared his wings and wheeled away from the blinding radiance. He heard the shrieks and squeals of his students as they fought to protect their eyes. When his eyes adjusted, Sorgi peered beneath the shelter of his wing to see several heavily armored humans holding the ends of Narix and Remus's chains.

"Get out of here!" Sorgi howled in panic. "Back to the Valley!"

The young dragons screamed in terror, running over and colliding with one another in an attempt to escape.

Sorgi weaved his way through the children as they scattered, intent on using himself as a shield to guard their escape. With a deep, guttural roar that shook the cavern, he let the calm exterior that he possessed as a teacher fall away, and the menacing, primal animal that lurked within took its place. The complex biological mechanism that produced the ever-present spark of warmth within his chest swelled one hundred fold. That spark welled up into a churning swell of flame. With a jerking thrust of his head, Sorgi threw open his jaw and forced forth the super-heated air at the defenseless humans.

They didn't flinch.

Instead of the air catching fire as Sorgi expelled it from his lungs, a painful cloud of black smoke poured from his mouth. He coughed painfully on the caustic fumes and then slammed a balled fist against his chest. With a strong snort, he cleared out the remaining smoke and growled at the humans. Unsure what went wrong, Sorgi tried again to manifest enough internal heat to breathe fire. This time, the spark was gone. The warrior dragon stood dumbfounded in the face of his mortal enemy. *What's happened to me?*

From the brightly lit tunnel came his answer. A tall man

wearing a dark brown robe and a long cap drew near, uttering words in an ancient, foreign tongue. The sound was hypnotic. Each syllable swirled about in his brain, making him unable to focus on any other thoughts. Around him, his students grew calm. Oddly, he no longer felt the desire in his heart to fight, to turn these puny humans into charred hunks of flesh. He no longer had a thought of his own.

3

Rolling fields of tall, lush grass swept by Fenicus as he flew off in pursuit of his friends. Once again he had been picked to be "it" in what was becoming a daily game of Sky Hunter.

Competition, encouraged by their parents from early on, was a way of life for young dragons in Berathor Valley. It kept their talons sharp and their skills even sharper should the day come when they needed to defend their homeland. So everyone fed into the aggressive gamesmanship in the interest of both fun and personal improvement—everyone, that is, except for Fenicus. He did not take well to all the heated competition. Not that he was a slouch, but he just knew that he was wired a little differently from his friends. It was one of the reasons why he had let his discord with

Darius go on for so long without resolution. And Darius's anger toward Fenicus had made him even more apt to shy away from such dealings. It's one thing to be a little competitive while playing with friends. It's a completely different thing when someone is angry and out for blood.

Though Fenicus may have disliked competition, he absolutely hated the game of Sky Hunter. When they were little, it wasn't so bad. They played in the open air above the sprawling grasslands. Life was blissfully simple then; they just played for fun and everyone stayed safe. But as the years rolled by, the game turned downright treacherous. The better they all became at flying and aerial agility, the more cunning they grew when it came to concealing themselves. Eventually, the places that were once considered "out of bounds" became fair game, regardless of how unsafe or dangerous the terrain. And the more dangerous the hiding place, the more respect their skills earned within their little circle, especially when Fenicus was doing the chasing. No one was more agile or fleet of wing than Fenicus. His friends saw his skill as a challenge, and they met that challenge as of late by choosing the most hazardous playfield imaginable; a dense forest filled with fallen trees, broken branches, and unexpected changes in land contour. Coupled with the speeds at which they flew, it was a recipe for disaster.

The wide swath of woodland lay about a hundred flaps from the edge of the main village. Fenicus covered the stretch of sky with a casual pace, his eyes scanning the rest of the valley for his prey. Soon, the tops of the tall pine trees that populated the rim of the forest rolled into view. With an energetic burst, he increased his speed and closed in on the woodland realm. He soared up toward the forest canopy and hovered just above the treetops. There he had hoped to catch a glimpse of his playmates before they ducked down into the foliage, but they seemed to have smartened up since their last game. Fenicus sighed, flared his wings, and descended gingerly through the thick pine boughs.

Fenicus settled himself down carefully on the forest floor. A few twigs snapped underfoot and he cringed at the sound. Thankfully, nothing in the forest reacted to his presence. He hoped his arrival went unnoticed.

With a quick survey of his surroundings, Fenicus felt certain that his friends had taken shelter within the forest. Leaves drifted to the ground from trees he never touched. Many of them swayed as though they were struck by a large amount of weight.

Dozer would be the easiest to find since he rarely bathed and liked to play in the dirt. He was the one weirdo whom everyone seemed to like but couldn't stand to be around. Fenicus also knew that he would be hanging out near the ground since he was afraid of heights—a bit odd for a dragon. Taking careful steps, Fenicus tried not to snap any more twigs or branches underfoot.

A rather large mass of rock jutted up from the ground about twenty paces ahead of him. It appeared plenty large enough to hide behind. A sudden, gentle breeze rolled through the forest in his direction. Fenicus stopped in his tracks. Flaring his nostrils to take in as much air as possible, he tried to pick up on anything that might clue him in to where his friends might be. His mind raced to process the scents carried on the breath of the wind: the tingly scent of pine needles, the aroma of moist earth, a few drops of tree sap clinging to his snout, and a hint of pollen drifting in from the grasslands. Not a single noteworthy scent. Then he sensed the breeze shift slightly from north to northeast. Fenicus's eyes remained tightly closed in concentration as he continued to process incoming odors. An evil grin came across his lips and his eyelids snapped open with the recognition of one scent—*Dozer!*

Crouching down low on all fours, Fenicus crept toward the rock formation where the scent seemed to originate. But in his zeal to tag Dozer and end the game, he lost focus on his footing. His right foot slid on a mossy patch of rock, and he crashed into a heap of twigs and brush, making a loud series of cracks that echoed through the forest. Dozer uttered an obscenity and launched himself into the air. The game was aflight.

Fenicus immediately took to the air after him. Dozer flew close to the ground, weaving in and out of tightly clustered trees and making sharp turns. Fenicus kept up with little effort, though Dozer's erratic path had him questioning his heading.

Flying past two large maples, Fenicus caught sight of Talon and Laurel in his periphery and, for a moment, considered making an about face to go after them. But he knew that by the time he came about to give chase, they would be too far-gone to catch up. So Fenicus bore down on Dozer. Slowly but surely, he started to overtake his friend.

Dozer continued to lead Fenicus through a maze of fallen trees along the back reaches of the forest. The foliage was so thick that both dragons snapped branches with each thrust of their wings. Fenicus finally drew close enough to make a final lunge for Dozer when they flew over a nest of crumbling birches and then sharply down over them. Suddenly, Fenicus found he was no longer behind Dozer. Dozer was gone.

Fenicus slowed in his flight, working his head in all directions to find his prey. For the first time ever, Dozer had outwitted him. Fenicus then caught a glimpse of him scrambling out of a dank old cave and taking flight.

"Damn it!" Fenicus roared in frustration. With a growl he straightened his neck to face forward. His eyes snapped open wide in surprise. A nest of thick branches and leaves blotted out his view. Fenicus threw his arms up over his face as the branches lashed at him like a thousand little whips. His wings crunched against several tree trunks, causing him to spin out of control. No longer able to maintain his altitude, he crashed to the ground in a heap. Fenicus slid across the forest floor, scraping through patches of jagged shale and bone-dry dirt. He finally skidded to a halt just short of falling over a sheer rock face. A thick cloud of dust swirled about his motionless form.

Fenicus groaned. Though greatly weakened by the crash, he managed to push himself up onto his hands and knees. Each muscle vibrated intensely with effort. A thin stream of blood trickled from his mouth, pooling on the ground. A wave of dizziness swept over him and he collapsed.

The crunch of sharp talons grinding into the earth resounded in Fenicus's ears. Another dragon had landed next to him.

"Get up!" an angry voice growled. He heard the footfalls of the other dragon drawing closer. "I said get up!" the voice shouted again. A foot kicked at Fenicus's sprawled limbs.

Fenicus strained his neck to look up in the direction of the angry voice. Though three unclear images wavered before him, Fenicus managed to focus his eyes and mind long enough to discern that it was Darius who had found him. Now totally wiped of strength, his head slumped back to the dirt as more blood seeped from his mouth.

Darius yanked Fenicus up by his right wing and pulled him to his feet, wrenching the limb loose from its socket. The already anguished dragon cried out in pain. As if to silence his wails, Darius grabbed Fenicus by the throat.

Unable to stand on his own and certainly unable to fight back, Fenicus could do nothing to stop Darius's aggression. "Go ahead," he rasped. "Get it over with."

"Gladly!"

Releasing Fenicus's throat, Darius spun like a top, his tail slicing through the air before colliding with Fenicus's jaw. The crunching crack of bone against bone reverberated through the forest. Fenicus stumbled back on unsure feet toward the cliff.

Coming back around, Darius's eyes grew wide in horror. He lunged forward, reaching out for Fenicus as he stumbled toward the precipice. His talon-tipped fingers grabbed hold of Fenicus's tail as he tumbled over the edge, dragging Darius with him. He dug his feet into the dirt and stopped their momentum. Yet, Darius was unable to maintain his grip. Fenicus slipped from his fingers. Darius averted his eyes and turned away. With a crackle of broken tree branches and a dull thud, the young dragon crashed against the valley floor below.

Screaming voices drew near. Darius turned and looked into the sky. Laurel, Talon, and Dozer were flying straight toward him.

The three landed hot, skidding in the dirt and shale at dangerous speeds. Laurel flopped down on the ground, her long neck and head leering over the edge. Dense trees filled the ground below, hiding Fenicus from view. Talon and Dozer stood on either side of her, chests heaving as they too peered down into the valley.

Dozer turned to Darius, his eyes blazing. "What did you do?" Dozer howled as he rushed after Darius, grabbing him by the throat and dragging him to the ground. The two dragons writhed about in the dust, biting and clawing at one another.

Talon jumped into the fray to separate them. Taking hold of Dozer around his midsection, he fought to yank him off of Darius. Talon planted his foot on Darius and pushed off, successfully separating them. The two fell backwards to the ground. The weight of Dozer knocked the air out of Talon, but he did not let go. Gasping for air, Talon rolled Dozer over onto his stomach, straddled his body, and pinned his arms to the ground. "Cool it!" he yelled.

For a few moments, Dozer fought against Talon's grip. Then his eyes fell upon the huddled form of Darius lying curled up on the ground, shaking.

"Calm down, Dozer," Talon insisted, "before you kill someone."

After a few heavy breaths, the young dragon ceased fighting his restraints. Talon extended a hand to Dozer and helped him to his feet. The two approached Darius who now sat on his rump in the dirt, his head in his hands.

"What did you do?" Talon interrogated him. "You just had to keep pushing, didn't you? Didn't you?" his voiced boomed. Birds flew from the forest.

Darius sat there shaking his head. He pulled his hands from his tear-streaked, dirty face. "I didn't mean...I...it was an accident."

"What were you thinking?" Dozer asked, now much calmer. "Didn't you realize what might happen?

"I swear. I didn't do it on purpose." Darius rose to his feet. The three of them walked to the edge.

Through all of this, Laurel lay peering over the cliff's edge, sobbing. A soothing hand touched her wing, stroking it gently. Laurel pulled herself up onto her knees. "Why? Why couldn't you leave things alone, Darius? How many times did he try to apologize and you threw it back in his face? This didn't have to happen." Her watery eyes turned to Darius who stood next to her, his hand on her wing. She slapped it away in disgust. Laurel spun to her feet. "Get away from me." She shoved Darius away.

"I swear it was an accident. All I meant to do was hit him. I never thought he'd fall over the edge." He looked to all three of his friends. "You don't really think I would've done it if I knew what would happen?"

Talon responded very matter-of-factly. "It doesn't matter what you intended. It's what happened that matters."

For a brief moment there was silence. Then Dozer took a good look at the valley below. "Hey!" his voice broke the calm. "Could he have survived the fall? I mean, it isn't that far."

The other three looked over the edge.

Laurel's somber grimace began to ease. Her tears stopped. "Well, what're we waiting for?" She took off galloping toward a slope of stone that led down the face of the cliff.

"Whoa, what are you doing? Just fly down!" Darius suggested.

"The wind shear is too strong, you idiot. We'd never survive the landing," Laurel shot back. She then turned to continue her downward trek.

"Oh, wait!" Darius called out to her.

Laurel stopped dead in her tracks and turned back, seething impatiently.

"Shouldn't someone go get help?" Darius looked to the others for affirmation. "If he's still alive, he's gotta be busted up pretty badly."

Talon and Dozer appeared to consider the idea while Laurel rejoined the group.

"He's got a good point," Talon acknowledged. "Someone's got to get back to town and fetch the healer."

Dozer and Laurel nodded in agreement.

"I'll stay with Fenicus," Darius volunteered. "It's my fault he's down there. It's the least I can do."

The other three looked at each other. Talon nodded and added, "All right." He then motioned with his head for Dozer and Laurel to follow him. Taking a few swift steps,

Talon flapped his wings, leapt into the air, and rose into the sky.

Dozer followed right behind Talon, calling out to Darius. "Don't you dare leave him!"

Laurel shook her head disappointedly at Darius. "If you're lucky, maybe Fenicus will find it in his heart to forgive you. If," she paused for a moment before continuing bitterly, "he survives."

Before Laurel completely flew out of earshot, she called out to him. "We'll be back as soon as we can!"

Having watched her fly away, Darius returned to the precipice of the cliff. He scanned the ground below. Trees and jagged boulders littered every speck of ground. Darius located the path Laurel began to traverse and, with careful steps, started his own descent into the sunken valley.

The footing was treacherous. Each step brought with it the chance of a dangerous landslide. Swirling winds whipped at him, forcing him to keep a low profile to the ground while hugging the valley wall. After a significant amount of toil and time, Darius reached the midway point of the path. His friends had yet to return with help and the daylight was waning. He looked longingly toward the sky. "Where are they?" he wondered aloud.

Then a deep, somber tone resounded through the valley—the ringing of Berathor's warning bell.

Darius looked down into the valley and then back up the pathway. He closed his eyes, clenching his fists. "Damn!" he snarled. Leaping into the air, Darius fought the erratic winds to escape the valley and flew back to the village.

4

Fenicus awoke with a start. Inky blackness surrounded him. Bringing his hands to his eyes, he felt a crusty seal covering them. He strained to open them, but they wouldn't budge. Rubbing at them frantically, the substance gave way and he opened his eyes. Bringing his fingers to his lips, he tasted some of the residue that clung to them. *Blood!*

Lying flat on his back, he saw a gap in the canopy above where he had made his painful entrance into the valley. Several branches were snapped off of the trees and strewn about in a painful heap beneath him. Finger-shaped clouds drifted across the face of the moon while a misty halo encircled it, adding an eerie air to its visage.

His newly liberated eyes drifted to his right where he caught sight of a jagged boulder that protruded straight up from the forest floor. At that moment Fenicus realized just how lucky he was to have survived his plummet from the cliff face.

Rolling over onto his belly, he tried to take stock of his injuries. Other than some minor bumps and bruises, he felt pretty good. He dug his talons deep into the damp soil to establish a solid footing. Taking a deep breath, he pressed hard against the ground. His body began to gradually rise until he sat resting upon his hands and knees. There he paused to catch his breath. Moving his right foot flat upon the soil and his right hand onto that very same knee, he did his best to stand up. When he straightened his neck, flashes of light sparked in his field of vision like tiny black fireworks surrounded by sunbursts. A shot of pain seared through his head. He grabbed at the source of the discomfort to find a deep gash near his ear. An overtaxed artery pumped below his scales. He braced himself against the rock, waiting to either vomit or for the dizziness to pass, whichever came first. Taking several deep breaths, he managed to reverse the wooziness.

Judging by the height of the moon in the sky, Fenicus calculated that he must have been unconscious for close to eight hours. For the life of him, he couldn't figure out why no one had come looking for him yet. Surely his friends went home by now and told someone what happened. Even if they thought him dead, they still should have sent out a party to recover his body. He sat there puzzled. It was as if everyone just forgot about him. *Maybe they don't really care about me anymore.* "Nah!" he barked aloud, remembering the priceless amulet his uncle bestowed upon him. *The amulet!* He no longer felt its weight around his neck. Fenicus grasped for the silver chain from which it hung. *It's gone!*

Fenicus frantically scrutinized the ground in search of the amulet. The moonlight that filtered through the treetops did not provide enough illumination to reflect off of its glittering surface. *Try not to lose it this time*, his mother's words rang like a gong in his mind. He promised her that he wouldn't lose it. He couldn't bear the shame of returning home without the one meaningful gift that his uncle had given him. Dropping down on all fours, he swept his hands over the ground, desperate to find it. Fenicus left no rock, twig, or leaf unturned as he groped his way along the dew-laden loam, praying that he might stumble across it. On the verge of giving up, his right hand fell upon a slab of cold metal. Fenicus scooped it up, slung the chain around his neck, and breathed a sigh of relief.

Back to his feet, Fenicus dusted himself off and flared his wings, ready to go home. He rhythmically flapped his wings until they generated enough lift for takeoff. With both wings supporting the full burden of his weight, a searing stab burned though his shoulder. The foggy memory of Darius dislocating his wing came back to him. The tendons and musculature that held the ball joint of his wing together couldn't handle the stress of flight, and the pain became too much to fight through. He dropped back to Earth.

Fenicus rolled the joint of his injured wing to work out the discomfort, but after a few painful, loud crunches, he accepted the fact that he would have to forego flying for a while. To get home he would have to do it by foot, and that journey would take some time. Fenicus navigated the trees and rocks along the valley floor until he found the small path that led back up top. He tucked back his wings, dug his talons into the rock, and began a slow ascent along the steep trail. When he reached the top, Fenicus used the moon to gain his bearings. The clouds that lingered in the sky were obscuring its glow, but enough light remained to guide his way. Fenicus turned east and headed back home.

At first, Fenicus thought little of the clouds, even though they seemed to grow thicker as he walked. A series of meandering streams that cut through the grazing plains told Fenicus that he wasn't far from home. Nervous sheep and cattle scattered at his presence. Leaning down, Fenicus lapped up some of the cool, crisp water, and then splashed some on his face to wash away the blood. The sensation of the cool water dripping off of his scales and filling his empty belly refreshed the young dragon. It was at that moment that his heart dropped in his chest like a landslide; as he looked to the sky, he saw a few thick, black plumes of smoke billowing up from the village square. Something big was on fire. Fear filled his mind and adrenaline surged in his veins. Fenicus dropped to all fours and galloped home at full speed.

He skidded into the village square and stood staring, jaw agape, at the destruction that lay before him. The entire village was in ruins. Large marble statues, erected in honor of the great dragons of the past, lay shattered upon the ground. The few buildings that stood around the square were nothing more than smoldering remains. The very earth itself had been ripped apart. Square-cut stones that once covered the ground were now replaced with gaping craters.

The shock of the situation sent Fenicus's mind into overload. He teetered on the edge of an emotional breakdown, unsure as to whether he should be overcome with sadness or filled with rage and hatred. At the far end of the village stood the remains of a framework dragon built of wood and lashed together by vines. And sitting on the ground before it were similarly fashioned Dragonian runes spelling out FENICUS. That night it should have been alight with fireworks to celebrate his hatching day. The whole of Berathor, all his friends and family, would have been gathered there to congratulate him.

Of all the thoughts that swirled about Fenicus's brain, one came screaming to the forefront—*family*. In a dead sprint, he made his way toward the southern outskirts of the village. The wind whipped at his face as he crested a small hill just beyond their warren. From what he could see, everything looked intact. He ran down the hill and trotted into his home through the open entryway. It was cold and dark. All the candles had burnt out, leaving behind only smoldering wicks. There were no sounds other than those of his rasping breaths.

"Mother?" he yelled. Fenicus frantically searched their warren. He made his way from chamber to chamber. It was empty. The smell of the soothing herb his father smoked still hung in the air. Fenicus breathed it in deeply with his eyes closed, finding some comfort in the aroma.

A crack of thunder brought Fenicus back to reality. He moved toward the nearest airshaft to peer at the sky outside. Dark clouds were rolling in. Bolts of lightning leapt from cloud to cloud, chasing one another in an age-old game. A booming crack shook everything, and with it came a gust of cold air.

A rustling sound came from a rarely used cavern that his parents hoped to use as a hatching chamber. Fenicus pushed aside the curtain that had closed it off from view. Behind it he saw something that caused an ache in his body a hundred times greater than the full wrath of Darius's anger. Dangling from wall to wall were braided vines: one strand was green and young, the other was coated in paint made of powdered gold ore and tree sap. Amidst them hung a banner that read, "Happy 109th Hatching Day, Fenicus!" He felt a breeze move past him through the warren that caused them to swing to and fro. That was the source of the rustling sound. He stumbled forward a few steps.

"They didn't forget," he whispered. His blood began to boil, bringing to life a small spark flickering in his chest. A loud roar burst from him, filling Berathor Valley with the sounds of rage and despair. As the last bit of breath left him, two white wisps of smoke flowed from his nostrils. The tears Fenicus fought back for so long finally crested through to the surface with the release of his pent up emotions. He staggered toward the center of the room where a conical arrangement of hand-sized eggs—109 of them to be exact—rested in little upward turned claws. He sniffled, wiped his eyes, and lifted the topmost egg; its shell sparkled in his hand. Written on its surface was the Dragonian rune for "zero." Cracking the shell open, an illusion swelled forth depicting the day that he hatched. His little head broke through the membrane within the shell, and his mother pulled him free. She held him lovingly; it was the start of his first year. Each of the remaining numbered eggs contained a memorable moment from that year of his life. *They fooled me. They were going to surprise me!* His limbs gave out and he collapsed to his knees. An anguished roar thundered from him. Sapped of all his strength, Fenicus fell into a heap on the floor where he lay sobbing until he fell asleep.

*   *   *

A single gray bird sat atop the egg tower, warbling a cheerful tune. The giddy arrangement of notes awoke Fenicus from his slumber. His achy, swollen eyes creaked open to reveal a haze-covered world. He rubbed at them with his knuckles and his sight cleared. The bird flew off at his stirrings.

The entire chamber was dark, except for a ray of sunlight that entered through an airshaft. A thin layer of dampness covered everything. Beads of dew clung to the streamers, the eggs, and Fenicus. An ominous silence lingered. He knew that the events of the past day were not some kind of incredibly realistic hallucination. He was, in fact, living a nightmare.

Everyone was gone. For the very first time in his life he was alone and he did not have a clue as to what he needed to do. It did not sit well with him. The natural emotional urge to cry began to rear its head again. Knowing those tears would do him no good, he swallowed his sadness and focused his attention on the situation at hand. *What happened? Where did everyone go?* It was a mystery that Fenicus knew would not be solved as long as he sat still. He had to start looking for clues.

Heading out into the daylight, Fenicus started back to the village square. There he discovered the shredded remains of a few pale-skinned creatures littering the ground. Most of the bodies were incomplete. Some of them were missing limbs while others were missing heads or huge chunks of their torsos. Others were totally unidentifiable-- torn apart or burned to a crisp. Black cloth and pieces of shaped iron plates covered most of the bodies. He had heard of such things from his uncle and saw drawings of human weapons and armor. These seemed to match up pretty well. He counted thirteen complete bodies before losing track. The first part of the mystery was solved; humans had invaded Berathor, and some of them paid for it with their lives.

Then Fenicus noticed that not a single deceased dragon lay among the dead. *They invade our home but don't claim a single life?* Something didn't add up. His hand instinctively drifted to the amulet around his neck as he thought about his uncle's lessons. As far as he knew, humans had no qualms about slaughtering dragons, so why would they take prisoners?

Fenicus spent the next few hours piling up the bodies, looking for anything among their limited belongings that might serve as a clue. The only thing he found was a band of silver that some of the men wore on their fingers. Fenicus removed one such band from a severed hand and examined it closely. It was a simple piece of jewelry that had no remarkable traits other than a symbol etched into its thicker, flattened side. Some sort of crest or symbol marked it. After looking at it from all sorts of angles, he realized that the symbol was that of a howling wolf head. With no other prospects, Fenicus placed all his faith in that image. Not knowing any other way to keep the tiny trinket safe, Fenicus opened his jaw and fitted the band around one of his slender fangs.

Finished with his gruesome task, Fenicus ripped some cloth from one of the dead bodies, wrapped it around a large splinter of wood, and lit it ablaze in one of the smoldering fires burning throughout the village. He tossed the makeshift torch onto the pile of bodies and watched as the flame grew into a roaring bonfire. It didn't take long for the pungent odor of singed hair and charred flesh to get to him. In all his days of witnessing deceased dragons being laid to rest in this manner, he never recalled such a foul odor resulting from their cremation. Dragons actually gave off an aroma similar to that of clover when they burned.

Walking away from the fire, Fenicus tried to make sense of the chaotic, mixed pattern of human and dragon footprints on the ground. With any luck, the humans led his fellow dragons out on foot. He knew that if the humans flew them out of Berathor, there was no possible way to track their movement. His only hope was an exodus by land. And after a thorough examination of the grounds, Fenicus finally found what he was looking for—a single file trail of both human and dragon footprints leading into the mountainside caves.

Fenicus came about and made his way to the cave where

his father stored the luminous moss juice. The place was a shambles. Searching through the rubble, Fenicus recovered a long, smooth rod with a glass orb affixed to its top and a small barrel of moss juice. Taking the pole in hand, he grabbed the small piece of cork that plugged the top of the orb and removed it. Then he filled the orb with the bluish-green liquid inside the barrel. Filling it to capacity, he replaced the cork and set the barrel aside.

Fenicus then made his way toward the mouth of the cave where the footprints led. Taking a deep breath, he mustered his courage and stepped inside. With nothing but blackness before him, Fenicus shook the shaft of the pole vigorously. Initially, the orb produced a soft glow that merely lit up his face. Then a rapid a chemical reaction occurred within the orb, and the liquid produced a blinding flash, bathing the entire cavern in light. Fenicus averted his eyes until the initial burst subsided. Slowly, the intensity of the light subsided. The glow of the torch provided the perfect illumination to explore the cave. Looking to the floor, the trail was difficult to pick up. So many feet trampled through there on a daily basis that discerning one set of prints from another was incredibly difficult. But the one thing that separated one trail from the other was the presence of the small human footprints. They wore some kind of coverings over their feet that did not leave typical prints with toe and nail marks in the soil. It was those markings that would be his guide.

5

Several hours had passed since Fenicus first disappeared into the system of caves that threaded through the Tatra Mountains. The path was long and difficult to navigate. Just as the moss juice began to lose its power, he saw a spark of sunlight in the distance and knew this part of his journey had come to an end. Tossing the glowtorch aside, Fenicus made his way through the last hundred or so paces of the cave. The sunlight from outside grew brighter with every step. His eyes had grown so accustomed to the darkness of the cave that the bright sunlight conjured up an instant headache.

There he stood on the precipice of fate. Fenicus didn't want to take another step further from his home. Since the time of his birth, he had been isolated from the outside world and taught to fear it. The caves, to some degree, were a familiar part of life from as far back as he could remember. So as long as he stayed in the confines of Berathor, as long as he stayed right where he was, he was home, kept company by memories and familiar surroundings. Once he stepped one foot outside the cave into the open, he would be on his own and unprotected in a place where he didn't belong. But Fenicus knew that staying put wasn't an option; he had to follow the footprints until they led to those responsible for the disappearance of his friends and family. And if he couldn't set them free, he'd rather share their fate then live alone. Fenicus looked down as a wave of depression swept over him. He sighed and took his first step into the unknown.

Brilliant rays of sunlight shone through numerous breaks in the thick, puffy clouds, basking the Earth in their warmth. Lush, green grass covered the ground as far as the eye could see. It bent and swayed at the behest of a cool breeze that rolled across the land. Fenicus breathed in a deep helping of the refreshing air. The fragrant aroma of pollen, lifted from the wild flowers, teased his nostrils.

Fenicus made his way on all fours into the open field. After a few steps, his feet felt as though they were sinking into the ground. Looking down, he realized he was walking in thick, soupy mud that cut a trail through the grass. Within that muddy path lay the unmistakable footprints of both dragons and humans.

For hours and hours he followed the trail. At times he attempted to busy his mind by calculating just how many men were in the party that had invaded his homeland. He always counted up to around fifty or so different footprints before he lost track. As the day progressed, the realization came to him that at his current pace it might take forever to catch up to them. On foot he was no faster or slower than those he pursued. Fenicus knew he had to give flight another try.

Fenicus bit his lip pensively, unfurled his wings, and flapped them up and down. Generating enough vertical thrust for takeoff, he rose up on his hind legs and then into the air. Again, the sharp pain that he felt back in the sunken valley shot through his wing. Though he winced, he refused to set down without trying to work out the ache. After a few moments, the pain dulled to into a throbbing sensation that he could endure. Looking down, he found that he now hovered far above the ground and the muddied trail. Its dark brown color stood out in stark contrast against the vibrant green grass. He smiled a wide, toothy grin.

Fenicus corkscrewed and somersaulted through the air. An unusual feeling of freedom washed over him, and he couldn't get enough of it. There were no walls, no mountains, nothing to hold him down or rein him in. It was exhilarating. But as much as he loved the way he felt, his mind never wandered too far from what led him to this point. The swelling and discomfort in his wing served as a reminder of the past day's events. While his wings were able to support his weight in flight, he could not bear the discomfort any longer. Short of breath and lightheaded, Fenicus flared his wings and floated along the wind on a gentle approach to the ground, covering as much territory as possible along his descent. *Tomorrow*, he thought, *I'll try again.*

As sunset approached, Fenicus found a small cluster of trees some distance from the worn path. The density of the foliage provided thick enough cover to hide him from the eyes of any passerby. After feasting on a few of the wild creatures that inhabited the countryside, he found a comfortable enough clearing within the thicket and settled upon the ground, curling up into himself for warmth.

*   *   *

Fenicus awoke from a restful night of sleep. His whole body felt much better than it had in days, and he was eager to resume his course. Fenicus decided to start out on his feet rather than attempt flight again so soon.

As the sun reached its apex in the sky, Fenicus noticed that the very shape of the land began to transform. The rolling hills lessened in grade, the grasslands gave way to patches of sand, and the trees had all but vanished. Fenicus then caught a whiff of salt on a breeze floating in from the north. He thought it odd to taste such things on the wind. Curious, he pushed onward. Just as he made his way to the top of a sandy hilltop, his quest was dealt a vicious blow. The changes in the landscape and the salty air meant that he had reached the sea. Before him flowed an endless body of water unlike anything he had ever seen. A new hopelessness took hold. Fenicus sprinted to the shore in desperation. Peering at the ground as he ran, he watched the last remnants of the trail vanish into the rolling tide. He ran straight into the surf, kicking and punching at the water, yelling at it to bring them back. But it was no use. He was too late. There was little chance he could ever trace their path over such a vast body of water without a trail or scent to follow. Fenicus stumbled back onto the soggy sand of the beach and fell back onto his rear.

"Great!" he bellowed. "Now what am I supposed to do?" Fenicus grabbed at a small pebble and chucked it into the sea. It skidded along the surface before disappearing beneath a wave.

"Sitting on yer bum isn't gonna help now, is it?" a low, guttural voice barked at him brusquely.

"Wonderful," Fenicus concluded, shaking his head. "I'm losing my mind." *Lost my family, lost my home, why not?*

"Hey there," the voice came again. "Over 'eer!" A loud splashing sound came from the same direction as the voice.

Fenicus followed the noise to his right. His eyes grew wide in amazement when he saw what looked like some sort of gargantuan fish lying awkwardly upon the shore, half in the water. It wallowed about, flapping its long, flat appendages in the water.

"Do you think you could lend a hand, lad?" the bizarre creature pleaded with Fenicus in a thick, odd accent. "I seem to be a wee bit stuck, if you know what I mean." It flapped around some more in the water, demonstrating its inability to free itself.

Fenicus strode over to the peculiar beast, a bit curious as to what it was. A few feet from it, Fenicus stopped and scanned over its length. It was at least three times longer than Fenicus, bluish in color, and had many of the features similar to the fish he caught in the streams back home. It seemed to have fins, though they looked more like wings with their tremendous size. Near the top fin in particular, he noticed a distinctive white patch in the shape of a crescent moon. Fenicus could not figure out for the life of him the nature of this creature. The most puzzling feature of all was its eyes. They were set just behind its jaw hinge. Fenicus turned his head almost completely upside down trying to figure out if it was upside down.

Frustrated by Fenicus's obvious confusion, the oversized fish vented, "I'm right side up! I'm right side up!" It screamed out the words in a flurry.

Fenicus reared back alarmed and apologized, "I'm sorry. I was just trying to figure out what you are. I've never seen anything like you before."

"The feelin's mutual, lad. Apology accepted." The creature responded in a much softer tone this time. Its extremely low voice rumbled Fenicus's guts. "Help me outta 'ere an' we can exchange pleasantries later."

"What do you need me to do?"

"Help me push meself back in. Me limbs are too far outta the water to get any leverage."

Fenicus nodded. "I'll see what I can do." He extended his hands toward the creature, but he wasn't sure where to place them. He kept searching for the right place to push off without hurting the beast. He doubted he even had enough strength to push its massive girth back into the deep with nothing but loose, wet sand beneath him. "Where should I push?"

The creature's oversized eyes rolled about in their sockets. A large plume of seawater and air shot out of a hole atop its head. "Lad, as long as you don't push me back ashore, we ain't got no problems, see. Just push as 'ard as you can."

Fenicus shrugged his shoulders. "Okay!" He moved to his right a few feet to get clear of the large fin or wing—he couldn't tell—that extended from its side. Huffing out a few breaths to gird up his strength, Fenicus waited for a wave to slosh under the beast and then he rushed at it with his hands extended before him. They made contact smartly with its large side (which was a bit slippery) and he began to shove. He pushed with everything he had, even lowering his shoulder into the beast while he pumped his legs hard against the soft beach.

The creature moved its enormous tail from side to side, creating gigantic surges of water in all directions. The waves nearly knocked Fenicus off his feet. Their efforts made little headway.

Fenicus finally gave up. He stood back and gazed along the length of the creature, trying to think of a way to gain more leverage. Nothing came to mind. He dropped down on all fours, shaking his head. "Now what?"

The creature looked Fenicus up and down. "What about those fancy wings on yer back?" it inquired. "What if you flap 'em real fast? Might that 'elp?"

Fenicus had totally forgotten about his wings; if he pumped them hard enough, he might be able to generate enough power to get the job done. Unfurling them, he made a few practice thrusts to test his injured limb. There was only the lingering hint of discomfort. "I'll give it a try. Cross your fingers."

The creature shot him an irritated look.

"Sorry," Fenicus replied in earnest through a shudder of laughter. "Ready?"

"Ready."

Fenicus rammed into the beast with his hands and shoulder once more and pushed against the sand with his legs. But this time he beat his wings in horizontal thrusts, causing the creature's hulking body to move. It was only a few meters but it was working.

"Beat 'em harder, beastie," hollered the creature. "Don't give up now!"

Fenicus felt every vein in his head and neck pressing to the surface as if ready to burst. That dreaded feeling of lightheadedness came over him again. Just as Fenicus began to see bursts of light, he fell forward into the surf as the beast slid off into the deeper part of the shore. Pulling himself up out of the sea, he watched as it gaily maneuvered its way through the water, whooping and hollering as it swam.

The creature ducked out of sight below the surface of the water. Fenicus feared it swam off. He turned away, saddened that a possible friend in this lonely world was gone. But as he plodded his way back out of the water to dry sand, he heard a loud "Whoohooo!" and whirled about to see the creature cresting through the water and smacking down flat on its back. A huge spray of seawater shot in all directions and rained down on Fenicus. The beast swam back toward the shore.

"What are you?" inquired the young dragon.

"I'm a whale, lad. The name's Seamus, an' I owe you a debt of gratitude. If it weren't for you, I'd likely be dead soon."

Fenicus felt like a fool. It wasn't a fish. It was a mammal. Sorgi told stories in class about the noble giants of the sea known as whales, but he never imagined he would ever come face to face with one. Fenicus remembered how Sorgi talked about them being some of the largest creatures to ever inhabit the Earth.

"Pleased to meet you, Seamus. You're the first whale I've ever met. Never thought I'd see the day."

"An' yourself lad, what're you supposed to be?"

"I'm a dragon," he said sadly. "By the looks of things, I'm afraid that I'm the last of my kind. My name's Fenicus, Fenicus Flint."

"Fenicus, eh? A good, noble name. Glad to make your acquaintance." He sat looking thoughtfully at Fenicus for a spell. "Well, lad, I hate to burst yer bubble, but you aren't the first of yer kind I've ever seen."

Fenicus's gaze locked questioningly upon Seamus. "What do you mean? I'm not the first you've seen?"

"Until this mornin' I'd never seen anything like you before. But a whole bunch of yer kind were taken aboard ships by 'em blasted humans."

A sudden rush of adrenaline surged through him. Fenicus had thought that he was completely out of luck. That faint glimmer of hope that was dashed upon the waves of the shore began to shine once again. He rushed toward Seamus. "What did you see?" he begged.

"A great host of dragons were loaded onto massive ships. That's how I got meself stuck here. I let me curiosity get the best of me, an' when I swam in to get a better look, I realized

I'd gotten meself into a bit of a bind. When the tide came in, I kinda hoped that it might free me from the shore, but it wasn't enough to do the trick. Those ships, though, sailed away with ease. Thankfully, you came along just in time to save me sorry arse." Seamus laughed warmly.

"Seamus," Fenicus's voice shook with nervous excitement, "do you know where they took my family?"

"I'm pretty sure I do, lad. I can help you find 'em. After all you've done fer me, it's the least I can do."

Fenicus nodded with eagerness. "Please."

6

The village of Falterton had a life all its own, especially in the marketplace where merchants sold all manner of wares to those with loose coin. Anything a person wanted or needed to get by could be bought or sold here.

One man carried an awkwardly bent hoe to the smithy to work it back into shape after he mangled it on rocks in his garden. The smith just nodded with a smile and went to work repairing the familiar farming tool. With the job finished, he sent the farmer on his way, refusing to accept payment. It was a good neighbor's deed.

Along the inner track of the marketplace were more traditional shops where housewives and farmers sold their goods on a much smaller scale. Some of the merchants sold vegetables and freshly picked fruits from the first harvest of the spring. Others sold animal skins from hunting and trapping that they fashioned into clothing and blankets. One woman in particular sold baked goods. She was an old grandmother who made goodies of all sorts. Her stock was usually the first to run low each day. Crowds of villagers would be there at the break of dawn to buy up all her delicious baked goods. There wasn't a single recipe that escaped her. On a small hand-drawn cart that she labored from her home each day, she displayed her goods for all to see. The aromas that wafted off her freshly baked rolls lingered through the marketplace making noses rise up and heads turn in her direction. Though most people in town who visited her paid the nominal fee she requested for her labor, there was one person in particular who cut into her profits.

A small boy of twelve years wandered through the village. His skin was pale and blotched with dirt. A tangled mess of sunny blond hair sat atop his head. No other children in town appeared as needy or untidy as this boy. He was a castoff, a street urchin—an orphan.

He weaved his way in and out of crowds, threading himself through the busy marketplace on a very specific course. Carefully, the boy strode behind a man who gnawed hungrily on a turkey leg while walking hand-in-hand with his daughter. As they walked, she turned to look behind her. Her gaze fell upon the boy. She smiled at him warmly. He smiled back and began to walk very formally, mimicking her father's gate and mannerisms, one hand behind his back and his head held high. She giggled and turned back to face the direction her father was leading them.

Finally, the moment the boy waited for arrived. Only half eaten, the little girl's father tossed the turkey leg lazily over his shoulder. Before it could reach the ground, the boy snatched it out of the air and ran off behind the nearest longhouse to gnaw off the remaining scraps. Having not eaten for days, the boy gobbled up every strand of succulent meat until a bare bone was the only thing left.

Though satisfying, the turkey wasn't enough to fill his empty belly. He decided to pay a visit to an old friend whom he hadn't seen in days.

Making his way through the shadowy alleyways between homes and shops, the boy slunk toward his target. Rounding a corner, he surveyed the area. A gang of villagers gathered around the very same kiosk that he hoped to liberate of some of its goods. The people appeared to be making small talk with the owner, asking for recipes and cooking secrets that she refused to divulge.

His timing couldn't be more perfect. The boy slid into the ebb and flow of market patrons, cutting across the midway toward the kiosk. Having reached his destination, he carefully stood perusing the marketplace to see if anyone was watching him. With his back to the patrons, who were becoming even more insistent that she relinquish her secrets to them, the boy took a few steps to his right toward the edge of the gathering. Through the narrow gaps between people, he concentrated his attention on the owner's eyes. Finally, one of the men who had been haggling with her for some time decided to purchase a loaf of bread. Her attention drifted to the man's purse as he offered up payment for her goods. Without hesitation, the boy thrust his arm between two men, snatched two fresh rolls from a basket, and took off at a full sprint.

She screamed as loud as she could. "Thief! Thief! The little bastard's stolen from me again!" Everyone standing around her turned to watch the boy flee through the crowded streets, knocking into people and causing quite a ruckus. She begged and pleaded aloud for someone to grab the dirty little boy, but no one could catch him before he escaped through the village gates. As he had all too many times, the boy vanished into the thicket of trees across the clearing, leaving the old woman a few coins short in her purse.

Settling down with his back against an old oak, the boy stared into the wispy clouds that streaked across the soft blue sky. He wiped the sweat from his brow with an already soiled sleeve and heaved a few deep breaths to calm himself down after his getaway. Deep down, the boy hated taking from her, but she was one of the few people he could easily take advantage of since she couldn't run too fast. He cheerlessly tore a hunk from one of the rolls and stuffed it in his mouth. The boy took his time savoring every delectable bite until nothing was left. With his belly now full, he stretched out on a thin layer of leaves and grass and nodded off to sleep.

*   *   *

A crack of thunder in the distance awakened the boy from his slumber. He snapped up from the ground, his heart pounding in his chest. When he had set himself down to sleep the sun was still high in the sky. It was now close to setting, and the sky had grown dark with cloud. The foul weather that loomed a short distance away made the boy pause with concern. While the thicket of trees offered only minimal protection from the rain, he had grown accustomed to sleeping outdoors. Thunder and lightning, however, was another story.

The only safe place to hide would be back in the village, but the townspeople were swift to send him on his way once they realized that he had made camp under one of their overhanging roofs. A few drops of rain descended from above and onto his arms. The boy pulled his knees close to his chest and huddled into himself for warmth. For now, he decided, he would take his chances where he was.

Thwap! Thwap! The raindrops fell from the sky and collided with the leaves of the trees. At first, the drops fell here and there with only a few falling on him. But with the storm clouds closing in on the village, the gentle sprinkles that descended grew into a crescendo of pelting rain that created swells of water on the ground. Several large puddles collected not too far from where the boy sat under the large oak. The rain was cold against his skin, causing painful chills to race up and down his spine. He peered with blinking eyes into the falling rain to try and assess if he was in for a long night. There was no visible break in the gloomy clouds that overcast the sky. The boy decided to make his way back to the village where he would take his chances with the townspeople.

He rose to his feet just when a brilliant bolt of lightning struck the ground on the far side of the village. He blurted out an obscenity of shock before a fierce rattle of thunder shook the ground. The boy stumbled backwards, tripped over an exposed root, and fell flat-backed into a deep puddle. Water splashed up all over him. Soaking wet, he sat deflated in his own little lake of self-pity.

Another rumble of thunder crackled across the countryside. This rumble, however, did not fade away like the other one; instead it lingered. The boy felt small tremors vibrate through the ground all around him. There was a definite rhythm and patter to the thudding. He noticed ripples traveling through the pool of water that he sat in.

He pulled himself from the puddle and stood still, hoping to hear where the sound was coming from. The heavily falling rains and crashes of thunder all around him made it difficult to ascertain the direction from which the static thumping originated. He took a few footsteps further into the thicket. The pulsating tremors seemed to be getting stronger with each step. But beneath the din, intriguing new noises met his ears. The boy swore he heard the subtle *dink* of chains swaying in the wind along with random snapping sounds like miniature thunder claps.

Moving further from the village, the boy began to feel a bit uneasy. Though he knew he should be heading back in this foul storm, he found himself compelled to move toward the source of the tremors. Coming upon the other side of the thicket, the images he witnessed made him gasp. He covered his mouth with his hands to muffle himself. The boy dropped to a crouching position behind a few sparse bushes to peer between the branches.

Through the cold, driving rain he watched a long line of giant creatures being led on chains by a host of men. The rain falling in his eyes made it difficult to see just what the creatures were. He shielded his eyes against the onslaught of rain with his hand to get a better, unobstructed view. He had never seen anything like them before. Each of the creatures was as tall as four men and about half as long as a modest sized karvi. Golden scales covered them from their snout to the tip of their tail. Their undersides appeared to be covered with a softer manner of flesh, whitish-pink in hue and arranged in horizontal bands. Bony appendages protruded along the length of their spines like some kind of giant armored lizard. But it was their large wings, bound by massive entanglements of chain, which made these creatures quite amazing in the boy's mind.

The thrashing crack of a whip drew his attention back to the men who urged them northward along the muddied road. The barking of harsh words accompanied each thrash of the leathery weapons. They looked like masters driving cattle. They traveled along the highway that ran the length of the island, moving northwards away from the harbor at Gotland's southernmost tip. The boy watched as the long line marched past him. He could hardly believe what he was seeing, but he knew he was not imagining things. The procession seemed to go on for quite a while. At one point, he gazed up and down the length of the road and saw nothing but the bizarre parade.

Another bolt of fierce lightning cleaved the sky into shards. A deafening boom filled the air as wind rushed to fill the vacuum left behind by the bolt. The boy flinched back fearfully, not knowing what direction was safest. He scanned his surroundings, looking for an area that might provide enough safety from the storm to allow him to watch the mysterious procession. Yet, there was no safe ground to be found other than the sheltering walls of the village. Ignoring the danger, he decided to hunker down and watch, despite the danger.

A deadly exclamation point, however, marked the end of his stoic perseverance in the storm. Just as he was about to settle himself into a crouch, a knotty pine to his right became the unfortunate target of a humming bolt of lightning. The tree's trunk split in two with a terrifying crack. Flame burst from the torn timbers, and shards of scorched wood exploded into the grass and underbrush. The flash of light lit up the thicket as if a thousand suns shined upon it.

The boy screamed in anguish as the black-on-white silhouetted image of a shattered tree burned at the back of his eyes. He spun away from the incandescent glow and rubbed at his eyes furiously to drive out the pain, but it would not subside. Another exposed root caught his ankle and he tumbled backwards, splashing down in a puddle of mud. He scrambled to his feet and groped his way to the nearest tree. Taking a few deep breaths, he waited for his sight to clear. Through his blindness, he began to see enough of the world again to discern the outline of the village. Slipping and sliding in the soft earth, he made his way back to the safety of Falterton.

7

Seamus drove his massive flippers against the salty seawater of the Baltic. Waves splashed along his sides and onto the draped legs of the queasy, lethargic dragon slumped over his back. Having never sailed or journeyed by water before, Fenicus found it difficult to keep down the handfuls of fresh fish that he had eaten earlier in the day. It was the up and down, chopping motion of the sea that made his insides churn. With every bob of Seamus's long form, Fenicus felt the urge to throw up, but he fought hard to keep it down. Sitting there, he felt chunks of food trickle up his esophagus, which he swallowed down behind tightly clenched teeth. A caustic burning from stomach acid itched at the back of his throat. He let his jaw hang agape and breathed deeply through his mouth. The cool sea air offered a bit of relief. To his surprise, a bubble of air rose from his stomach and pursed his lips in a spasmodic burp. The released air brought even more relief to Fenicus. He carelessly began gulping down huge breaths of air, hoping to replicate the effect of the first burp. After a few tiny expulsions of air, Fenicus sensed the presence of a massive air pocket trapped in his stomach, waiting to come up. Opening his mouth as wide as possible, he pressed the air from his belly. What came up this time was not air but a river of half-digested food. It splashed squarely across Seamus's back.

"What was that?" Seamus inquired with a rather annoyed tone. He looked back at Fenicus, but the young dragon did not answer.

Fenicus looked around for a solution to his embarrassing predicament. He tried wiping it away with his hands, but that only seemed to spread out the mess. Unsure of how to tell his friend what happened, he uttered a few more unclear responses. Then he remembered that he was surrounded by millions of gallons of seawater. Using his thigh muscles to hold onto the whale's back, Fenicus reached his hands into the water and scooped a few handfuls onto Seamus, washing away the frothy mess.

"Is there a problem?" Seamus asked. He slowed in his pace as he waited for a response.

"No problem. You just had a dry spot. I think you've been out of the water too long."

"You're right, lad. Hold on!" Without giving Fenicus a chance to brace himself, Seamus dove beneath the waves, dragging his reluctant passenger with him.

"Oh, no!" Fenicus screamed as the salty water filled his mouth. Seamus barrel-rolled beneath the surface. All the young dragon could do was hold on for dear life. Seamus finally rose back to the surface.

Back above water, Fenicus slid down Seamus's right side. He groped for a handhold and narrowly grabbed onto the whale's right flipper, his bottom half wading in the sea. Seamus looked back at the seasick dragon drooping over his limb.

"Next time yer gonna heave," Seamus commented, "don't do it on me back."

Another rush of air pressed itself up Fenicus's throat as he tried to answer. "No problem." A gurgling burp eked from his mouth.

"If your havin' such a hard time, why don't you fly fer a bit?"

Fenicus nodded his head in agreement. "Good idea."

Flaring his wings, Fenicus caught a sea breeze and lifted into the air. Back in his natural environment, the sickening feeling swirling within his stomach subsided. Looking down upon his traveling companion and not preoccupied by sickness, Fenicus thought about Seamus and how, like himself, he seemed alone in a vast world.

"Seamus?"

A plume of water shot from the whale's blowhole and fell as mist upon Fenicus. "Yeah, lad?"

"Where's your family?"

Seamus's large brown eyes fell away from Fenicus and toward the water where his gaze lingered. "They're gone," he answered sadly.

"I'm sorry."

"Ach." Seamus waved off Fenicus's sympathetic remark with a flap of his flipper. "It's okay. I've been on me own now fer a few years, ever since I was weaned. Before that it was just me and me mum since I came into this world. We humpbacks aren't all that social, if you catch me drift. We like it that way."

"Really?" It was a concept Fenicus struggled to understand. In a world so large, he couldn't fathom living alone and being happy about it. But Seamus's matter-of-fact attitude made him realize that not all species valued family and camaraderie as much as the dragons had come to value it in the centuries following their exile. *It must be a terribly lonely life*, he thought of his new friend's existence.

"Absolutely. I was actually on me way to find meself a mate when I got hung up on that shore." Seamus blew another shower of water through his blowhole and rolled his eyes. "Me mum warned me about gettin' too curious to human tinkerings. I think she was more worried 'bout me being caught by one of them big hunting ships rather than getting stuck ashore though." Seamus laughed and then looked to Fenicus flying just above him. "But I'd hate to think where I'd be without yer help."

Fenicus smiled back at his friend, which said everything that needed saying.

With a keen eye on the horizon of seemingly endless blue, Fenicus realized a distinct change come over the seascape; several broad masses of land came into view. It was the first time he had seen land in at least a day. Fenicus started to feel some of the darkness that had surrounded his heart dissipate. If Seamus was correct that the boats that abducted the other dragons came from this region, then there was a real chance that he might be able to find them and set them free.

"Thank you, Seamus."

"Fer what, lad?" Seamus asked, seemingly confused.

"For what? I'd never have made it this far without you. I'd still be sitting on that beach feeling sorry for myself. If you're right about this place, I'll be able to set things right."

"Aye, but don't get ahead of yourself," Seamus stressed. "Finding land is one thing, finding those ships is another. You still have a long journey before you. Which reminds me that this is about as far as I can go."

Suddenly, a new sorrow washed over Fenicus. Though he had known Seamus for little more than a day, the humpback was his first friend that wasn't a dragon, and he wasn't ready to say good-bye. Yet, he understood that this dilemma was his responsibility to shoulder, and Fenicus had taken up enough of this kind creature's time.

"I'll never forget what you've done for me." Fenicus flew down to the surface of the water and rubbed his hand on Seamus's head in big circles right behind his eye.

"Me sentiments exactly." Seamus grinned.

"Good luck, Seamus. I hope we meet again someday." He patted him a few times in the spot he was rubbing and then rose up a bit in the air directly in front of the whale. "Take care," Fenicus bid his new friend as he took off.

Flapping his wings, Fenicus flew toward the landmass that accented the horizon. As he drew closer, he saw that it was in fact several bodies of land that fell across the sea like giant claw marks. Though his mind was focused on searching for his family, a nagging, worrisome feeling pecked away at his brain, eager to be noticed. He tried to shake it off, but it persisted nevertheless.

Pulling up and rounding about on the open sea, Fenicus hovered in place. He searched the surface of the water for Seamus, worried that things weren't well with his new friend. The setting sun in the west reflected off of the sea, which made it very hard to discern waves from a wet whale. Squinting to peer through the glare of the setting sun on the water, Fenicus barely noticed the form of his friend plodding westward. Seamus was still in one piece. He shook his head, feeling foolish for thinking such stupid thoughts.

When he turned to resume his course, however, Fenicus caught sight of something unfamiliar that appeared to be trailing Seamus from a distance. Zeroing in on it with the eyes of a hunter, he quickly surmised that the object was a manmade, seafaring vessel of some sort. It looked amazingly sleek in comparison to the ships that Seamus described. It possessed a narrow beam and keel that allowed the vessel to slice through the water without generating much wake. It glided along, gaining on Seamus quickly. Several men moved about the ship, adjusting the sails and moving about the deck in a state of excitement. And it was the men at the bow of the ship that caught Fenicus's attention. It was not the ship itself that posed danger to Seamus but an oversized, crossbow-like weapon at its bow. The man who operated it took a long, tethered harpoon and affixed it to a slot on the top of the weapon. He was preparing to fire it at Seamus.

Fenicus now knew that the bells and whistles chiming off in his head were not false alarms. This crisis, unlike when he discovered his village in shambles and his people missing, did not drive him to tears or fear. One thought surged within Fenicus's mind—fight. Adrenaline rushed through his body in preparation for combat. Snorting a dense cloud of black smoke, he flared his wings and raced full force in the direction of the threatening ship. Banking hard to his right, Fenicus set himself into a downward, sweeping dive on an intercepting course with the vessel.

With a thud the harpoon fired through the air. Its braided tether hissed in its wake. Fenicus traced the weapon's arc as he closed in on Seamus; it was a perfectly targeted volley. He cut across its path and hovered between his friend and the vessel, casting a shadow across Seamus. The humpback came about with a slap of his tailfin as Fenicus caught the harpoon in midair. The deadly projectile meant to take the whale's life sat clutched in the young dragon's hand. Seamus watched with slackjawed awe.

The rhythmic fluttering of Fenicus's wings blew gusts of air at the hull of the vessel making it tip and sway awkwardly on its side. Its crew, alarmed by the sudden and unexpected presence of the dragon, attempted to come about and escape. Fenicus leered at the ship with an devilish grimace etched upon his face. With one swift motion, Fenicus snapped the harpoon in two under his thumb as though it were nothing more than a matchstick. He let the roped end of the weapon fall away into the water and flipped around the tipped end so it sat in his hand like an oversized dart.

Rearing back, Fenicus unleashed the tip of the harpoon with all his fury directly at the ship's hull, just below the waterline. It shattered through several strakes. The ship rocked unsteadily as it started to take on water. Fenicus and Seamus watched as the humans abandoned the sinking vessel.

To emphasize his message to the heartless crew, Fenicus landed on the doomed ship and began dismantling it, tossing pieces of it at the men in the water. He bit right through the mast, snapping it in half. His claws ripped through the hoisted sails, shredding them into ribbons. His tail smashed downwards through the deck and then swung powerfully from side to side, decimating the gunwale into splintered shards. Enjoying the moment, Fenicus put on a show. The dragon beat at his puffed chest with balled fists, roaring a bloodcurdling war cry. His victims screamed wildly as they swam toward the shore.

With his friend's life no longer in danger, Fenicus's anger subsided. He lifted off into the air again just before the vessel vanished below the surface of the sea. Fenicus laughed uproariously at the humans. "Look at 'em go, Seamus. Not so tough, are they?"

"Glad yer on me side, Fenicus."

The whale's voice turned Fenicus around. He was glad to see his friend alive and well.

"Thank you. Looks like I owe you again."

"No repayment this time, Seamus," Fenicus answered, waving him off of another debt. "Friends have got to look after one another."

"Your family'd be proud of you, you know, for what you

did today."

"Thanks, Seamus." Suddenly, Fenicus thought about his mother, father, and sister. Somewhere they waited to be rescued along with the rest of his kin. Having now confronted mankind by himself and succeeded, he believed that if he could somehow find his friends and family, he could set them free. After all, he saved Seamus just in time. But could he get to them before it was too late?

"Well, on your way, Fenicus. Yer family's waiting fer you."

"Are you sure you're all right?"

"Aye. Best ye go now." Seamus waved him off with his flipper.

Fenicus bid his friend a final farewell with a simple nod and resumed his trek toward the islands to the north. Though he doubted he would ever see Seamus again, the young dragon felt that he had made a valuable friend he would always cherish.

*　　*　　*

Beneath the waning sunlight, Fenicus maintained a low flight path over the sea, skimming over the surface of the water. As he came around the southeastern tip of one of the long, finger-shaped landmasses that broke up the expanse of blue water, his eyes scanned the shorelines for any signs of the seagoing vessels described to him by Seamus; he knew that they were much larger that the whaler he destroyed, possessed several tall masts with massive sails, and their bows were adorned with the figurehead of a howling wolf.

The sun fell below the horizon, leaving the land in shadow. Fenicus did not mind this one bit. With nighttime falling upon the land, there would be few humans out and about. He could fly along the coast unnoticed under the soft glow of the moon.

For hours he searched unsuccessfully. Along the way he examined hundreds of watertight vessels, none of which fit the size parameters or description that Seamus offered. The majority of the ships he found had only one mast that carried a single sail made up of vertical panels sewn together. And most of the ships' figureheads were wooden carvings of human women and sirens. But there were no wolves.

Fatigue came upon Fenicus as the night wore on under a cloudless sky. The desire to sleep pressed down upon him like a landslide of stone. Though he wanted to continue on, the day's events left him with insufficient reserves of strength to push on much farther. Desperate for a place to settle down and rest for the night, his attention fell upon a modest island to the east where a bank of thick clouds spewed forth a maelstrom of rain, wind, and deadly lightning that illuminated the landscape. At the southernmost tip of the island, he could make out a harbor where several seaworthy ships bobbed in the tide. Figuring he could exhaust one more possibility before resting for the night, Fenicus broke from his coastal flight pattern and headed toward this new island.

The stars in the night sky flickered wildly around the moon, lighting Fenicus's way. Nearing the ships, he coasted in quietly and set down gently upon the dock. The wild storm that tore through the land still rumbled to the north, but it had long since left the island's southern coastline.

Around him were seven ships secured to the tie-downs along the length of the dock. These ships were drastically different in shape and size from the whaler he encountered earlier that day. These ships looked like they were designed for hauling large loads of cargo.

Fenicus looked at the ship to his left. *Check the figurehead.* Moving carefully toward the bow of the ship, his foot cracked against something hard that protruded from the deck. Fenicus crumpled to his knees and grabbed his stubbed toes. He gritted his teeth and tried to massage away the pain. Slowly, the pain faded to a dull throb and he got back to his feet. Looking down, he found the object he tripped over; a plank that connected the dock to the main deck. Checking to see that no one heard his little accident, Fenicus followed the dock the rest of the way until he stood beside the bow of the ship. There before him, carved out of a single piece of wood, hung the figurehead. The light slap of seawater against the hulls of the ships and the subtle creaking of their timbers echoed in his ears as the ship rose and fell gently with the ebb of the tide. Fenicus stared at the figurehead, trying to make out its shape in the blue moonlight. His eyes grew wide and he pulled loose the ring he had placed upon his tooth. Holding up its flat side so that it could be compared side-by-side with the carving upon the bow, he concluded that the two figures were identical. Each one showed the visage of a wolf.

"Yes!" he called out excitedly. Fenicus quickly clapped his hand over his mouth, momentarily forgetting himself and his situation. He hunched down and scanned the rest of the harbor for signs of movement. His ears listened for the faintest out-of-place sound. Nothing.

Fenicus relaxed his lungs. He breathed out a breath he didn't realize he was holding and shook his head. *Idiot.*

Even though he knew his friends and family were somewhere on this island and he knew he had to head inland to find them, morbid curiosity caused him to focus his attention on the ship itself. Backtracking along the deck, he relocated the gangplank that led to the main deck, and he climbed up. Upon first inspection, the main deck didn't offer much in the way of satisfying his curiosity. Three large sails, like the ones described by Seamus, sat furled upon the masts. A wooden railing encircled the entire deck. Glancing up the deck toward the bow, he noticed a dark hole that appeared to lead to a lower deck in the flooring near the forward mast. Fenicus approached the opening. Standing beside it, the opening was in fact a stairwell leading down, but it was far too small for him to squeeze himself into.

"I'm not getting down that way." Fenicus sighed. Turning around, he moved in the direction of the stern and examined the deck as he walked. He strained his eyes in the poor lighting trying to find another way to get below deck. If these were indeed the ships that carried his people away, he knew there had to be another way to get into the cargo hold.

As he reached the rear mast, Fenicus saw a series of ropes rigged to pulleys. Each rope rose upward, threaded through another wooden pulley attached to the mast, and then fastened to the corner of a wooden platform that rested upon the deck. Next to the platform were two long doors built into the floorboards with two iron handles affixed along the sides of each. The size of the handles surprised Fenicus when he reached down to grab them. They were so small he could barely slip a single finger into the gap to grab it. He was not used to the size of humans relative to himself. Still, he worked the tip of a talon beneath one handle on each door and swung them open, revealing the lower deck. From within, a dim light illuminated the chamber below. Placing his hands upon the doorframe, he lowered his head inside the opening. A few weakly burning lanterns remained to light an enormous lower deck. It most definitely had enough room inside to transport numerous dragons. But how would he get down there?

Then Fenicus remembered the platform lying next to him on the ground. It seemed just the right size to be lowered into the opening. For a moment he inspected the rope and pulley apparatus attached to it. Fenicus surmised that the humans might have used the ropes to lower each dragon into the hold below. Knowing how much he weighed (never mind an adult dragon), it must have taken four or five men on each rope to operate the lift.

Gathering up all four of the ropes into his hands, Fenicus stepped onto the platform and tugged at them. With little effort on his part, the platform rose a few feet into the air and swung over the opening. "Hmm." He grunted and looked up at the clunking parts of the lift. "Smart little buggers."

Letting the rope slide slowly through his hands, Fenicus lowered himself to the next deck. The platform touched down with a thud. He hopped down from the platform and examined the cargo hold. Bolted to the very framework of the vessel were chains and shackles far too large to hold any human. Their locking mechanisms lay open. With each step, Fenicus's mind flooded with visions of what it must have been like to be trapped in here, chained up like some kind of wild animal or slave, not knowing if you'd ever see your home again or how the ordeal would end.

Fenicus stopped moving and leaned against a support beam where a pair of shackles hung. He then knelt down and examined the pair. Taking hold of one cuff, he laid it over his hand and started to close it. The scratchy feel of the cold iron against his wrist and the sharp edge biting into his scales enraged him. The shackle fell to the deck with a loud clunk. Rising to his feet and turning about, he slammed his fist against the hull. Loud thuds filled the cavernous belly of the ship with each punch. Having worn his knuckles raw, he stumbled backward and fell against the same support, his fists clenched. When his feet settled below him, they landed in something sticky and wet. Fenicus pulled a lantern from an overhead hook and held it close to the puddle. It was a thick, dark green liquid. Dipping his finger into it and drawing it up to his nose to inhale its scent, the little flame that began to flicker in his chest back in Berathor suddenly grew a little brighter. The puddle of liquid was blood—dragon blood. He now understood that this was no longer just about rescuing his family and his species; to him it was war. Feelings sparked off inside of him that he never knew existed. The rage that welled within him fought to loosen itself upon every human he could find. Smoke bellowed from his nostrils. His heart beat in his chest like a war drum.

Never judge a species by an individual. Uncle Balthazar's words fought to reason with him. His uncle preached that idea to him many years ago when he asked why the dragons didn't just wipe out the human race. As much as humans had done to their species, they weren't all evil. They were words Fenicus didn't want to listen to at that moment. All he wanted was to rip every human he could find to shreds. Fenicus had always believed they were inherently evil, and he'd seen nothing in the last few days to make him believe otherwise.

Using the lift to bring himself back to the main deck, Fenicus followed the gangplank back down to the dock and headed inland. A muddied road met his feet when he stepped down from the dock. Still weary and no longer possessing enough energy for flight, he dropped to all fours and followed the road in search of somewhere to rest. The long walk north seemed to lead him through relatively flat country. Some hills and valleys broke the monotony of his journey, but it was otherwise unremarkable country. Every once in a while, however, he saw the faint glow of candlelight coming from a human dwelling.

Unable to keep his eyes open any longer, Fenicus found a thicket of trees dense enough and big enough to protect him from view while he slept. Though it was a little too close to a human village for his liking, it would have to do for the night. He was too tired to find a truly suitable hiding spot. He stumbled through several bushes and over small trees which snapped underfoot. He winced with each sound, worried it may rouse nearby humans from their slumber. Within he found that most of the ground was sopping wet from the night's storms. There were large puddles everywhere he looked. Having found a relatively dry patch of ground, Fenicus collapsed upon the damp loam and fell fast asleep.

8

A single, unyielding bead of water hung from a wooden support rafter that stretched across a cavernous underground chamber. More water gathered to its cause, seeping through the saturated soil while pouring rains pelted the land above. The bead of water got larger and larger until it gave in to the pull of gravity and plummeted toward the ground. The drop of water fell headlong into a bucket of collected rainwater with a plunk, sending subtle sound waves through the underground chamber. It bounced from timber to timber, wall to wall, eventually striking the eardrums of the chamber's reluctant prisoners. The reverberations acted like an antidote to the charm that lay upon their minds.

Farimus Flint's eyelids creaked open. His eyesight was

much like trying to peer through a heavy fog. All aspects of the room around him seemed covered in a fuzzy light. The deadening fatigue that lingered in his mind and limbs made him feel as though he had slept for ages. But his stomach, only suffering from mild pangs of hunger, told him it had not been so long since his last meal. Farimus blinked his eyes. Slowly, his vision cleared.

Farimus was not alone; all around him were the other adult dragons, bound and chained, whom survived the assault on Berathor. Most of them did not stir. A few, like Farimus, seemed to be awakening from their slumber. Whispering voices, unintelligible mumbles, and agonized moans bounced oddly through the poorly lit chamber.

The cold, damp floor beneath his body gave Farimus chills. His eyes scanned the length of the floor he knelt upon. Hundreds of flat, square stones covered the soft ground.

Tssss!

The odd sound attracted the dragon's attention. His eyes fell upon a dimly burning torch that hung upon the nearest wall. Its bracket appeared to be fashioned out of finely polished brass. The drops of water that flowed through the ceiling's rafters struck the flaming tip of the torch, making it hiss and smolder but not extinguish. The rest of the chamber possessed numerous torches and brackets of the same fashion.

Wanting to rise from his kneeling posture, Farimus tried to pull his hands around to his front only to find he couldn't move them. Craning his neck around to his backside, he found that a pair of shackles had his arms bound at the wrists. Another length of chain anchored him to the floor. Anger bubbled up inside Farimus. He heaved at his fetters, hoping to wrench the chain free from the floor, but the anchor held strong. Again and again Farimus jerked the chain, using what limited strength he could rally to his cause, but none of his efforts caused the anchor to shudder in the slightest. The bubbling inside Farimus turned to rage and he filled the chamber with a blood-curdling roar, which roused the other incapacitated dragons from their slumber.

The shouting voice of instinct inside his head urged him to take flight, to escape his imprisonment. The muscles and tendons that spanned his upper back flexed beneath his scales, trying to unfurl his tucked up wings, but nothing happened. Frantic, he turned his head left and right to find the nearest dragon. Farimus immediately found Balthazar nearby, pressing himself against the wall for leverage as he struggled to right himself. His vision locked on the simple workings of the fetters that encircled his brother-in-law's wings. Shackles, similar in fashion to those that held his own wrists immobile, encircled the muscle-covered humerus bones that extended from both of Balthazar's shoulders to his wings. A short length of chain linked the two bindings together. Attached to that chain was another shackle that held his tail in a fully upright position, disabling the limb completely.

Whoever had imprisoned them in this chamber did their best to neutralize every natural weapon they possessed. Every weapon but the most important one—fire breath. Farimus sneered savagely as he clenched his jaw, urging his internal temperature to rise. All his thoughts centered on lighting the entire chamber ablaze. In his mind he envisioned each timber crackling under the stress of a great conflagration, the very flames licking their hot tongues at the wood before biting into them. Farimus, strangely enough, could not feel the heat of his internal furnace warming the blood within his veins. As hard as he tried, his blood remained cool, unable to superheat the air in his lungs to the point of incineration.

"Arggg!" Farimus blared.

Drained of energy and feeling defeated, Farimus collapsed against the cool stonework. The clank of a previously unnoticed shackle caught his attention. This fetter encircled his neck, yet it had no length of chain attached to it. Since it was not tight enough to choke him, it seemed to serve no other purpose than a simple adornment. Glancing about, he found that the other dragons all wore the same type of fitting. Bending and flexing his neck at all angles, Farimus tried to inspect the shackle, but he could not get a good look at it.

"They're enchanted," Balthazar announced.

Farimus whipped his head around to his brother-in-law. "What are?"

"That iron band around your neck. They've got some sort of extinguishing spell on them."

Farimus gave Balthazar a sideways glance. "How do you know?"

"Can you breathe fire?" he asked sarcastically. "No one can. It's also the reason why you don't feel its weight."

"Can you do anything to break the spell?"

"I don't think so. I tried a couple of things and nothing

seems to help." Balthazar shook his head. "It's wizardry well beyond my skills." A worried look overcame him as he seemed to fall deep in thought.

"What's wrong?"

Balthazar snapped out of his momentary quizzical stare. "I didn't think there were any wizards left among the humans. We wiped them out before we went into exile. I've got a bad feeling about this."

Farimus clenched his jaw. Mariel's brother was the foremost authority on history and magic, and his concerns struck Farimus hard. He could not recall how they got to where they were, let alone how the battle of Berathor ended. All he knew was that it appeared as though all the adult dragons sat imprisoned in this chamber. To have accomplished such a feat, whoever was responsible for their imprisonment was not to be trifled with.

All the *adult* dragons. The words shot through Farimus's head. Where were their children? A dread panic surged within. Horrifying possibilities swam through his mind. All he could think of was the safety of Fenicus and Ariel. Sitting back on his heels and stretching his neck as high as he could, he called out to Mariel.

"Farimus?" a weakened voice answered from across the length of the chamber. "Where are you?"

Her tired eyes met his. A little weight lifted from his heart, but not all of it. "Where are the children?"

"I don't know," she cried back. "I tried to protect Ariel, but she collapsed in front of me. I remember reaching out for her and then everything went black."

"What about Fenicus?"

Mariel shook her head, her shoulders bobbing with the motion of her sobs. She did not answer back.

Angry, Farimus repeatedly muttered *no* to himself.

"No one knows what happened to them?" Balthazar pleaded with the rest of their number as he looked upon his forlorn brother-in-law. No answer came forth.

The creak of greaseless door hinges emanated from behind Farimus. All the dragons within earshot contorted their arrested frames to glance in the direction of the disturbance. Many of their number gasped audibly as a human man dressed in a white blouse and brown trousers passed through an open pair of double doors at the far end of the chamber. Around his shoulders he wore a cape crafted out of animal fur. Brown leather boots covered his feet. The cheekbones of his face were carefully etched as if chipped from stone by a master sculptor. His pin-straight blond hair hung to his shoulders, and he wore a carefully trimmed goatee of the same brilliant color.

Two other humans followed behind him and took positions at opposite sides of the doorway. Each of them brandished a long, dangerous looking polearm that they held pointing upward with the butt of the weapon resting against the ground. The hair of the two men appeared to have many snags and snarls unlike the first human's finely groomed look. Each man wore a grimy white kirtle that lay tucked beneath baggy black trousers at the waist. Frayed, brown leather belts held their trousers tight to their hips. Crude animal hide boots covered their feet and rode all the way up their calves to just below the knee.

The blond-haired man moved along a portion of the

floor stonework cast in tan rock rather than the gray stone the dragons rested on. As he traversed the walkway, the dragons around him lashed forward to the extent of their leashes and snapped their toothy jaws at him. All attempts fell just short of their target. Nearing the end of the tan stones, he called out, "So, how are my guests feeling today?" He spoke to the dragons in their native tongue.

Farimus and Balthazar cast confused glances at one another. The chamber was alive with chatter.

"No human can speak our language," Farimus grumbled at the human.

Turning to face Farimus who knelt a short distance away, the man looked him up and down.

"A foolish assumption." The man spoke down to Farimus as if he were a dog. "Clearly, I'm speaking your language. Your race apparently didn't get any smarter over the past four hundred years, did it?"

The man's scathing tone infuriated Farimus. He thrashed at the man in vain, stretching his anchor chain taut and baring his teeth. A loud hiss escaped his lips. The man looked with a childish curiosity at the dragon whose jaws snapped in his face.

Unable to break the tether of chain restraining him, Farimus recoiled back onto his haunches. "What's the meaning of this?" he shouted. "Why have you brought us here?"

"You're in no position to ask questions, dragon. If you want to see your precious children again, you'll do exactly what I tell you."

The weight of his words fell squarely upon Farimus.

When he first realized that their young stood unaccounted for, Farimus had hoped that the children had escaped capture and fled to the Golden Vale, the last human-free region on Earth. But at hearing this human's words, those hopes were dashed. The anger within Farimus grew ten-fold. "What have you done with them? If you've hurt them I'll..."

"You'll what?" The human cackled. "I've taken away every weapon you possess. No fire-breath, no claws." His eyes broke from Farimus to glance at the edge of the tan colored stones and then pointedly back to the dragon. "And you can gnash your foul teeth at me all you want, but you'll never reach me." He smiled wryly at Farimus. "To put it plainly, your children are my hostages."

"What makes you think you can get anything out of us by threatening our children?" Balthazar inquired coolly.

The blond-haired man rounded on Balthazar. His words were quick and boastful. "I've spent my entire life studying your species: every legend, every myth, every artifact. Eventually, all the pieces of the puzzle fit together, and now I know everything. It's how I discovered your precious valley, and it's how I know that the safety of your children is paramount to your species' survival. Without them, you have no future."

Balthazar looked at Farimus. The helpless grimace on his face said everything. They were at his mercy. Farimus acquiesced for the moment. "What do you want from us?"

"Ah," the human said, clasping his hands together. His tone calmed and his talking pace slowed. "What do I want from you?" He paused as though in deep thought and smoothed his goatee with his fingers. Then he began to pace across the end of the tanned stone path. "Well, it's very simple. When your kind turned tail and fled into hiding four hundred years ago, you left behind massive collections of golden ore and coin for which you have no use."

Farimus felt the urge to address the man's misinformation, but a wide-eyed glance from Balthazar warned him off. "Get to the point already," he snapped at the man.

"I was content to leave your pestilent race alone in your little enclave, hoping that I could find your abandoned gold stores. But when my men failed to locate them, I had no choice but to bring you here." The man stopped pacing. "Tell me where you've hidden your gold, and I'll send you back where you belong."

From behind Farimus, a new voice spoke out. "Who are you?" Galadorn, the eldest dragon left on Earth, interjected. All the other dragons bowed their heads when he spoke. Though he was not their king, he still commanded great respect from the entire community.

Without pause or hesitation, the man rendered his answer. "I am Kell, son of Aaron, Chieftain of Gotland. I serve as protector and leader to those who serve me." Kell moved slightly from side-to-side, trying to find the dragon who spoke. "Who are you?"

"My name is Galadorn." The venerable old dragon rose to his full height, standing proudly in bondage as if no chains could ever hold him captive. A sense of dignity exuded from him. "I speak on behalf of my kind."

"So you're their leader." Kell spoke so low that his voice was nearly inaudible. "Good, you'll answer me then. Where's the gold?"

Galadorn shook his head. "Not so fast. What do you need gold for? Are you just another greedy human bent on thievery and a lust for riches?"

Kell's frame stiffened. He combed his fingers through his hair. "This has nothing to do with lust or greed. My people are lost, leaderless. Centuries of tribal warfare have torn us apart. If we aren't killing each other to allay the boredom of life and increase our plunder, then we're trying to satisfy thankless gods who give nothing back in return. My people need someone to lead them, someone to point them in the right direction. Your gold will allow me to do that."

"How?" Galadorn scoffed. "Gold isn't power."

"Maybe not in your world, dragon," Kell argued back, "but it is in mine. I've already gathered many warriors to my cause by offering them hope and something real to fight for. They recognize true leadership. But the others, their allegiance can be bought for the most part, especially in these dark times when day-to-day survival is so uncertain. Your gold will allow me to gather them to my banner, helping to unite our clans under one leader and stop the mindless bloodshed. We'll finally be at peace."

Galadorn narrowed his eyes and said, "A noble cause, I suppose. But you insinuated that most men can be bought. What about the others?"

Kell shrugged his shoulders, seemingly quite aloof. "Those who can't be reasoned with or bribed can only be swayed by a show of strength. With superior numbers, no one will be able to oppose my rule. The fools who try will be crushed."

Balthazar snorted. "So you'll use more violence to end the violence? Such hypocrisy."

"Balthazar," Galadorn barked, silencing the historian.

Balthazar looked to Farimus and Mariel, but their eyes fell away from his stare immediately. He slumped to the floor and curled up into himself as best he could.

Galadorn turned his attention back to the human. "Did you ever consider that the reason you never found our old gold was because others of your kind had already plundered it by now? That's probably why your men never found it. It was likely the same men whom broke our treaty and tried to wipe us out." Galadorn narrowed his eyes and stared at Kell in disgust. "Men just like you."

"Let me make one thing very clear," Kell interjected. He pointed a single, emphatic finger at his accuser. "I'm nothing like those who dishonored the treaty." His tone and body language shifted abruptly to one noticeably more subdued and diplomatic. "I'm doing this for my people, nothing more."

The wily old dragon needled him further. "If your cause is so noble, why didn't you come and ask for our help instead of attacking us without provocation?"

Kell nodded. "True, I could've come and asked for your help, but given the history between our two races, would you have listened?"

"So you assume your only recourse is through conquest?" Galadorn asked sharply. "We hid ourselves for a reason. All we wanted was to live in peace, out of the way of mankind. But you couldn't leave well enough alone, could you?"

"You didn't answer my question, dragon."

"To be quite honest, I can't guarantee that we would've helped you had you come to us. But by resorting to the methods you've chosen, I find it hard to see any reason why we should help you, even if we had the gold you claim we have."

Kell scratched his head for a few seconds. "The way I see it, I don't think you have much of a choice in the matter. Tell me, how often do dragons reproduce, every two hundred years or so? Being a species struggling to survive, do you really think you can afford to risk the lives of your children?"

"So you're telling me that if we don't comply with your wishes that you'll murder our young?" the great dragon questioned, a look of fear upon his worn face.

"Your children are your greatest weakness. If I need to expose that in order to bring peace to my people, then I'll do so without reservation. I leave the decision up to you. But know this—if you don't help us, I'll drag your precious children in here one-by-one and slaughter them before your very eyes until you see things my way."

"You vile, despicable coward!" Galadorn shouted, finally unable to maintain his own diplomatic posturing.

"I give you one day to make your decision. After that, I'll waste no time showing you just how serious I am." The human whirled about on his heels and started for the dungeon entrance. Just before he took his leave of them, he paused and turned back toward his captives. "One day!"

Standing between the two doorway guards, Kell whispered to them. Finished speaking, he passed by them and into the same passageway from which he came. The two guards followed closely behind him, closing the two doors behind them.

Azriel knelt a few meters to the left of the closed doors. The 207-year-old dragon rubbed his face up and down aggressively upon a few sharp-edged rocks that bulged from the dungeon wall. Flakes of skin drifted through the air to the floor. A wide strip of shed scales along his cheekbones peeled back farther with each pass upon the rocks.

"So now what?" Azriel pondered aloud. "We can't just sit back and let this lunatic hold our young under the knife! The gold he's looking for means nothing to us anymore. We've hidden more than we could ever need back home. We must give in to his demands." When the last syllable left his mouth, he returned to his feverish scratching. Green blood dripped from the raw, irritated flesh and down the wall.

Throughout the dungeon, the other dragons fired back assertions of vehement agreement with Azriel. Soon, the entire chamber filled with booming voices all pleading with Galadorn to make a decision.

"Silence!" Galadorn howled. Everyone obeyed. His powerful voice then grew calm. "I don't intend to let this madman harm our young. My children may be grown and on their own, but I feel as you do." Looking in Azriel's direction, Galadorn nodded to him. "Azriel's right. The gold that we left behind in our warrens is of no use to us anymore. As long as we have Andvari's ring, we have a limitless supply that will sustain us forever."

"But why don't we just give him the damned ring," a dissenting voice leapt from the back of the dungeon. "The dwarf's curse would end his pathetic existence just as it did all its previous owners. Then we can pick it off his carcass and be on our way."

"It's too risky," Balthazar interjected. "If Kell's wise enough to discover our homeland and learn our language, then he may know enough about the ring's curse to use it without incurring its wrath. Then we'd be totally at his mercy."

Many muted murmurs circulated the chamber. When the last sounds died down, Galadorn addressed his flock. "Then it's decided. We give Kell what he wants. But first we must all swear the most sacred of vows. Every one of us, regardless of what happens, must keep the ring and our dependence on gold a secret, even if it means a few of us surrender our lives in the process. While Kell does seem to know a great many things about us, it appears as though he's unaware of our greatest frailty. I fear that if he learns of the ring's location and our need, he'll likely take it and any other gold we've hidden and enslave the lot of us. Besides, if we can escape this place, we can't survive in isolation without that ring. And without isolation, our kind will surely perish."

Once more, all the dragons nodded in agreement. The second point, however, seemed to leave Galadorn's lips with less eagerness.

"Second, if we do manage to find our way to freedom, we

must abandon Berathor Valley and make for the Golden Vale."

An eruption of dissenting voices hit Galadorn's ears.

"Please, everyone!" Galadorn pleaded. "Calm down!"

His words, though, did not quiet the masses. They had the opposite effect. Their voices grew to an angry crescendo.

The voice of Vorgil, the commander of the sentry, erupted over the noisy throng. "Quiet!" He looked around him as the others subjugated their voices in favor of his. "With all due respect, Councilor," he leered at Galadorn, "I believe I speak for a great many when I say that there's no reason for us to leave Berathor. Everything we need to survive is at our fingertips. We have enough food to last ten lifetimes, all the gold we'll ever need, and beauty all around us. It's where most of us were raised, where our children were born, where our elders passed over. We can't abandon it! It's our home!"

The voices thundered again in support of Vorgil's speech.

"Vorgil, even if Kell is telling the truth and sticks to his word, Berathor Valley's no longer safe. Others, maybe even more dangerous than this one, will follow the same steps he took and discover where we're hiding. Sooner or later we'll end up paying the ultimate price for being so shortsighted. Look how easily they conquered us. We must go where we'll be safe. I know it won't be easy for any of us, but we can't afford to call Berathor home anymore. Does that decision meet with everyone's approval?"

Though not a single dragon spoke out against the

decision, the somber faces surrounding him told the story. They were not ready for this contingency. They never thought this moment would ever come. And like anyone forced to leave behind everything that they knew, that they had built with their own hands, the idea was difficult to swallow. But if they had learned anything from being a species on the run, they had to try to survive at all costs.

9

A loud, cackling bird woke Fenicus from his sleep. His puffy, swollen eyelids snapped open. Two bloodshot eyes rolled about in their sockets as they strained to focus on the blurred image before them. The landscape slowly cleared to him, revealing an image of the early morning sun peeking over the horizon. He lay curled up in a ball with his long tail wound around him for warmth. A thin layer of dew rested upon his scales. Though he wanted to close his eyes and drift off to sleep for a few more hours, the existence of a nearby town and a bright, sunny day ahead meant he must forego rest and be on his way before someone found his hiding spot.

He rose lethargically on all fours, not quite awake enough to balance on his hind legs alone. The muscles in his neck and shoulders were stiff from sleeping in such an awkward position all night. He twisted his long neck like a washrag to wring the fatigue from it and get the blood circulating. Loud pops sounded from his vertebrae. Fenicus grabbed hold of a nearby tree with both hands and then rolled his shoulders forward and backwards together. A few more cracks emanated from his back.

Fenicus groaned, feeling some of the tightness and soreness dissipate. He noticed that the nagging ache of his injured wing did not fade with the rest of his soreness. The heavy dose of flying the day before had taken its toll. Walking would once again have to be his primary source of travel.

Fenicus's attention then turned to his empty stomach. Through the wall of his belly, his stomach shouted obscenities of all sorts at him. A sickening feeling rolled over him from a lack of nourishment. He gave the immediate surroundings a quick once-over for something edible at neck's length. There were little more than twigs, grass, and moss littering the floor of this small wooded area, and none of the trees offered any kind of meaningful fruit to satisfy his hunger. Fenicus was out of luck.

He decided to seek better fortunes elsewhere, but just as he was about to move on, a quiet rustle of leaves behind him alerted Fenicus to the presence of something else in the thicket. His cover was blown. Fenicus spun around on his hind legs toward the source of the disturbance, bearing his teeth and claws in an offensive posture. He expected to find a few pitchfork-wielding humans from the town standing behind him. But what he discovered both surprised and dumbfounded him. Covered in dirt from head to toe stood a small human, partially hidden behind a tree. It didn't seem to be too scared by the flashing of Fenicus's teeth and claws. In fact, it seemed more curious than afraid. In a further attempt to scare it off, Fenicus stepped forward hard into the mucky ground and growled toward the small human. The intended result did not occur. Though it drew back behind the tree a bit more, its eyes stayed locked on Fenicus. It remained stoic and unflinching in its posture. This human, Fenicus thought, was either very brave or incredibly stupid.

"Hello," Fenicus said using a common tongue that humans were known to understand. He was unsure of what kind of a response he might induce. The human appeared taken aback by his words and revealed more of its diminutive form from behind the tree. Coming into view, Fenicus noticed that this human's clothes were tattered and quite filthy. The men he assaulted at sea wore garb of a higher quality. They were also not nearly as disheveled as this one. A brief, downwind breeze of the human alerted Fenicus to just how dirty it was. The scaled skin atop his snout furled in response to the unpleasant odor. *Ugg. It smells worse than Dozer!* Fenicus lifted his head well above the height of the human to avoid another wisp of its pungent stench.

Fenicus asked, "Who are you?"

It made painful facial gestures in an effort to speak. The small mouth upon its face opened slightly and then shut several times without speaking a word. Finally, an almost inaudible word squeaked from its lips.

"Malkolm," the human whispered. A certain kind of shyness marked its speech. "My name's Malkolm."

Fenicus hardened his voice and squinted in a cold stare. "Malkolm?" he questioned, having never heard such a strange name before. "What kind of a name is that?"

A few more difficult words stammered forth. "It's a...um...boy's name?" Malkolm didn't seem too sure about his answer.

Fenicus gazed at him curiously. "Are you a child?"

"Yes, I am. What's your name?" Malkolm asked bravely. The dirty boy took a few steps toward Fenicus, showing the dragon how little he feared him.

Fenicus withdrew a bit from the boy, unsure of his intentions. "My name's Fenicus. I am a dr—"

Malkolm interrupted Fenicus. "A dragon!" he shouted.

"Yes." Fenicus found himself fighting the urge to show any kind of emotion toward the human boy. The energy and enthusiasm he showed amused Fenicus. It was quite an exhibition of satiated childhood curiosity.

"Are you a boy or a girl?" Malkolm inquired. He started to walk brisk circles around the dragon, looking him up and down. The boy's curiosity seemed to have no bounds.

Fenicus stood very still while he watched the boy inspect him. He felt secure that Malkolm was far too small to pose any real threat. As far as he could tell there were no other humans in the vicinity either. If this was a trap, it was a well-disguised one. Fenicus answered the boy.

"I'm a male dragon." Fenicus's eyes followed the boy as he moved. *Why isn't he afraid of me? The men on that ship were.* He shook his head, confused. The strange paradox made him a bit uncomfortable. Holding his breath, Fenicus leaned in toward Malkolm. "Aren't you afraid of me, boy?" He turned his head from one side to the other while he stared down the small human, trying to figure out what it was about him that was so different. "Aren't all humans afraid of dragons?"

Malkolm settled down upon a flat rock. His eyes locked on Fenicus in an awestruck expression. "Not at all. Why should I be?"

The boy's response struck a chord with Fenicus. He was right. *Why should he be afraid of me?* Malkolm neither carried any weapons Fenicus could see nor made any kind of threatening gestures against him. Fenicus was beginning to understand that the boy was not stupid, as he previously wondered. He was actually rather brave. In fact, he displayed a kind of purity that puzzled the dragon. The smile that fought to show itself on Fenicus's face could not be denied this time. Fenicus scratched his head as he tried to make sense of this boy. He went against everything Fenicus had ever learned about humans. All the stories his uncle told him were about how humans hated dragons because of their strength, their power, and most of all, their gold. The idea of a human portraying none of these characteristics seemed farfetched. Finally, the most logical reason Fenicus could think of as to why a lone human might fear dragons came to him.

"I'm not sure why you'd be afraid of me other than the possibility that I might eat you." Fenicus leaned closer and smiled. His massive, gleaming teeth reflecting back Malkolm's image.

Malkolm's eyes grew wide. Subtle tremors traveled through him. "You'd eat me?" His breathing shuddered as he spoke. He squirmed away from the dragon's gleaming teeth, moving backwards across the rock. Malkolm fell right off the back into a deep puddle. A wide splash of mud erupted upwards in all directions. Malkolm floundered about in the brown water. Small whimpers came from him.

Fenicus laughed to tears at Malkolm's reaction. Before the boy could run off or hurt himself, Fenicus grabbed onto the back of his shirt with his talons and lifted him out of the mud. The boy screamed, thrashing his arms and legs about. Blood curdling shouts of "Don't eat me!" rang out. What had been humorous for a moment had become a serious problem. Malkolm's screams were loud enough where the townspeople might hear him and come running to his aid. That was the last thing he wanted.

"Shhh!" he whispered nervously to Malkolm. "I'm not going to eat you. Shhh!" Fenicus tried desperately to calm the boy, but he would not relent. Knowing little else to do, Fenicus dropped the boy on the ground. He landed hard on his rump.

"Owww!" Malkolm grabbed at his hindquarters and rubbed vigorously. The ground, though damp from the previous day's rains, was not soft. Numerous tree roots and small rocks littered the ground, and he landed right on top of one. "Wha'did you do that for?" Malkolm whined.

"Sorry." Fenicus felt horrible, but he was glad that the boy stopped yelling. Kneeling down, Fenicus extended a helping hand toward Malkolm. "Are you all right?"

"I don't think anything's broken," Malkolm replied, his

eyes squinting painfully. Water collected in his eyes, yet no tears fell.

"I had to do something. You were yelling your head off and I didn't want company. The last thing I need is a bunch of villagers running after me with pitchforks and swords." Fenicus puffed out a hot breath of relief and dropped down upon the knotty ground. The rocks and roots jabbed painfully at his soft, fleshy rear. An achy snort muttered from Fenicus. "I guess the ground is pretty rough, huh?"

Malkolm nodded. "There isn't anything for you to worry about, by the way."

"What do you mean?"

"With the townspeople. They wouldn't have helped."

"Why not?" Fenicus inquired.

"I'm an orphan."

"An orphan?" The sound of the word was completely foreign to Fenicus. Though the boy's language made sense to him, in his native tongue there was no equivalent word. It sounded like nothing more than garbled noise. "What's an orphan?"

Malkolm stared at the ground. "I don't have a family. I'm all alone."

The second it hit his ears, the idea sounded like the most ridiculous thing that Fenicus had ever heard. "Oh come on, that's crazy." He chuckled. "Who doesn't have parents?" The curt laugh that rumbled in his chest began to fade when the boy's melancholy countenance did not break. His tone grew more serious. "You're kidding, right?" The somber shaking of Malkolm's head gave Fenicus all the answer he needed. "How can that be? Where's your family?"

"I don't know. I never knew them. My mother left me on an old woman's doorstep when I was just a baby. She cared for me until she died, just a few years ago. Once she was gone, there was no one left to take care of me. I've been on my own ever since."

The concept swirled about in Fenicus's mind. Grasping it took every ounce of mental agility he could muster. The idea that this boy's family, his parents, his own flesh and blood could abandon him so heartlessly was a totally alien concept. Since his earliest days, Fenicus's memories were filled with his family and friends always around him and a part of his life. And even those members of his community who lost their family knew they could rely on their neighbors to take care of them in a time of need.

"What about the rest of your village? There's no one else that could take you in?"

"Times are bad for everyone," Malkolm answered very matter-of-factly. "For a while, I begged the old lady's neighbors to help me, but they told me they had a hard enough time getting by on their own and didn't need another mouth to feed."

The bond between mother and father, brother and sister, parents and children, knew no limits in Berathor. Perhaps, Fenicus thought, in his world where life was a precious commodity, being there for one another was of paramount importance for their species to thrive. Unfortunately for Malkolm, life was the least sacred of all gifts in the world of humans. Fenicus felt deep sorrow for this poor boy who knew nothing but loneliness. The sorrow he felt for Malkolm became concern for himself. A sudden, sinking feeling moved through his guts, tearing him down from the inside out. Chills raced along his spine causing him to shiver. Looking at Malkolm and trying to understand his lot in life brought rise to a dreadful realization. If Fenicus should fail in his quest to liberate the others, then he too would suffer the same fate as this boy. While Malkolm lived in a world where he had no family, Fenicus would find himself in a world where he would truly be alone, the last of his kind. The worth of his life quickly came into view. He knew he had to succeed or die trying. A renewed sense of urgency stirred his blood to a boil.

"I'm sorry, but I must be on my way," Fenicus declared. A look of desperation washed over him.

Malkolm watched Fenicus turn and walk away. Then he leapt to his feet and cut off the dragon's path.

"Where are you going?" Malkolm raced around to face Fenicus, but the dragon kept on walking right by him, nearly walking over him in the process. "Are you looking for the other dragons?" The words snapped sharply from his lips. A sudden sense of confidence marked his voice.

Fenicus stopped dead in his tracks. His chest heaved powerfully as adrenaline shot through his body. He snatched up Malkolm in his hand. "You've seen them?" The forlorn grimace that previously sat like a toad on Fenicus's face lifted. An air of optimism, of hope radiated from him. Small butterflies fluttered in the pit of his stomach. "Please tell me you saw them!"

A few nearly inaudible words passed through Malkolm's lips. "I did." His skin was now a deep shade of purple. "You're crushing me," he wheezed.

Taking a good long look at Malkolm, Fenicus realized that the deep purple tone of his skin was no more a natural look for humans than the layer of dirt covering him. He was squeezing the life out of Malkolm in his excitement. Not knowing what else to do, Fenicus unclamped his hands. Once again, Malkolm fell toward the ground.

"Oops!" Fenicus snatched the boy out of the air within inches of him hitting the ground. "Sorry, I got a bit excited." Carefully, he set him back down upon the ground and delicately straightened his ruffled clothes as if he were handling a delicate heirloom.

He found himself in the unenviable position of begging a human, the sworn enemy of his kind, to help him in a moment of need. Fenicus settled on his knees before Malkolm in a subservient posture. Deep down, his instincts told him that this boy was unlike the stereotypical humans that he was warned of since infancy. There was honesty in his eyes and an untainted view of the world. He neither feared nor hated the dragons for being different from himself. There was even a sneaking suspicion threading around the recesses of Fenicus's mind that perhaps humans weren't evil at all. At the very least, something told him that this boy was worthy of his trust and worth the risk.

"Malkolm," Fenicus implored, "where are they?"

"Come with me." Walking around behind Fenicus, Malkolm broke through the short bushes into a wide clearing. The light of the sun bore down hard on both of them. A light fog that covered the land began burning off. Amidst the fog, a clearly defined road led northwards beyond the limits of sight. Malkolm pointed to the roadway.

The dirt was a dark brown, still damp from the morning dew.

"I heard a loud noise coming from this direction. When I looked out over the bushes I saw something I never thought I'd see. There were a lot of them, like you, chained to one another." His arm lowered and he looked up to the dragon that towered over him. "They were led north along this road in the rain. I thought I was dreaming or that I was seeing things until I met you this morning." He paused for a moment. "Was that your family?"

A somber look crossed Fenicus's face as he looked down at the boy. "Yes, it was." Fenicus lumbered over to the road while Malkolm hung back and watched him. At the road's edge he stopped. From one end to the other, Fenicus searched the road for signs that Malkolm's story held water. Though nearly washed away by the rains, rough outlines of dragon feet and human feet littered the ground. All the prints led in the direction Malkolm said. Fenicus peered back at him.

"Do you know where they were headed?"

"At first I wasn't sure where they were going." Malkolm drew closer to Fenicus. "But then I overheard some people in town talking about a fortress being built around the town of Valstena. That's where our chieftain lives."

"What's a chieftain?"

"Some kind of ruler." Malkolm then pointed to Fenicus's mouth and the ring secured around his tooth. "That ring bears his mark, the mark of the wolf."

Having almost forgotten about the ring, Fenicus pulled it free from his tooth and held it in his hand, examining it.

Malkolm continued. "Everyone's been telling stories about how he's building an army to conquer his enemies. What do the dragons have to do with it?"

"I don't know," Fenicus admitted, shrugging his shoulders. "They invaded our homeland and took everyone away. And other than this ring, I had nothing else to go on." He looked to Malkolm with a scornful grimace. "I'm the only one who got away, Malkolm. I've got to do something. Whatever the reason is for kidnapping my friends and family, I've got to figure it out." Fenicus knelt down on one knee into the mud. In his hand he tossed the ring up in the air, caught it, and tossed it again. "How do I find this place, this Valstena?"

Malkolm took a few steps toward the road and said, "C'mon, I'll show you," but Fenicus didn't follow.

Fenicus shook his head sharply. "I'm sorry, Malkolm, but I can't ask you to go where I'm going. It's too dangerous for you."

Malkolm stomped fitfully at the ground. "No! Please take me with you. I have nothing here. You're the first, um, person that's ever taken the time to talk to me, not yell at me. The first to show me any kindness at all." Lowering his head, his shoulders started to bounce subtly with the onset of muffled sobs. A long, golden finger carefully lifted his head upwards. Lines of tears streamed down his face making clean marks along his cheeks.

"Malkolm, where I'm going, there's a good chance I'm not coming back." Fenicus grinned at his small friend. "You're more than I ever hoped to find in any human, and I could never live with myself if anything happened to you.

This is my war, not yours." He laid a comforting hand on his shoulder.

"But I can help you," Malkolm insisted. "I'm a lot smaller than you, I can sneak into tight spaces. I won't get in your way, I promise. Please, let me come with you."

"I'm sorry, Malkolm. I have to do this on my own. How do I find the village?"

Malkolm kicked a stone across the ground. "Just follow the road until you come to a walled village with a tower on top of a hill. That's Valstena."

Fenicus rubbed Malkolm's head, ruffling his hair worse than it already was. "Thank you. You have no idea how much you've helped me. I hope we meet again, Malkolm."

Fenicus turned away and began his journey north. His lumbering form moved cautiously across the road. Though his shoulders were broad, the burden of his responsibility was bearing down on him. Fenicus glanced back at his new friend, but Malkolm was gone. He was alone again.

10

Two dungeon guards pulled at the chains around Galadorn's neck while another kept a sharpened polearm held firmly against his spine. Its tip poked at him, urging him forward. They led him down a long, dark passageway deep underground. There were too many twists and turns along the way for Galadorn to figure out exactly where they were taking him or how to get out if he broke free.

The small procession came to a halt at the end of the passageway. Two heavy, wooden doors on iron hinges loomed before Galadorn. An eerie creak groaned from the doors as they swung open from the inside. A flood of light bathed the dragon, blinding him. Once his eyes adjusted to the brightness, he saw another chamber similar to the one that Kell was using to imprison him and the other adult dragons. Yet, this room was much smaller. To Galadorn's shock and dismay, two of the younger dragons, Isabelle and Talon, hung splayed against the rear wall, unable to move. Crudely fashioned iron bindings kept their limbs stretched taut. Blood seeped from their wrists and ankles where the jagged edges of the shackles cut into their flesh. Neither of them looked very healthy, but at least they were alive. Remembering Kell's promise, Galadorn understood why they brought him to this chamber.

Kell stood before the children along with a peculiar-looking man with white facial hair and tattered brown robes. The chieftain glanced over in Galadorn's direction with a cheerful grin as though he was welcoming a friend to dinner. He strolled toward the dragon.

"Ah, Galadorn. So good of you to join us. As you can see, I've brought a few of your friends to join the party. Please, have a seat."

A stinging jab from the polearm in his back sent Galadorn stumbling into the well-lit chamber. To his right a large pile of hay covered the floor. Kell gestured to Galadorn to take a seat there. Afraid he might put the youngsters in further danger by fighting back, he conceded to Kell's request. He lumbered proudly to the designated spot and waited while his tormentors anchored his restraints to iron fittings in the walls and floor.

"Why are they here?" Galadorn demanded, motioning his head in the direction of the young dragons. "You gave us your word that we'd have one day to make our decision."

"I gave you no such word. I told you I'd use them as leverage to get what I want, and I intend to do so. They're here for insurance."

"I don't understand."

"It's time to decide the fate of your species, dragon. Your gold or your children, it's your choice." Kell paused for a moment, looking to the younglings and then back to Galadorn. "And to make sure you do the right thing, I've decided to give you a gentle nudge in the right direction." His words came out cold, calculated. "A little preview, if you will, of what will happen if I discover treachery in your midst." Kell leaned down and picked up a coiled whip that sat upon a stool. Holding the handle, he let the weapon unwind itself, its tip resting on the ground. Then he lifted it high above his head and wheeled it into motion before bringing its painful tip to bear on young Talon.

Crack!

The whip opened a gash several inches long upon the soft tissue of Talon's snout. A single trail of green blood seeped from the wound. The young dragon gritted his teeth but did not wail.

"Stop this immediately!" Galadorn pleaded. "You can have the gold. Just let them be." His words fell on deaf ears.

Kell's tendril-like weapon traced another wide circle in the air before it lashed this time against Isabelle's exposed belly. She cried aloud for a brief moment before biting down hard on her lower lip to quiet herself. The young dragon aimed a hateful glare at Kell through tear-filled eyes.

Grunting, Kell unleashed another parabolic swing of his whip. Its fierce bite made its mark this time upon young Talon's abdomen, tearing away a strip of flesh. Once more, his only reaction was a visible wincing. Talon then spat at

Kell and began a pained laugh.

Kell nodded his head. An evil grin curled the corners of his lips. "So that's the way you want to play, huh?" he barked. "Fools! Have it your way." Wheeling back his arm, Kell initiated a ruthless barrage of lashings upon the helpless bodies of the two young dragons. One after the other he struck out at them, waiting for some sign of their crumbling will. But neither succumbed.

Galadorn looked on helplessly from the other side of the room. He ground his teeth to fight back the rage welling inside. *Crack* after *crack*, the report from the whip echoed through the chamber. Galadorn winced and clenched his fists with each successive lashing, more so than Isabelle and Talon. Though all he wanted was for their torture to stop, it was their bravery and strength that kept him from pleading further. While the method of torture was cruel and painful to watch, it did not pose a serious threat to their lives. So as long as they could withstand it, Galadorn decided he must withstand it too. Otherwise, their sacrifice would be wasted.

So, Galadorn continued to watch in disgust for some time while Kell unleashed lash after vicious lash upon the two children. After a while, he grew sick to his stomach. The voices inside his head begged him to give in, to call an end to the incessant abuse. But each time he looked to the youngsters for a sign that they could take no more, they bravely shook their heads at him to hold his ground. Their lips remained locked tight, unwilling to allow one more whimper, one more cry to pleasure Kell's ears.

As minutes passed, Kell grew noticeably fatigued. The

looks of displeasure he shot at Galadorn could burn through solid rock. He yelled furiously, hurling the whip across the room at Galadorn and then slamming his fists down onto a rickety table nearby.

Galadorn laughed heartily at his frustration.

"Damn you!" Kell screamed at the amused dragon.

Behind him, the man in brown robes cackled hideously. Kell rounded about to face him. A gnarled smoking pipe dangled from the corner of his mouth while his laughter faded to a mere snicker.

"Calidin!" Kell bellowed.

The robed figure leaned forward and drew in an elongated, concentrated breath of the sweet smelling smoke before blowing it straight at Kell. The smoke formed a hazy cloud around the chieftain's head. Kell choked hard and waved his arms to disperse it.

Through the smoke, Kell leered at the two young dragons chained to the wall. Zigzagging cuts and gashes riddled their soft undersides, yet Talon and Isabelle remained stoic. Kell barked at Calidin, "Make them understand the meaning of pain."

Calidin rose from his seat and took hold of a wooden staff that leaned innocently against the wall. Once his fingers wrapped around its length, the small sapphire nestled atop the staff took on an unnatural glow that pulsated like a heartbeat. With slow, deliberate steps, Calidin crossed the chamber until he stood right between the two young dragons and only a few feet away. He thrust his staff into the air and brought it down hard against the ground. A loud thud echoed through the chamber.

Lowering his head, he commenced a queer uttering of words. The pulsating glow of the staff quickened. His voice grew in volume, resonating oddly as it bounced from wall to wall.

The sound of Calidin's voice pressed at Galadorn's mind like someone was squeezing his head in a vice. He clenched his eyelids shut and shook his head as he struggled against the mysterious sensation. For a brief moment, Galadorn opened his eyes to see a blinding ball of shimmering light encompass Calidin and the young dragons. Through the glowing sphere, he watched the simple, innocuous wounds on the young dragons swell into gaping sores from which blood gushed. The two screamed in anguish. Galadorn struggled to his feet and thrust himself forward only to be impeded by the limit of his chains. The game had suddenly turned far too serious.

"Stop it! They've had enough!" Galadorn begged.

Kell rushed to the other side of the room and stood just beyond the reach of Galadorn's chains. A savage grimace marked his features. "Have they?" he yelled at the dragon. The veins in his neck bulged to the surface.

Galadorn jerked his body hard against his chains and snapped his jaws centimeters from Kell's head. "To Hell with you," the elder dragon growled.

"Have they had enough?" Kell screamed in response, his tone reaching a menacing volume.

Galadorn glanced at Isabelle and Talon writhing in pain. He could no longer ignore his duty to protect their lives. "Yes! They've had enough. Stop hurting them!" he pleaded.

"Are you sure?" Kell turned to look in the direction of

Calidin and the young dragons. He rubbed his chin as if he were in deep, reflective thought. He turned back to Galadorn, bringing his face a hair's distance from the snapping jaws of the dragon. His whole demeanor turned calm and creepy. "They don't look it."

Galadorn growled fiercely, frustrated by his vulnerable position. With great reluctance, he spoke words he thought he'd never hear himself utter. "Whatever you want, all the gold, it's yours." His voice grew desperate. "Just stop, please!"

"You just don't get it, do you? It's not just the gold I want. I want you on your knees, dragon! I want you to beg—beg for mercy and swear your subservience to my will."

Galadorn scowled at Kell, his hatred for him intensifying with each callous action against dragonkind. Stripped of his pride, Galadorn dropped hard to his knees. The shame was so unbearable he could no longer hold his head high. He slumped to the floor, his spirit bent but not broken. Reluctantly, he obeyed his orders. "I beg you, show them mercy. I and the rest of my kind are yours to command, to live and die by your will."

A satisfied look overcame Kell. He turned to face his powerful assistant. "Calidin!"

He showed no signs of acknowledging Kell.

"Let them be."

Calidin lifted his head and the pulsating sphere of light collapsed back on the staff. Talon and Isabelle, free of the spell's influence, fell slack against their fetters, unconscious. Calidin rolled his head slowly, causing all sorts of grotesque popping and cracking sounds to eminate from his neck. Where moments before he strode confidently to the center of the room, he now withdrew sluggishly back to his bench. He appeared to be worn out, needing to lean on his staff for support. Each step took seconds to complete. He slumped forward, shaking his head.

"As you can see, Galadorn, my wizard is a force to be reckoned with." The whip Kell threw across the room rested at his feet. He bent down to pick it up. When he returned to his full height, Kell wheeled the whip about his head one more time and laid a viscous strike to the side of Galadorn's face, which cut deep into the flesh covering his cheekbone.

The dragon didn't flinch. His forked tongue slithered from the corner of his mouth and lapped up the free flowing blood that crawled from the wound.

Kell laughed while he strode toward the double doors that led out of the chamber. Before he departed, he glanced back one last time to face Galadorn. "If any of you try to escape or deceive me, I'll make sure every single one of your children die a slow, agonizing death while you sit and watch." With that, Kell exited the chamber.

The three men who accompanied Galadorn to the chamber reentered, pulling two long wooden carts behind them. Together, they positioned the carts against the far wall, one beneath each of the two young dragons. With the carts properly positioned, the smallest of the three guards cut across the room and pressed a release switch on a small, iron hand-crank. The chains slackened that held the dragons splayed against the wall. Both of them fell unmoving onto the carts. The only sign of life from them was the nearly imperceptible rising and falling of their chests as they breathed. The men worked quickly to tie them down before they awoke. Calidin stood nearby, monitoring their progress. Having completed their task, Calidin and the guards headed for the doorway, leaving Galadorn alone to contemplate the circumstances surrounding their captivity.

Before exiting the chamber, Calidin paused, turned, and then walked toward Galadorn. The dragon growled at his approach, but the wizard did not flinch. In fact, to Galadorn he seemed sad. Stopping just outside the dragon's reach, Calidin raised his head slightly and peered with pained eyes at the chained beast. "I'm sorry."

Galadorn's stature softened, unsure if he heard the wizard's words correctly. Before he could speak in return, Caladin lowered his head and shuffled out of the chamber.

* * *

The moon, full and glowing, hung in the sky along with all its tiny neighbors. The light it reflected from the sun bathed the countryside around Valstena in a soothing blue light. Several small fires burned inside the bailey of the walled village, helping to keep the nighttime guards alert and warm through the silent hours of the evening.

From atop the tower, Kell leaned over the balcony of the railing and surveyed the state of his dominion. The growth of the village over the past few months pleased him. Nearly every aspect of his plan was coming to fruition. Still, he understood that much work had yet to be done, and until then he could take nothing for granted.

He lifted a clay goblet of warm tea to his lips. The liquid

was piping hot. Sinewy tendrils of steam rose into his nostrils. The soothing aroma washed over him. He blew a few concentrated breaths at the tea before he took in a small sample.

The sound of bare feet padding along the wooden walkway told Kell that Calidin drew near. Being the only one of his men crazy enough to go around in bare feet at all times, the wizard's gait was unmistakable.

"Good evening, Calidin."

"My lord," the wizard moaned in a weary voice.

Kell glanced out of the corner of his eye to see Calidin's hood drawn up over his head and his hands hidden in the gaping sleeves of his robe. Not a single feature of his face could be discerned through the shadow the hood produced. He always roamed about like a specter at night, creeping along the hallways of the fortress and the streets of the village, scaring the wits out of anyone who might be awake. The bizarre fellow never slept, or at least not that anyone ever noticed.

"Making the rounds?" Kell inquired humorously.

Calidin stood silent, ignoring his master.

After blowing a few more cooling breaths on his tea, Kell took another drink from the goblet. He then leaned back against the railing and sized up the wizard. "That dragon-tongue enchantment is working perfectly. They can't see past the ruse."

Calidin, again, stood silent.

Fed up by his standoffishness, Kell returned his gaze to the land below with a grunt of frustration. "Tell me what you want and be off with you." He placed his drink down upon the railing. "I have no time for your games tonight."

"Don't get too carried away with yourself." There was a raspy coldness to his tone. The words seemed to spill from the very air around them and not from Calidin's mouth.

Kell swallowed hard at hearing the blunt remark. He refused to even look at him. "Make your point."

The wizard took a deep breath of the crisp night air. "I would be remiss in my duties if I didn't warn you of a premonition that has come to me in my meditations." There was an indistinguishable reluctance to the tone of his voice.

Kell aimed an aggravated stare at the wizard. "What is it this time?"

The intonation of Calidin's voice continued. "We did not capture every dragon in Berathor, m'lord. One escaped our grasp."

"That isn't possible," the chieftain asserted. "You must be mistaken."

"I'm not mistaken. It's a young dragon, and it's headed this way."

Kell rubbed his chin, considering the possibilities. "Does it pose a threat to us?"

"Alone?" the wizard paused momentarily. "No. But he's aided by a small boy."

"What kind of damage are we talking about?"

"I can't foresee that far into the future. But what I've seen is enough to unsettle my mind. This rogue dragon, I fear, may destroy Valstena."

Kell shook his head in disbelief. "I think you've been in the bottle again old man."

Calidin loosed his hand from the robe and grabbed at a golden necklace tucked beneath Kell's collar. A golden amulet dangled from the chain. On one side it depicted the silhouetted form of a human, and on the other side, a dragon.

Kell reached out and ripped the amulet free from the wizard's grasp before tucking it back beneath his shirt.

Calidin shook his head. "You've no idea what you're dealing with, do you?"

From his waist, Kell pulled free an ornate scepter, crowned by a brilliant sapphire. Many of its settings where other jewels once rested were now empty. Several large gashes existed along the length of its shaft. The very base of the shaft too seemed melted and reformed several times. Kell attempted to prod Calidin with the sapphire tip of the scepter, but the wizard drew back away from his gesture as though he feared or loathed the object.

"Do not forget your place, wizard," Kell barked angrily. Sensing the fear in Calidin, he resorted to just pointing the scepter in a menacing way toward him. "I set you free from that miserable prison of yours, and you'll serve me 'til the end."

Calidin turned his head away from his master. He paused for a moment before responding. "You released me to provide counsel, to protect you from that which you can't see. I'm telling you now, if you aren't careful, you'll pay for your arrogance and thirst for power with your life and the lives of all those around you."

Kell did not want to hear his words. He leaned out over the balcony and away from Calidin, only barely able to view him in his periphery. "You're mistaken, wizard. I set you free to bend the will of the dragons, not to enlighten me with your wisdom."

As usual, Kell felt the need to put Calidin in his place, to keep him in line. "Besides, your wisdom never served you well. All it ever got you was a sentence of eternal damnation in a prison bred of your own malice." His eyes dropped down to the courtyard. "So be mindful of your place. If you fail me, you'll find yourself back in Hell."

Turning back to leer at his slave, Kell was astonished to find that Calidin was nowhere to be seen. He was alone on the balcony again. He swore so loud that his voice echoed through the countryside. In his fury, he slammed his fist against the railing. The goblet that balanced there bounced into the air from the force of his strike and tumbled to the ground, shattering into tiny fragments.

Kell leaned his head back to gaze at the stars. After a few breaths, he left the balcony and turned in for the night.

11

Calidin paced back and forth between the mouths of two adjacent stone passageways that led in opposite directions. At the foot of the more roughly hewn of the two entranceways, he paused and closed his eyes. Concentrating all his mental focus on his sense of hearing, he listened for any subtle reverberations that might speak to him. Even the most trivial resonance packed nuance vital to his survival. The plunk of a drop of water, a slight breeze rustling up a cloud of dust, a rock tumbling loose from the cavern walls— each added vital brush strokes to the canvas in his mind.

Calidin's eyes snapped open. He shook his head and paced back toward the other passage. Unlike the first passageway that appeared to have been formed by the natural flow of molten rock through the mountain, this one was smooth to the touch and more perfectly formed. Closing his eyes once more, he eavesdropped on the passageway's secrets. His eyelids tightened more and more with each passing moment as he concentrated. Slowly, his eyes opened and he cautiously backed away from the passage, leering at it. He cocked his head to the side with a snide glance and narrowed his eyes. A power unlike any he had encountered before waited within. Feeling his nerves get the better of him, Calidin drew in a deep breath of air and pressed it out of his lungs. The butterflies tickling his insides settled for the moment.

He started to traverse the length of the passageway. Calidin paid close attention to every aspect of the floor, walls, and ceiling, desperately trying to avoid any pitfalls or booby traps. His journey seemed to take an eternity before he came face to face with a high-ceilinged arcade hewn from the mountainside. Ornate etchings adorned the façade of each column, forming vertically arranged pictographs of Dragonian history. It was a sure sign that he had chosen the proper passageway.

Raising his sense of awareness to a new level, Calidin ventured gingerly into the arcade. The series of archways that passed overhead made him feel uneasy, fearful, like he was caught inside the rib cage of some behemoth. Even though the area was open, the air itself became oppressive and claustrophobic, pressing in all around him. With each step, his desire to escape the danger that he sensed ahead grew steadily. Unable to move any farther, he paused to calm his mind. His fear could not be squelched. It hung on him like a hideous, disfiguring scar that one might seek to hide from view. Though he thought himself to be superior to mere mortal men, he could not peel off enough layers of his humanity to achieve the cold-blooded stoicism and courage necessary to face Weylark, the king of dragonkind. Angry with himself, Calidin focused on the task at hand and continued onward.

Calidin approached the final archway. The ceiling sloped down at a sharp angle and melded seamlessly with the wall. Another passageway lay before him. Its outer design and stonework were quite similar to the one he entered back at the forks. Something about it, though, struck him as being unique. All around him, the soft blue light that radiated from the sapphire crown of his scepter lit up even the darkest corner of the arcade. Yet, its light could not penetrate the darkness that obscured the passageway no more than a meter or two ahead of him. *Why can't I see what's inside?* An idea sprang to mind.

"*Ignis-lingua!*" Thrusting his scepter forward, he called forth a blast of white-hot flame that spun and whirled toward the opening of the passage. As the flame-tongue met the darkness, sparks of brilliant blue energy attacked Calidin's spell, snuffing it out as easily as a breath upon a single lit match. Pain seared through him. He snapped back the tip of the scepter and broke off his spell. The brief connection that his enchantment forged between himself and the darkness gave him insight into the level of sorcery that attempted to block his path. For once, he felt power akin to his own and the very thought of it caused chills to prickle down his sweaty back. The only thing holding back his immediate entrance into the passageway was the pain the connection brought him, making him wary.

Refusing to be deterred by the dragon's guard dog, Calidin urged the light within the sapphire to grow with great strength and intensity until it nearly blinded him with its brilliance. Calling forth his courage, the wizard stepped forward. Calidin felt a suppressing force close in around him. This was not the type of darkness easily extinguished by torch or tinder, but a magical darkness that felt like the weight of ten thousand hands pressing in on him from all directions, attempting to suffocate his power. He tried to push through it, hoping it would dissipate. Yet the further into the shadow he pressed, the dimmer his own torchlight shown—its energy melting away with each step—and the tighter the ethereal vice squeezed his body. Some unknown energy field was not only snuffing out his magic but also making him physically weak and disoriented at the same time. Unable to cope with the dampening field, he stumbled back to the safety of the arcade. The inky blackness that smothered his magic and threatened to rob him of his consciousness eased its grip. Slowly, Calidin felt his power return.

Feeling fully recharged, the wizard mulled over his memorized enchantments but was at a loss to find one potent enough to disperse the anti-magic conjuration filling the passageway. In his mind the wizard knew that Weylark awaited him on the other side of the darkness, comfortably resting in his protective gossamer of sorcery. *His power is indeed great,* Calidin admitted to himself. *He must've foreseen my coming.* The protective measures were far too intricate to be meant for simple humans. Though most mortals would fear insufferable night, he understood that the vast complexity and power of these security measures would only be truly appreciated by a fellow sorcerer, and therefore they logically must be meant to dissuade him or any other wizard from invading this dragon den. Calidin understood that it was only a matter of time before the dragons realized someone had violated the peace accord. What surprised him, though, was that they had not only learned of the treachery, but they understood the means by which they were being slaughtered. Whether or not they knew of Calidin, in particular, was yet to be seen.

Knowing the battle that may ensue within, Calidin steeled himself mentally and remembered a method by which he might be able to penetrate Weylark's outer defenses. From the depths of his knowledge he willed forth a translucent shell, growing forth from the tip of his scepter and engulfing his entire body. Sparks of white-hot electricity pulsed across the surface of the protective globe.

Calidin stepped forward toward the darkness, his body perfectly centered within his spell. A shockwave passed through him at the very instant his magic crossed the threshold into Weylark's enchantment. The fingers of electricity that raced along the surface of his protective charm immediately came under attack by an opposing force composed of similar but more intense sparks of red energy. Calidin felt the power of his enchantment being sucked away. Though the force at work beyond the wizard's enchantment threatened to neutralize his power, Calidin willed himself to go on, to press through the darkness until he could go no farther. The shell began to shrink around him. His feet no longer took sturdy, confident steps forward. Instead, he plodded through the soil as the last of his energy reserves passed into his spell before being sucked away by the darkness.

With nothing else to give, Calidin watched the veil of black that tore at the remnants of his meager defensive spell give way, and he fell into a motionless heap upon the floor.

Completely drained, the wizard struggled to lift his head to survey his new environment. His tired eyes observed an open chamber, dimly illuminated by beautiful bubbling fountains of lava that outlined the perimeter. The rounded walls of the chamber were golden and smooth in appearance like the inside of a giant egg. The only visible flaws in its form existed where the lava flows sprang up too close to the walls and melted away shallow alcoves.

Calidin's eyes then fell upon the one aspect of the chamber that made his insides knot up; coiled up in the center of the chamber lay a golden, slumbering titan. It was like a creature spawned from the wizard's very nightmares as a child. The sight of it stole away his ability to move or think for a short time. All Calidin could do in his state of extreme exhaustion was stare at its sheer magnificence and size.

Weylark exceeded his kin in size two fold, dwarfing them like a parent to a newborn. Strong, sinewy muscles lurked beneath his flesh, adding girth and power to his gargantuan frame. Protecting all that lay beneath was an adornment of perfect, armored scales that shimmered in the light of the cavern like a million newly minted gold coins. The talons that extended from each bony finger possessed edges keener than any sword or blade forged by mankind. Its perfectly white fangs protruded from its lips like the jaws of a portcullis lifted into the open position—a mere suggestion of the body-wrenching anguish they might imbue if lowered without warning.

The last physical characteristic Calidin gazed upon were the dragon's closed eyelids. The left side of Weylark's head lay directly before the wizard. Looking more closely, he noticed that the outer lids were slightly ajar, revealing the milk-white membrane that covered the delicate eye beneath. As long as the eye remained closed, Calidin could finish his work.

Some of Calidin's physical strength began to creep back into his muscles in dribs and drabs, but he was still fatigued. Nevertheless, he struggled to right himself into a kneeling position, his feet folded under his buttocks. Sparks of light snapped off in his field of vision with the sudden rush of blood to his head. He felt his body teeter. Placing his hands on his thighs, Calidin steadied himself. His head hung low while he breathed heaving breaths, trying to allay the lightheadedness. Unable to procure enough oxygen, he tilted his head back, closed his eyes, and breathed in deeply. The sensation gradually subsided. His eyes opened to find the dragon still slumbering soundly. Moving his hands away from his thighs, his eyes grew wide with a surge of terror.

The scepter! Where's my scepter? The catalyst of his sorcery was no longer in his grasp. He was so weary from traversing the passageway that he did not realize when it escaped his grasp. He feverishly surveyed the room from his kneeling position, looking for his precious possession.

Search as he might, it was nowhere nearby. The scepter seemed to have vanished. Then something caught his eye. The dragon's head rested alongside its left forearm. Nestled there beneath the outside edge of Weylark's palm lay the scepter.

Alone, Calidin possessed the ability to twist and contort only meager amounts of magical energy to fit his will. The scepter, though, unlocked the floodgates to unimaginable sources of dark energy that even he did not completely comprehend. And without it, the wizard knew that he could not slay the dragon. If the wizard dared stand toe to toe with the behemoth that lay before him, his power would be no more effective than trying to take down a siege tower by lobbing pebbles at its wheels. He had to get it back to stand any chance.

Calling upon the wisp of power that Calidin had regained, he centered his mind and reached out with ethereal fingertips to try and coax the scepter from under Weylark's hand. The tip of the handle bounced and wiggled under his influence, but the overbearing weight of the appendage lying atop it prevented it from being pulled free. The harder Calidin urged it to move, the more it bounced against the fleshy outer portion of the dragon's hand. Not wanting to rouse the slumbering beast, Calidin released his control over the invisible servant that he commanded. He swore angrily under his breath.

Too weary and tired to safely make his way out of Weylark's home, Calidin decided to take his chances. If he could get his hands on the scepter, he believed he could neutralize the dragon before it had a chance to tear him to ribbons. Taking a deep breath, the wizard rose to his feet and tiptoed toward the slumbering dragon.

An unexpected, ear-shattering rumble filled the chamber. Calidin slapped his hands against his ears to shut out the deafening tone. A few seconds later, the sound receded. Pensively, Calidin let his hands fall from his ears only to thrust them back when the thunderous clamor erupted again. The very ground shook beneath him. Examining the chamber for the source of the disturbance, Calidin's gaze fell upon the dragon's chest as it breathed out a slow breath. Watching its nostrils vibrate as it exhaled, the wizard realized that the dragon was snoring. He shook his head in frustration.

Then it hit him. Keeping his hands clasped protectively over his ears, Calidin watched Weylark's chest expand until it was full of air. At the onset of the next snore, the wizard began to creep across the floor, moving inch by inch until the chamber fell silent once more. Still too far away from his scepter to make a play for it, he waited patiently for another rumble. His heart thundered so loudly in his chest that he wondered if Weylark could hear it.

Tiptoeing the rest of the way, he found himself uncomfortably close to the dragon and mere inches from his scepter. Holding his breath, the wizard lowered himself down into a kneeling position beside Weylark. As a final rumble of breath fell silent, Calidin exhaled and made his move.

The wizard's hands quickly slipped from his ears and reached for the handle of the scepter. Before his hands could grasp the shaft, Calidin sensed something was gravely wrong. Raising his head, he came face to face with his own reflection staring back at him from a pool of inky blackness. His insides sank with a thud. It was no pool of ink he stared into but Weylark's massive iris. A flash of golden scales then closed down over the eye and pulled back to once again reveal a sharply expanding and focused pupil that lay locked upon him.

Calidin dove desperately for the shaft of the scepter. A wall of sheer power slammed into the wizard, swatting him away like a pitiful fly. He somersaulted through the air. Completely unprepared to defend himself, the wizard collided flat-backed against the chamber wall. His skeleton crunched under the force of the impact. Nearly unconscious, he slid down the wall between two fountains of molten lava and lay there helpless. He watched in horror as Weylark rose to his full, alert height, towering over him. With one clawed hand the dragon lifted his broken enemy up off the ground and stared ruefully at him. Calidin could barely keep his wavering line of sight focused on the dragon as the pain of his shattered form overcame his senses. Blood trickled from his nose, mouth and ears. Each limb dangled loosely from his body.

"Whatever you're going to do, dragon," Calidin spat in wincing tones to his captor, "get it over with. Death doesn't frighten me." And why should it? At that moment, he was certain that his death was inevitable. Besides, a quick death at that point would have been welcomed. Unfortunately for Calidin, Weylark had other plans in mind.

The dragon drew the wizard close. "I have no intention of permitting you the luxury of such a merciful deliverance.

The atrocities you've levied against my kind demand another brand of justice."

Calidin felt Weylark violate his mind, examining every callous act of injustice that he brought to bear against the dragons. Image after image passed by his mind's eye without any regard for the wizard. Finally, the connection broke.

Weylark picked up the scepter in his free hand and held it just beyond Calidin's reach. "This trinket, this tool of destruction you hold so dear, shall be your prison for lifetimes to come." The dragon leered at Calidin and growled menacingly. "From this day forth, I commit you to the sapphire that powers your malevolence. There you shall remain, ever awake, insatiably hungry, ceaselessly weary with no recourse or hope for pardon. All your days and nights will be filled with your hideous memories, played out before you in all their gruesome glory. You will never escape them until fate has determined that you have paid the price for your crimes. And if that day shall ever come to pass, you must serve the bidding of your liberator until their dying breath or yours, whichever comes first."

Then Weylark began to utter some sort of conjuration in ancient Dragonian. Calidin felt the last wisps of his power leach out of him. Slowly, a tiny vortex began spinning and whirling from the tip of the scepter's sapphire directly at him. As its mouth closed in on the wizard, every fiber of his physical being was stretched in unimaginable ways, far beyond the bounds of reality. The discomfort raging inside Calidin caused screams to pour from his tortured lips. A flash of light burst from the tip of the scepter, and it was over.

With one swift movement, Weylark thrust the shaft of the scepter into the floor of the chamber. He drew close and peered into the sapphire that adorned its tip. There was Calidin writhing in pain, tortured by his own demons, his own evil, with all eternity to contemplate the repercussions of his actions.

* * *

"NO!" Calidin screamed as he woke from his slumber. His torso bent upwards, bringing his head toward his crooked knees. With both hands he grasped at the sides of his throbbing head, hoping to rub away the memories that haunted his mind. His fingers raked through the damp nap of hair that sat twisted and contorted upon his head. The pain regressing, Calidin took hold of the wool blanket that kept him warm and pulled it aside. Every fiber of the coarse fabric dripped with cold sweat. He could feel his heart racing in his chest. The nightmares, the memories of his four-hundred-year imprisonment couldn't be shaken. They were the reason he rarely slept. Only in his waking hours did he escape the demons that haunted his mind.

Though Calidin knew that the dream was over, that his timeless torture had come to an end, his servile duties precluded him from letting go. He was the servant of Kell until death or vow of freedom released him from his bonds. And as much as he wanted to help the dragons, to make amends for what he did to them ages ago, he had no choice in the matter. It was fate, he decided, cruel fate that made his liberator a man whose sole purpose was the utter and complete destruction of dragonkind. And every cruel grimace, every arrogant word that came from Kell reminded Calidin of just that fact.

From the very start, Calidin tried to warn his new master of the dreadful consequences his actions would sow. With each day that passed since his liberation, the wizard's insight into the future grew clearer, his connection with the powers of the universe intensified. He knew that if Kell did not alter his course of action, every man who dared follow him into battle might pay the ultimate price. And being Kell's servant, Calidin did the best he could to warn his master of the foul harvest his inflexible ambitions might yield. While his warnings fell on deaf ears, he could not find the power to deny his duty; not out of respect or gratefulness for liberating him, but out of sheer fear. Disobeying Kell meant being sent back to Hell, to the nightmarish prison he would do anything to avoid returning to. He wanted to break free of his servile chains, but the memories of his imprisonment loomed so powerfully that he would unquestionably follow any order, cross any line in order to maintain his freedom. Or so he thought.

12

Under the cover of night, Fenicus surveyed the village of Valstena for any evidence that his family and friends were imprisoned there. From the brambles and bushes that lined the edge of the Heldark Forest, Fenicus kept a keen eye on the comings and goings of each human being as they retired to their dwellings for the evening. For the most part, Valstena resembled many of the small settlements Fenicus noticed from the road; many homes and buildings with frames constructed of wood, held together by wooden pegs and covered by thatched straw roofs. The *clunk* of drop shutters falling into place over the windows could be heard everywhere, like subtle drum beats out of rhythm. And as each fell into place, the flickering candlelight that was visible between the slats of the shutters went out and the village became a bit quieter. The only visible sign that life continued within each dwelling was the spire of smoke that billowed upward from the stone chimneys. In appearance they reminded him of the small trails of misty breath that escaped his nostrils in the crisp night air. The village, he felt assured, slept soundly.

Fenicus then turned his attention on the rest of the village and a rather unique characteristic that separated it from all others he had seen in his travels. Part way through the village, the main dirt road that Fenicus followed northward came to a sudden end and dove downward at a steep angle into a ditch. Beyond that ditch, a whole new village rose from the ground, and it could not have looked more out of place. Hundreds of felled trees stuck straight out of the dirt in a side-by-side fashion, creating a wall nearly six meters high. The tips of each timber had been cut and shaped into a fine tooth-like point—a forbidding warning to any would-be invaders that might consider scaling the perimeter. The wall stretched all the way around the backside of the village and back again. And across the ditch from the end of the road, a drawbridge stood locked in the upright position, preventing anyone from passing through. From Fenicus's vantage point, the only visible structure that stood beyond the protective wall was a mighty watchtower that stood atop a giant mound of earth, looming over the entire village. The tower was the only portion of the village that was not fashioned from some type of wood. It appeared to be wholly constructed of chiseled stone with the top of the structure accented by a parapet. Just below the parapet, a wooden balcony wrapped around the outside.

Fenicus yawned wide. Though he tried to stay vigilant, fatigue had begun to get the better of him. The village had grown cold and silent like a grave. A comforting heaviness seeped into his eyelids, urging him to sleep. Each time he sensed the world darkening around him, Fenicus fought to stay awake. He thought he had won.

Screeeeeech!

Fenicus's head shot up with a start. His eyelids peeled back fully to reveal bulging, bloodshot eyes. He had fallen asleep.

"What was that?" he whispered to no one. All around he searched for the thing that made the startling noise. His eyes ranged high and low but he could not find it. Sitting upright, he listened patiently for the sound to come again. The adrenaline that pumped through his body withdrew as the seconds passed by without another disturbance. Again, his eyelids grew heavy. Satisfied the noise was nothing more than a dream, Fenicus finally decided to give in and sleep. He returned to his restful position on the forest floor. After a few deep breaths, he started to drift away.

Screeeeeech!

The high-pitched shriek caught Fenicus's full attention. His ears honed in on the sound immediately, directing his eyes toward the odd bird that sat perched in a nearby tree. The look of it intrigued the dragon.

Its brilliant yellow eyes glowed in the pallid moonlight. A rounded head rested upon its thick neck, almost indistinguishable from the rest of its body. The entire bird modeled gray feathers with specks of black and white mixed in. It sat rather modestly upon a branch while its head swiveled in all directions. The fat little bird produced another trilling call before it leapt from its perch and glided toward the ground. Fenicus watched its slow descent. The claws of the bird wrenched at a small rodent scurrying about in the underbrush, lifting it into the air and carrying it away. Fenicus marveled at the bird's sharp reflexes and acute vision. Watching the rising path of the bird brought Fenicus's field of vision back to the village of Valstena where he caught sight of a shadowy figure threading its way through the streets of the village. The figure had a familiar shape, but Fenicus could not place from where he knew it. The action he had hoped for all night finally came to pass.

Picking himself back up off the ground, Fenicus watched the figure's erratic movements. It seemed to be searching for something. Finally, the shadow stopped moving in front of the drawbridge. There it remained for sometime, measuring up the closed roadway. Fenicus had a strong suspicion as to the identity of the mysterious shadow sneaking around Valstena. Being cautious not to make any noise, Fenicus emerged from the forest and took flight.

*　*　*

How am I supposed to get past that? Malkolm wondered. He spent a great portion of the night searching for a way to penetrate the outer wall of the fortress. Unfortunately, the raised drawbridge was the only way in or out. Wanting to get a better view, he stepped on some loose dirt at the edge of the moat and slipped. He hit the ground below with a thud. The feel of the wet dirt on his skin encouraged him get up and brush off. He crossed the bottom of the empty moat. At the base of the other side, he secured a better footing and climbed up onto the narrow bank. There was barely enough room to shimmy along the wall once he got up there.

Looking through the narrow gaps between each of the timbers, Malkolm saw several buildings arranged in a circular fashion around a courtyard and a longhouse nestled in the middle of it all. From the courtyard, Malkolm took notice of a promenade that ascended diagonally up toward the top of the earthen mound where another palisade surrounded the stone tower that overlooked the land below. All the rumors he had heard back in Falterton were correct. There was indeed a great fortress being constructed to the north. Whether or not Fenicus's family was being held prisoner within these walls he did not know. He resolved to find out as much as he could before sunrise. If he proved his worth to Fenicus, perhaps, he might let him tag along.

Malkolm closely examined the portion of the wall in front of him. There were a few places where he thought he might be able to get a firm grip and climb up—a protruding knot here or there and stumpy remains of hewn branches. Grabbing hold of two of those knots, Malkolm pulled himself up and began his ascent. His feet found two other knots jutting out from the timbers. In the middle of searching for another set of handholds, Malkolm felt a tremendous shot of pressure in his back that pressed all the air from his lungs. A loud grunt escaped him. Without warning, a snapping tug at his shirt ripped him away from the wall. His eyes watched as the ground raced away from him. He tried to scream but there was not enough air in him to make any sound. Shock gave way to relief when he looked up to see that Fenicus had grabbed him. The village shrunk to miniature and he felt the sweep of leafy branches brushing against him as he descended into the forest. Malkolm waited for the inevitable moment when Fenicus would drop him smartly on his rump, but the moment never came.

Setting Malkolm down gently, Fenicus scolded him. "What are you doing here? I told you to stay put." The dragon's frustration was obvious from his body language and his speedy talk.

"I'm sorry," Malkolm gasped, trying to catch his breath. "But I couldn't just sit back and let you do this all by yourself. Besides, how did you plan on getting inside?" Malkolm sat down on the moss and pulled his knees up to his chest with his arms wrapped around them. "You'd be kinda hard to miss trying to sneak in there."

Fenicus settled himself down onto the mossy ground and stared at Malkolm for a short time, shaking his head. He looked toward Valstena and then back to Malkolm and sighed. "So what's your plan?"

13

Eventually, Fenicus and Malkolm fell asleep. Though it was not a lengthy slumber, it was a refreshing one. Fenicus awoke slowly, rolling about on the forest floor in a vain attempt to keep sleeping. He finally gave up. Lying on his side for a moment, he stretched his limbs with a great yawn. His eyes caught sight of the budding leaves beginning to unfurl in the warm spring sunlight. A few birds chirped overhead in the branches. His fat feathered friend from the night before was nowhere to be found. Fenicus then realized that Malkolm was, likewise, nowhere to be found. He bolted up and went off in search of the small boy.

Having yet to bathe since Fenicus met him, Malkolm's potent odor wafted toward him on the breeze. The scent led him to a small stream that snaked through the forest. He searched up and down its shoal and soon found him. A little to his left he found the boy holding a pared sapling in his hands; a length of string dangled from its tip into the water. Fenicus lumbered on all fours over to his friend. He sat down in the sand next to him and stared in wonderment at Malkolm.

"What are you doing?" Fenicus inquired with a healthy dose of curiosity. In the clear water he saw a small, silvery hook attached to the end of the string. There was something brown wrapped around it that a few small fish seemed intent on pecking at. None of them had mouths large enough to wrap around the hook, but they fought ravenously for just a nibble of whatever it was Malkolm dangled in front of them. "Are you trying to catch them?"

Malkolm nodded without taking his attention away from the fish and the hook. Whenever one of the bigger of the bunch tried biting the brown thing on the hook, Malkolm jerked the pole. "Damn!" he hissed as the fish swam away.

The entire process intrigued Fenicus immensely. "What do you have on the end of that hook?" Fenicus leaned forward so that his face was only a few feet from the water, watching the action below.

"Just a worm," Malkolm replied nonchalantly.

Fenicus seemed in awe at the concept. "You use one animal to catch another?"

"Yeah. Why?"

Eyes wide, Fenicus shook his head in disbelief. "I've just never heard of anything like that before." He shuffled back on his hindquarters to lean against a nearby tree.

In the midst of his position shift, the sapling that

Malkolm held bent violently and the line stretched taut. Malkolm erupted into a flurry of excitement, trying to corral the fish pulling against his grasp. Fenicus didn't know what to do. The moment took him by surprise. He leaned forward to get a closer look at the battle going on in the water. The little blue and green fish fought hard to resist the boy's tugs. Finally, Malkolm fell back hard in the sand with the sapling still firm in his hands. The fish shot out of the water, landing next to him. It flopped around convulsively in the sand, bending and twisting as it slowly suffocated outside its natural environment.

"What're you gonna do now?" Fenicus hated to watch the poor thing suffer. He understood the order of nature and that more evolved species prey on the lesser, but his people always believed in a quick, painless death whenever possible.

Malkolm lifted the fish up off the ground by its tail and slammed its head upon a rock along the shore. A hideous cracking of bones struck the dragon's ears. He winced as though feeling the animal's pain, but he felt some relief in seeing that the fish no longer moved. Its suffering was over.

"Hmm. A big one too!" Malkolm held it up in the air like a trophy. "This ought'a fill me up." Laying the fish down on the rock, he started gathering up twigs and dried leaves and piled them up on top of each other in the sand. Then he took two of the twigs and began rubbing them together until a spark lit the kindling on fire. Malkolm glanced at Fenicus and rolled his eyes. "I did all that work when I could have just asked you to cook it for me." Malkolm did his own comic impression of a dragon breathing fire.

Fenicus laughed at his impression. "That's pretty good, but to be quite honest, I can't breathe fire yet."

"Why not?" Malkolm asked in a dumbfounded tone. "I thought all dragons could breathe fire."

"I'm not old enough yet. I've got about twenty more years before I can do that." Embarrassed by his inability to live up to Malkolm's expectations, he shrugged. "Sorry."

"That's okay. You've dropped me so many times I was afraid you might accidentally light me on fire next. One less thing for me to worry about."

The two had a good laugh for a minute before Malkolm went back to building his small fire into a blaze large enough for cooking. Watching him, Fenicus's stomach began to gurgle. His eyes focused on the small fish lying on the rock. Though it was completely insufficient for his needs, he could not help but salivate thinking about it. His stomach had completely bottomed out, and he needed some nourishment of his own. To try and quell the bubbling going on in his belly, Fenicus placed his right hand over his abdomen and massaged it.

"You're hungry too, huh?" Malkolm looked wide-eyed at Fenicus's belly. From the pile of gathered twigs, he picked one up, sharpened it to a point on a rock, pushed it into the mouth of the fish, and twisted the fish down upon it until it was securely in place. Then Malkolm lowered it over the crackling little fire. "Do you want my fish, Fenicus?" he said as he raised it from the fire in the dragon's direction. "I can catch another, it won't take long, really."

Fenicus smiled at the generous offer but humbly

declined. "You'd need about a hundred of those to feed me, Malkolm. It's okay." He gathered himself up and shook off the sand. "I'll go find something to eat. I'll be back in a bit."

Fenicus lifted off into the early morning sky.

* * *

The bloody carcass of a lamb dropped through the tree branches and crashed down in the sand. Malkolm looked up from where the animal came from to see Fenicus hovering overhead. He froze at the sight of it, his teeth sunken deeply into the side of the fish.

Fenicus landed right next to the dead animal and immediately settled down, ready to eat. Not thinking about his companion, the dragon ripped a leg clean off the lamb and started gnawing on it. With a few moist shreds of bloody mutton in his mouth, he became aware of the fact that Malkolm was staring at him. His jaw slowed in its motion until the boy's gawking got on his nerves and he stopped chewing completely.

"What?" he snapped at Malkolm.

Malkolm shook his head. "Nothing," he replied a bit hesitantly, his mouth full of food. His stare narrowed on the bloody leg of lamb Fenicus held. "I've just never seen anyone eat like *that* before." Malkolm then looked away, and he continued to eat his own meal while looking everywhere but at Fenicus.

A sudden realization came over Fenicus. While Malkolm cooked his fish before he ate it, it wasn't necessary for Fenicus to do the same with his catch. For Malkolm, perhaps, watching someone chew on an animal whose blood was still warm from living and not cooking didn't sit well with him. Fenicus decided to suck it up while in the company of his human friend and forego the pleasure of rare meat. He slid the meaty end of the lamb leg over the fire to cook it.

Malkolm could once again look in Fenicus's direction with a smile.

After a short while, Fenicus and Malkolm had both finished eating and were ready to begin the first stage of their mission. It was nearly ten o'clock by the time they approached the edge of the forest. Having found a safe spot where a few trees and some dense brush hid their prying eyes, they began to watch the village as it stirred.

Unlike the night before, the village was now alive and full of energy. The locals went about their business like any other day. A small group of children ran in and out of crowds and in between buildings while they played a game of tag. Their laughter echoed through the countryside. One of the boys ran right into a young woman trying to buy some dried fish from a monger. Offended at first by the rude collision, she laughed it off and chased the child away with a smile on her face. There appeared to be a light air to the people whom inhabited this village.

While the ebb and flow of life in the village interested him, Fenicus needed to find out if infiltrating the palisade of the fortress would require stealth and guile or simply walking over the drawbridge. Shortly thereafter, the answer to his question came forth.

Atop the gate tower, a guard moved out into the sunlight from his walled observation chamber before making his way to a pair of vertically positioned wheels with large wooden handles. Taking hold of the handles upon the rightmost wheel, he slowly cranked the wheel toward the front of the gate, lowering the drawbridge. The burden of the task appeared to be physically taxing on the guard; it took all of his body weight and strength to keep from losing control of the wheel. With each crank, the gate moaned as the ropes that controlled the mechanism strained against the weight of the heavy drawbridge. With a ground-shuddering thump, it came to rest upon the other side of the dry moat.

Having completed that task, the guard moved to the other crank wheel and pulled the handles toward himself this time, which required an equal amount of exertion to operate. The reinforced portcullis that provided a second barrier of defense rose languidly from the ground with each pull on the crank. Moments later, the guard finished his duty and staggered back to his station.

Almost immediately, a group of kids playing in the streets sprinted across the drawbridge without so much as a peep from the guards. Behind them, people of all sorts filed into the bailey. A man in his late twenties pulled a rickety wooden handcart inside. His cargo appeared to be a vast array of animal pelts that he must have collected from trapping over the winter months. Quite some time later, the man came back across the drawbridge. His cart was now filled with generous supplies of dried food and grains that must have been kept in storage somewhere behind the palisade.

Watching the order of life unfold in the village, Fenicus

began to understand that this "chieftain" who watched over these people took great care of them. None of them dressed in rags or looked to be of ill health. And everyone who brought something of value within the outer wall came away with what they needed: damaged tools reworked by blacksmiths, new clothes fashioned by tailors, and dried food procured from the winter storerooms. Outside the palisade, the villagers grew all sorts of crops, raised foul and cattle, trapped for furs, and caught fish. The villagers had everything they needed to not only survive but also to live happily. It appeared to work to perfection. But a question still lingered in Fenicus's mind.

"I don't get it," Fenicus muttered to Malkolm, shaking his head.

"What?" Malkolm broke his gaze from the village to glance at his friend.

"This human looks after his own people so well." Fenicus's eyes narrowed while he scanned the village. "Yet, he's heartless enough to invade my homeland, destroy it, and kidnap my friends and family. They all probably revere him. Like I said, I don't get it."

"Maybe," Malkolm added, "it's because you're not human."

Fenicus nodded. "Maybe." He thought back to all the stories his uncle told him about their battles against mankind and the gross destruction each race wrought upon the other. To dragons, humans were like a swarm of insects, faceless and easy to destroy. And to the humans, the dragons were a race of giant monsters that ruled the skies. They shared nothing in common. There was no empathy between the two races. Each side felt bitter hatred toward an enemy they didn't really understand.

Then Fenicus shifted his thoughts. When it came to his own personal struggle against Darius, he found it harder to fight. The face he saw was so much like his own reflection. When it's your own kind, things *are* different. Perhaps there was another side to the story. "I guess it's easier to destroy something that doesn't look the same as you."

"Yeah," Malkolm responded, "I guess you're right." He paused for a moment before continuing. "But if he cares so much for the villagers, then why wasn't that wall built around all the homes and shops?"

In an instant, almost everything started making sense to Fenicus. He told Malkolm that he thought the design of the village was rather ingenious. While the villagers would likely be welcomed within the protective wall of the fortress if they ever came under attack, it did not serve that purpose alone. The design of the fortress allowed for all major survival and military resources to remain strategically protected within the palisade. All the shops, farms, and homes outside the palisade could be easily rebuilt again after fending off an invasion. And from what Malkolm told Fenicus, the construction of the fortress occurred in the last year or so. The fortress, other than the filling of the moat, was complete. The building process took place quickly and covered only the bare necessities. There were no luxuries of note. Only the most essential needs were protected. The chieftain was preparing for war, for some kind of conquest.

One thing still did not make sense. Fenicus found himself suddenly consumed with thoughts of his friends and family. If they were indeed the chieftain's prisoners, what plans did he have for them? Did he intend to use them for military might, for an airborne army, or were his plans more sinister? Either way, he did not intend to find out by sitting back and letting their fate be decided for them. He conveyed the contents of his mind to Malkolm who did his best to understand it all.

"Well," Malkolm paused while he scratched the side of his head. "I guess I should go see what I can find out."

"Are you sure you're still okay with this?" Fenicus asked, terribly concerned. "Maybe this isn't such a good idea."

Malkolm shook his head. "There shouldn't be any trouble. The villagers are pretty used to me by now and I've even talked to some of the kids before. I can take care of myself. After all, I've done it for this long." He patted the dragon on the leg with his small hand. "What about you? Aren't you gonna fly around the village or something?"

"I'm going to wait until dark to do that. I want to make sure you come back in one piece. Anyway, it will be harder for them to see me flying around at night than in the light of day."

Malkolm squirmed about apprehensively.

"Are you absolutely sure you want to go through with this, Malkolm?" Fenicus looked over Malkolm, sensing his nervousness. "I'll keep an eye on you as best I can from here." He tried to sound convincing. "Just keep your head on a swivel. Get in, find out what you can, and get out. If you run into trouble, I'll try to find a way to rescue you."

A long, nervous exhale escape Malkolm. "All right." He took in a deep breath and pressed it out. "Here goes nothing!"

Fenicus placed part of his hand on Malkolm's shoulder as he started to leave. Malkolm looked back to his friend.

"Good luck!" Fenicus bid with a hopeful smile.

Malkolm nodded, broke from the cover of the forest, and made his way into the village.

*　　*　　*

Standing at the foot of the drawbridge, Malkolm peered within. Beyond the palisade he saw several buildings, much like the ones that lined the streets of the village. Though he did not fear what awaited him within these walls, a looming sense of dread hung on him. No matter how much he wished to turn around, to head back to the safety of the woods and his friend, he knew that he must go forward. A lump rose in his throat. He swallowed hard, trying to knock it down. Malkolm picked his right foot off the dusty ground. He felt his foot shaking. Slowly, he stepped onto the wooden planks of the drawbridge and drew in a deep, calming breath. One foot after the other, he made his way into the bailey beyond the wall.

Once inside, Malkolm began to feel more at ease. A sizeable throng of both soldiers and civilians mingled about within the bailey, just like back home. Knowing he always did his best work when the streets were at their busiest, Malkolm disappeared into the crowd. Using the villagers and soldiers as shields against the watchful eyes of the tower guards, he began taking notice of anything that might prove useful to their cause.

In general, the collection of buildings and structures did not strike him as anything special: a few weapon smiths, an armory, two soldier barracks, a great hall, and the storehouses for food and grain. They were all things he expected to see inside such a formidable fortress.

An eerie moaning sound spilled forth from within the bailey. Malkolm stopped dead in his tracks as the shrill groan grated against his ears. He looked about hesitantly for the poor tortured creature he thought must be making the sounds. His eyes then caught sight of the culprit; at the other end of the bailey, a massive wooden walkway ascended upwards toward the top of the great mound of earth where the watchtower stood. The very base of that walkway broke away from the ground and began to rise into the air like a giant drop-shutter being propped open. Clumps of mud fell from the timbers. Two hefty oxen, urged on by men with firm switches, pulled their tethers through wooden pulleys, lifting the ponderous section of the walkway into the air. The groaning Malkolm heard came not from the oxen but from the timbers and rope strained by the burden placed upon them. Having reached its apex, the walkway ceased in its movement. Beneath it, a sturdy wooden footbridge led to two gargantuan doors at the base of the mound. After a few odd thuds, the two doors swung inwards on their hinges where massive forms lingered in the darkness.

Malkolm strained his eyes to peer inside the shadowy opening, but the bright sunlight drowned out his ability to pierce the darkness within. Then, one by one, fifteen dragons walked into the sunlight. Some of the dragons were similar in stature to Fenicus while others were much larger. Each dragon stood chained to the next one in line. Unlike the first time Malkolm laid eyes on the dragons, this time their hands were not bound. At first he thought that someone foolishly forgot to shackle their hands and they'd soon break free. Then he noticed that their wings were still immobilized to prevent them from flying and their feet were limited to a narrow gait due to the short length of chain that connected them. Though their eyes no longer held the white-eyed, blank stare, they still seemed to be kept in check by some sort of power. The only way he could explain the somber countenance on their faces was that something had driven fear into their hearts and that fear alone made them servile. If that wasn't enough, if any dragon stood still for too long, several hard-handed men drew near and began lashing them with studded whips.

Leading their procession was a man who seemed to walk on a cushion of air. He wore a brown hooded robe that covered every part of him but his face. Though he had the look and posture of a young man, his skin showed signs of either extreme age or a life of hardship. Locks of gray hair and a beard of like color obscured his sharp features.

When the man drew near Malkolm, the boy stepped aside as if guided by some power other than his own will. The boy stood by in awe of the spectacle that marched past him. Malkolm winced at the crack of another whip, breaking him out of his trance. He saw the mark left behind by the biting teeth of the leathery weapon on the underside of an ill-looking, defenseless dragon. Though he knew there was nothing he could do to save them at that moment, the desire to tear the whips out of their hands and use them against their masters whirled about in his mind. Malkolm also began to wonder the pain that Fenicus must be dealing with if he saw what was happening from the brambles along the edge of the forest.

Though he knew this venture was dangerous, Malkolm decided to follow the procession anyway. He understood that Fenicus, in some way, would eventually need to rely on Malkolm and therefore he could not afford to get caught. But he also believed that by keeping a close eye on the dragons, he might be able to gain useful information from them. It was a risk he had to take.

Malkolm took up a careful gait in pursuit, making sure he stayed a good twenty paces behind the procession while they made their way through the streets of the village. Here and there he ducked behind buildings whenever someone looked back.

Eventually, the marching dragons reached the outskirts of the village. Malkolm ducked behind a few wooden ale barrels and watched the men drive the dragons forward. The group eventually split in two. Half of the dragons were led by the robed figure to a spot a few hundred meters north of the village. The other half of the dragons took to their knees and began digging at the ground with their talons. Their work quickly shaped into a trench that led from the edge of the empty moat to the other dragons.

Wanting a better look at the dragons that were led away from the village, Malkolm searched for another way to approach them without being seen. He then took note of the forest that stood some distance away. The curved edge of the tree line grew right alongside where the dragons toiled. Heading back around the other side of the village,

Malkolm entered the forest and stealthily moved up on their position.

As he got closer, Malkolm saw that a river ran through the woods. It was that river where the robed figure took the other group of dragons. He had them digging another trench, only this one led southward from the river toward the village. Deciding he had gone far enough for safety's sake, Malkolm knelt down behind some shrubberies and carefully surveyed the work done by the dragons and men.

What are they doing? Malkolm wondered. Then it struck him. Though the fortress was complete, the final defenses were incomplete. The final impediment to invasion, the moat, was nothing more than a six-foot deep dirt trench; it was hardly enough to stop anyone from scaling the walls. By digging a trench from the river to the moat, Kell planned on using irrigation to fill it.

Watching the dragons reduced to mere slaves, Malkolm sighed deeply. It was so obvious to him who should be the dominant race. If anything, it was humans who should be the slaves of dragons, yet it was not the case. The thing that made Malkolm feel worst of all was that he was certain that Fenicus too watched them from the other side of the forest. He chewed nervously at the corner of his lip, trying to decide if he should stay where he was to keep an eye on the dragons or head back to Fenicus to figure out some strategy to set them free. Moving slowly, Malkolm stood from his place behind the bushes and made his way back to his friend.

14

Kell stood brooding over his land through an open window that overlooked the bailey below. He watched intently at the collection of dragons slaving away outside the village walls. The last few rays of sunlight bathed his face in warmth. All his plans were coming together. He drew in one last breath of the cool spring air. Behind him, Kell heard a flurry of activity; his subordinates milled about as they worked to assimilate the information obtained from interrogating the dragons. He turned about on his heels to attend to the business at hand.

This chamber, normally utilized to convene meetings of Kell's military council, now had the appearance of a war room. A large, darkly stained wooden table took up a large portion of the center of the room. Covering the top of the table was an extensive map of the world sketched upon patched together pieces of yellowed parchment.

A young man carrying several scrolls entered the room. He immediately moved to the end of the table nearest the door and set down his load. As quickly as he entered the room, he exited.

Several men stood around the table with a sense of eagerness. One by one, the men randomly grabbed at the scrolls and investigated the contents. While some men seemed greatly excited by what they read, others seemed disappointed. Nevertheless, each man then grabbed hold of a small, gold painted rock from the pile stacked upon the other end of the table, wrote upon it the same number written upon the scroll, and placed it on top of the map. Each rock marked the location of another dragon's hidden gold hoard.

Kell approached one of his men who faced the other direction. He placed a hand upon his shoulder. The man turned around to face Kell. He was much older than the mighty chieftain. His face showed the wear and tear of a long life of conquest and hard times. His skin was nothing compared to his starkly gray locks of hair. The only other noteworthy characteristic of this man was that he had but one hand. At the end of his right arm, a series of cloth bandages encircled a stump where his hand once was. Though they cauterized the wound to prevent unnecessary blood loss, the bandages were still bloodstained from the blisters and sores caused by the burns.

"Sven, how're we faring?" Kell asked with a cheerful grin on his face.

"We've nearly got'em all," the elder barbarian stated with exuberance. "By sundown we'll know where all of it is. Yer queer friend has a way with them dragons."

"I meant yer hand."

Crooking his arm, Sven brought the stub into view. "It still stings madly, but it's better than bleedin' to death."

"Aye, it is." Kell raised his eyebrows in agreement. "Since you mentioned it, how much of their gold do you think we'll be able to recover?"

His assistant put his one good hand to Kell's back and urged him over to the table. He drew his chieftain's attention to the section of map that covered Western Europe and Scandinavia. He then waved his stub over the whole area in small, sweeping circles. "From what they've told us, most of their stockpiles of gold are hidden in mountainside caves all around Europe. They even managed to hide some of it in underwater caves during low tide. Nevertheless, they claim that most of these hoards are either used up or greatly depleted."

Kell appeared thoughtful, the corner of his mouth drawn taught.

"What's wrong, m'lord?"

Shaking his head, Kell responded. "Something doesn't add up. If they're indeed telling the truth, why would their stockpiles be depleted? What could they possibly have done with all that gold?"

"I'm not quite sure myself. It could be a ploy to dissuade us from pursuing it. I wouldn't trust a word of it m'lord."

Kell nodded. "Yer probably right, Sven, yer probably right. How soon till we'll be able to dispatch scouts to assess the feasibility of recovering these hoards?"

"We're gathering them as we speak. They're simply awaiting your dispatch command."

Kell rubbed his hands together, longing to feel the cold, gleaming metal in his hands. "Excellent!"

*   *   *

The outlook wasn't good. Fenicus and Malkolm sat at the edge of the stream tossing stones into its flowing waters. Every plan they devised to infiltrate the fortress had some flaw in its design. Each option was too risky, too dangerous to consider past its initial inception. Nevertheless, they kept searching for an answer to their dilemma.

"You could always swoop in and tear the place apart," Malkolm proposed. "Even without fire you should be able to handle them."

The look on Fenicus's face did not immediately show his dismissal of the concept. It was true. From what he remembered of attacking that whaling vessel and the lessons taught by his uncle, humans were soft, fragile creatures. They couldn't put up much of a fight against his razor sharp talons, teeth, and his nearly impenetrable scale armor.

A sobering thought then came to Fenicus. The confident demeanor upon his face fell away. "It won't work."

"Why?" Malkolm wondered.

"This is the same group of humans who invaded my homeland. If all of that remains of my race couldn't defeat them in battle, how could I ever hope to succeed? They at least had fire on their side. I don't even have that."

Malkolm too shook his head. "I'm sorry. It was a stupid

idea."

"No, it wasn't," Fenicus consoled Malkolm. "It was a good try. Besides, we can't afford to ignore any idea." He smiled at his friend. "If I knew that I could get to the other dragons before the humans overpowered me, I'd do it. But if I fail, any chance there is to set them free is gone."

Malkolm snapped his fingers. "Wait a minute. What if I sneak in and free them? I mean, after all, my kind go in and out of there all the time. I'd certainly have an easier time slipping past the guards unnoticed than you would." Malkolm gazed at Fenicus with a hopeful grin. "What'ya think, huh?"

Fenicus mulled over the idea. He knew Malkolm was different from the rest of his kind; he could be trusted. Yet, none of the other dragons knew Malkolm. That was the wrinkle within the plan. "I, uh," he mumbled while shaking his head. "I don't think that will work either."

"Why not?"

"Malkolm, your kind kidnapped my friends and family. And given the history between our two species, I doubt they'll be willing to put too much trust in any human."

Malkolm's voice whined. "But I'm different. I'm not like the rest."

"I know. I know you're different, but they know nothing about you. They'd be more likely to chew you up than accept any help from you."

A frustrated sigh escaped Malkolm. His head and shoulders slumped. He fell silent.

Fenicus too shared in Malkolm's despondency, but he could not remain silent. "I can't believe I've come this far only to fail." Fenicus slapped his tail hard against the ground, pulverizing fallen branches and twigs that lay there. The impact sent tremors through the ground. A growl, muted only by his fear of being discovered, rumbled through his clenched teeth. "There has to be something we can do."

Malkolm shot back sharply. "But the only way to break them free is to get you inside and there's no way for us to get *you* inside." He stressed Fenicus's massive size with his hands, demonstrating the root of their problem. Malkolm shook his head and dropped to his rump upon the forest floor. "It's hopeless."

Fenicus could not deny that he was their biggest roadblock. Any dragon seen wandering through or flying around the village would immediately draw attention to itself and that would bring an end to any sort of rescue attempt. The operation would only succeed if they operated in secret, unseen and unheard until it was too late to stop them. Staring at Malkolm, Fenicus felt his frustration reach its peak. He couldn't help but wish, if for a short time, he was like his small friend—an unassuming human who could slip beyond the defenses of the fortress and liberate his imprisoned friends and family. It was a wish he knew was pointless, but he couldn't control it as it raced through his mind. "I don't think I've ever wanted to be human so much in my life." No sooner had the words spilled from his lips then he realized that Malkolm was not paying any attention to what he said. Rather, he seemed hypnotized by something. He lowered his head to the boy's level and placed a hand on his back. "What is it?" his voice edged with concern for his friend's health. "Are you okay?"

Malkolm's dirty arm rose mechanically from his side until it aimed directly back at the dragon. His index finger extended to point out the source of his wonderment. "Look," Malkolm whispered.

"What's wrong?" Tracing the line of Malkolm's arm and finger, Fenicus gazed upon on the amulet that hung from his neck. There it hung in the air, levitating freely against the pull of gravity. It oscillated wildly. The raised figures upon it had become a blur. And from the blurred core of the amulet grew a dazzling blue light, as if a distant star in the heavens had fallen from the sky to hang upon his neck. It grew with intensity until the brilliance consumed the whole amulet. Then the light vanished without warning. The amulet fell limp, hanging perfectly still. Then the amulet attached itself to Fenicus as though magnetized to his scales. The side left exposed was the one depicting the human form. And tracing the outline of that form ran a singular spark of blue light, which left a glowing trail in its wake.

Then, as the spark finished outlining the human silhouette in its lingering glow, the same brilliant blue light erupted from Fenicus's fingertips, flashing into Malkolm's eyes and blinding him temporarily. A cry of pain escaped him. Crouching to the ground, Malkolm covered up his face with his arms and cowered away from the radiance.

Pulling his outstretched hands toward his face, Fenicus watched the light recede to a shimmering aura that encircled the tip of each of his fingers. An odd tingling sensation tickled at the affected flesh. Without warning, the glowing ring of light crawled across his hands and up his forearms, moving with growing vigor as it passed over each scale. In its wake, the light left his scales shimmering like water. He saw his own wavering reflection gazing back at him in his liquefied flesh.

The aura approached his neck with increasing vigor. Having reached his shoulders, the glow quickly enveloped the base of his neck and began its progression toward his face while it likewise swept over the rest of his body. The tingling within the muscles of his neck forced them to become rigid. As the corona of blue traveled over his eyes and to the end of his snout, he became suddenly aware of a dull ache that began growing inside of his body.

His visual spectrum altered drastically, Fenicus saw the world in a photonegative of blue, white and black. Taking notice of the aura as it passed over him, Fenicus watched the light complete its envelopment of his legs and tail. With that completion, he felt the subtle discomfort that pulsed within him balloon into anguish beyond comprehension. Fenicus's back arched violently in response to his physical distress, his limbs flailed outwardly. His eyes, shocked wide open by the overwhelming pain, watched as his liquefied flesh and bone shrunk back from each limb.

Finally, another brilliant flash of light ripped through Fenicus from the inside out and the painful ordeal precipitated by the amulet had ended, leaving him in a heap upon the forest floor. His body smoldered in the cool spring air. Though he was not sure how, he was certain that the power of the amulet had changed him in some way. Fighting through an odd sense of disconnection with the world around him, Fenicus lifted his head to examine himself. What he first laid eyes on, however, was Malkolm, standing over him with a look of complete awe. But it wasn't his look of amazement that Fenicus found strange; it was the fact that Malkolm *stood* over him. Something, most definitely, had changed.

"Are you all right?" Malkolm asked pensively. He very carefully moved closer to Fenicus, looking over him with each step.

Prying himself up off the ground to his hands and knees, Fenicus caught sight of that which amazed Malkolm. Where glimmering scales once adorned his stout frame, pale human flesh now covered a far smaller set of muscles and bones. Horror struck at his heart. Wildly, he scrambled for the river's edge, crawling right through their extinguished campfire in the process. Nearly falling into the water, Fenicus thrust his hands into the river. They sank deep into the sandy shoal. Having disturbed the surface of the water, Fenicus waited anxiously for the ripples that obscured his reflection to subside. After a few brief moments that felt like an eternity, the image cleared.

"By Weylark!" he gasped. "What've I done?" The reflection that looked back at him was one totally unfamiliar to him. It was the face of his enemy. It was the face of a human. His wishful thinking awakened the mysterious, slumbering power of the amulet. With a muddy, wet hand he grabbed at the trinket to examine it. Suddenly, the raised images that adorned its sides made sense to him. It was a metamorphosis amulet, one meant to change its wearer into another creature unlike itself.

Preoccupied by disbelief, Fenicus did not hear his

friend's footsteps closing in.

Slowly and with notably more concern in his voice, Malkolm repeated his question. "Fenicus, are you okay?" He laid a gentle hand upon Fenicus's bare shoulder.

The feel of Malkolm's hand snapped Fenicus out of his state. He whipped his head around in the direction of the hand that touched him. Looking at Malkolm, Fenicus realized the simple beauty of the situation he now found himself in. Thinking upon his own new form, the solution to his dilemma began to take shape. He took notice of the soot caked on his hands and knees from crawling through the burnt-out embers. A lightness of spirit came upon him. Fenicus erupted into laughter. He hadn't felt this good in days. Malkolm could not resist joining in. The two sat there amused with themselves for quite some time.

Once the laughter subsided to the point where Fenicus could catch his breath and speak again, he let Malkolm know what brought him so much joy.

"I've got an idea!"

15

Calidin and his assistants led the broken dragons back toward the underground keep under the dim glow of torchlight. Angry whips lashed at their hardened hides. While they did little damage to the others, poor Azriel felt the sting of every whip crack cutting into his softened scales. No longer did his body shed its aged skin that itched feverishly at him, nor did he receive the liquefied gold that his body thirsted for. His body succumbed to the effects of britasia. He lagged at the back of the train, barely able to carry the weight of his own body. The scales that covered him, once gold of hue, were now browned in small patches all over his body. His time grew shorter every day. If they didn't find their way to freedom soon, he would pay the ultimate price.

Another stern lashing across the outside of his upper leg released a trickle of blood. He moaned in anguish, unable to maintain his strong exterior. Darius, who walked just ahead of Azriel, fought the limit of his shackles to aid the ailing dragon.

"Az," Darius whispered to his withered companion, "let me help you." He contorted his head and neck to fit them through the gap between the sickly dragon's arms. With his wrists bound, Azriel needed no strength to hold on—the irons did all the work for him. While he weighed much more than Darius, the young dragon balanced the bulk of Azriel's weight upon his back and managed the load. The men who drove them on shouted in unintelligible tongues that were as wicked in tone as the lashings they unleashed.

Floating past them all on a cushion of air, Calidin signaled to the two guards stationed at the base of the stairway. Each man approached a small pen that stood nearest him. Within each pen rested an ox. One ox stood before a bounty of hay and water, feeding itself to satiation while the other ox slept soundly on a pile of straw. Bursts of vapor shot rhythmically from its nostrils. Around each of their necks hung a sturdy harness from which a long braid of rope stretched upwards into the air and continued through a series of iron loops and pulleys atop a stout wooden tripod that stuck out of the ground. The other end of the rope connected to another iron loop anchored firmly to the bottom of the stairway.

The crack of a wooden paddle smacking squarely against their hindquarters roused the still oxen in their pens. The sleeping ox sprang to its feet, snorting with displeasure while the other kicked at the dirt and hay. Both beasts followed their natural instincts to move away from the stinging pain. Immediately, the lengths of rope attached to their harnesses drew taut through the pulley mechanism. Another wicked smack provoked further progress. The oxen pulled hard against the heavy load attached to the other side of the rope. Though the softened dirt within the pens made for poor traction, the oxen's strength was more than a match for the relatively meager resistance provided by the walkway. A splintering crack filled the air as the base of the walkway broke free of the ground and began to rise. A little at a time, the oxen pulled their load forward. With each plodding step, the walkway rose higher and higher into the air. The massive weight of the breakaway portion of the walkway creaked under the strain. One last whack of the paddle brought the oxen to the end of the pen. With the walkway raised to the apex of its design, the two guards made their way to the front of the pens. Once there, each of them took hold of a short length of rope with smaller iron hooks knotted to each end. They hastily attached one of the two ends to a small hook on the top of the oxen's harness and the other end to a similar hook anchored soundly into the soil. Unable to move back or forward, the oxen dove their heads into a heap of straw placed strategically before them and chewed away mindlessly. With the stairway hoisted to its apex, the doorway beneath became visible.

The parade of winged reptiles and their vicious masters passed beneath the raised platform toward the massive double doors situated there. Calidin, still at the head of the procession, spread his arms wide before the doors. A spark of blue energy swirled from the end of his staff and pierced the narrow gap between the two doors. The edges of the doors glowed eerily in that same blue color before they swung open as though the hands of fifty men pushed at them. At the behest of painful lashings, the dragons slowly followed the wizard straight through the entranceway and into the underground keep.

The guards watched the hulking creatures plod past them. The one standing alongside the leftmost oxen pen smiled arrogantly at them.

Preoccupied by the dragons, he missed the fact that his belt became suddenly lighter. The faint jingle of metal caught his attention. The guard groped at his belt in the darkened bailey. His face turned bright red and contorted into a look of rage. He rounded about and scanned his surroundings. His eyes locked on a filthy, blond-haired boy standing a few feet away, dangling his money purse in the air like a carrot to a horse.

"Lose something, did you?" the boy laughed, swinging the purse back and forth from his fingertips.

The guard clenched his teeth. "You filthy scamp, give it back!" He lunged forward for his purse, raking his hand through the air. The boy snatched it out of his reach just a split-second earlier.

Sticking out his tongue, the boy taunted the older man and took off at a full gallop toward the smith's workshop. That was all the incentive the guard required. The guard lunged at the boy.

The guard who manned the other oxen pen turned his attention away from the dragons as the last one passed under the raised walkway. He then glanced at his companion, who was a good fifty pounds or so overweight, huffing and puffing his round body around the bailey in pursuit of his stolen purse. The guard had a good laugh at his companion's expense.

The younger guard brought his attention back to the oxen. An odd shadow slithered about near the open gateway. He looked in its direction and squinted through the darkness. Scratching his head, he concluded, "Bah, muss be seein' things."

After releasing both of the ropes from the ground anchors, the guard called out to the oxen to heed the pull against their harnesses and return to the back of their pens. He snapped at the anchor ropes when the one of the animals lagged behind, causing the walkway to bend and twist unnaturally.

A loud crash followed by the splash of water echoed through the night. "Son of a bitch!"

Twisting his head, the younger guard looked in the direction of the other man as he approached. He was quite a sight. Chunks of softened potato and half-rotted carrots clung to his face. A brownish gruel dripped from his body. He breathed heavily from the effort of the chase.

"What happened to you?"

"Very funny, maggot!" The older guard grabbed a handful of slop from his sleeve and chucked it at the younger man. "The little bastard got away. I tripped over one of the pig troughs."

The younger guard held out one of the anchor ropes to his messy companion.

"What're ye handing that to me fer?" the older guard barked harshly. He looked at the teetering stairway that was on the verge of breaking under the strain of its own weight. "Why should I help you with that?"

"If you don't help me lower the stairway, it'll be both our heads. Kell will be down here any moment fer the festivities an if he's got to wait fer us to lower the walkway there'll be hell to pay."

"Aye," the older man mumbled. "I guess yer right." He immediately lifted the tensed rope from his companion's hand and the two commenced lowering the stairway. Moments later, the walkway settled back against the soil. Life, for the moment, was back to normal.

*   *   *

The dark tunnels beneath the tower snaked about in all directions, similar to how the roots of a tree grow in the soil. Along the dirt floors, scattered hay worked to absorb the dankness of the underground keep. It was a maze of chambers, dungeons, and poorly lit hallways meant to disorient prisoners. But the shadow that crept about the halls was not a prisoner or a prison guard. It was an intruder. For quite some time it wandered the underground fortress, getting its bearings and searching for living gold. Pressing its back flat against the damp walls, the shadowy figure shimmied along the passageway. It approached a lit torch that hung from an iron bracket affixed to a ceiling support.

The shadow stopped abruptly. Men's voices, barely audible, began to grow in the passageway. Its head turned in the direction of the surging voices to ascertain if its safety was about to be compromised. Quite a distance back from where it came, the warm glow of a hand-held torch grew from around a crook in the tunnel. The head of the figure looked about feverishly for a place to hide itself away until the danger passed. Its gaze locked on an abandoned section of the keep that appeared as though it may have once been meant to be another passageway or the beginnings of a new chamber. Glancing once more to its right, it saw that the light cast by the torches of those who approached was nearly upon its position. Wasting no time, the shadow sprinted across the breadth of the tunnel and ducked inside the dig site. There it crouched quietly, patiently waiting for the danger to pass.

It knelt down into a tight crouch and hoped the light of their hand-held torches would not expose its hiding place. Eerie silhouettes created by the mingling of light sources danced about the floor. The slinking figure felt the looming fear of discovery close in on it. Now within a few feet of its hiding place, the echoing voices of the approaching men were close enough and clear enough for the stealthy figure to eavesdrop.

"Don't you think it would have been better to just enslave them and use them for some worthy purpose?" asked one of the men to his companion. "I mean, after all, wouldn't they make mighty steeds for our warriors to ride into battle? Imagine that, yer brother sweeping down upon an opposing army on the backside of a dragon. All men would tremble at his feet."

The other man laughed. "Aye, that'd be quite the sight wouldn't it, Bryar." His voice was coarse. He sounded like a much older man than Bryar. "An army of winged beasties at our command." He let out a big sigh. "Alas, Kell has bigger plans for them. Besides, who needs the creature when ye have a suit of armor crafted of their hides and their blood coursing through yer veins."

The feet of the men crossed before the den of the hiding specter. "I guess yer right." Bryar made an odd sound, like someone gagging.

"What's yer problem?" the other man groaned at the sound.

"Just the thought of so much blood," Bryar replied. "I've never been one for the sight of the stuff, Halbard. The thought of carving them up and draining them dry makes me a bit queasy. I've never been able to kill anything, not even a lowly squirrel."

The shadowy figure let out an audible gasp when it realized what the man's words meant. Its hand swiftly sought to cover its mouth. The sound of scuffing feet making their way down the passageway stopped. Fear gripped its heart in anticipation of being caught. It desperately waited to hear their conversation and fading footsteps resume.

Halbard and Bryar paused and looked about the poorly lit passageway behind them. Bryar moved the torch high and low, left and right to see where the noise originated from. Both men shrugged in uncertainty and began to make their way to their intended destination.

Another loud laugh escaped Halbard. He smacked Bryar across the back swiftly. "That's why yer a page lad. Ye can barely hold yer liquor."

"I know! It just doesn't feel like a fitting end for them. I mean, I've heard Calidin talk about how he doesn't believe it's our place to wipe them out."

Halbard stopped his companion again and lashed him verbally. "Ye never mind that crazy coot. He's trouble, ye hear me. Ye just do yer job and keep yer loyalty in check. Kell would never lead us astray. Now let's get going before we're late fer the feast."

Their voices faded into obscurity and soon their torchlight no longer filled the tunnel. The shadow emerged from its hideaway with a sense of urgency, making its way in the direction opposite Halbard and Bryar.

It was not long before the shadow came upon a crossroads in the system of passageways. Cautiously, the shadow hugged the wall and made its way toward the intersection. A few feet from the intersection, an odd noise struck its ears—a gurgling sound, like someone snoring away. Having reached the end of the passageway, it took a long glance along the rest of the tunnel, and then scanned the tunnel to its left. All clear. Taking in a deep breath and slowly pressing it out, the shadow peeked out from behind the wall to its right to investigate the source of the sound. Its suspicions were confirmed.

A rather portly, bearded man sat asleep at his post. His sword lay upon the ground beside him. To the left of his snoring head, a key ring held down a strip of colored fabric atop a makeshift table. Checking in all directions to make sure no one else saw its movements, the shadow crept from behind the corner of the passageway and stepped into the open. Its bare feet padded silently across the ground as it closed the distance between the dozing man and itself. The figure, now bathed in warm torchlight, investigated the man and his possessions. Wary of waking him, the shadow reached out for the key ring and the slip of cloth only to pull its hand back, having thought better of its actions.

Then the shadow took notice of something that it hadn't noticed before. An emptied bottle of strong-smelling liquor lay on the ground to the right of him, just teetering against his outstretched fingers. It was certain that this man wouldn't awake any time soon. Gathering up all its courage, the shadow extended its hand toward the key ring. The cold of the metal touched against its darkened flesh without any movement from the snoozing man. Swallowing hard, the figure pulled the ring up from the cloth it sat upon. The tiniest *clink* sounded from the key when it settled against the ring. Once more, the shadow exhaled another deep breath of tension. With the same kind of care and precision that a painter might take with a brush when detailing a fine line upon the face of a woman, the shadow pressed the key against the ring and closed his hand tight around it.

At first the figure thought to leave the slip of cloth behind but thought better of it and decided to give it a good once over before taking its leave of the drunken dreamer. Taking it into its hands, it saw that the colors were in fact embroidered lines of blue, red, green, white, and black, intersected and woven in strange patterns upon its surface. Though the shadow was unable to comprehend the words written on the cloth, it had no problems making sense of the woven symbols that resembled the heads of two distinctly different dragons—one breathing fire and one not. The strip of cloth was a map of the underground keep and those were the dungeons that held his kin.

The shadowy figure froze solid as the drunken man shifted and mumbled in his sleep. Over and over in its mind, the shadow prayed, *Just let me get away. Just stay asleep long enough for me to get away.* To its relief, the man's fingers continued to prop up the empty bottle. His eyes stayed shut. Quickly, the shadow attempted to make sense of the map. It did not take long for it to discern its location. It had to get to the lowest level, one floor down.

Keeping its eyes trained sharply on the man, the shadow backed away from him and moved back into the intersection. Turning right, the shadow rolled up the map, shoved it beneath the waist of its breeches, and took up a brisk jog toward the stairwell at the end of the passageway.

* * *

The sound of breaking glass captured the attention of the young dragons. Every pair of eyes leered at the entranceway, waiting to see the root of the disturbance. In the brief silence that followed, a noise that resembled a painful grunt slithered its way through the narrow gap between the doors. Another thud followed.

Creeeeeeek!

The dungeon doors slowly swung open. All eyes locked on the entranceway. In slunk a small, dark form. With both hands, it shoved the doors closed.

All the young dragons gazed oddly at the figure. It appeared to be a human, but one far smaller than those they had had dealings with since their capture. Stranger yet was its state of cleanliness. Dirt and soot covered it from head to toe. And while those other humans they had met moved with careful steps when around them, this human made its way across the dungeon floor toward them with an air of aloofness.

Ariel's soft voice called out to the human. "What do you want?"

A gleaming white smile shined like a beacon in the dark through its parted lips. It sprinted toward the dragon.

"Oh, Ariel," the human spoke with a sigh, its voice that of a young boy. "By Weylark's grace, you're alive."

Ariel shrunk away, seemingly uneasy with this human. Her tone grew impatient. "Who are you?"

The human looked over himself and then laughed as if suddenly becoming aware of some great discord between its appearance and its actual self. Holding up its hands in a gesture meant to temporarily halt her inquisitiveness, the human then pulled forth an amulet from beneath its blackened tunic and began to whisper. A stark, brilliant flash of light sprang forth from the human and bathed the dungeon in a blinding illumination. The dragons averted their eyes from the light. When the light receded, a well-known shape met their eyes.

"Fenicus!" Ariel cried happily. "We thought you were dead."

The rest of the dragons chimed in, calling out his name in disbelief.

Fenicus ran toward Ariel and they embraced. Reunited at last, he realized that all the things about her that he used to complain about were now quite trivial and meaningless. More so, he felt sorry for all the cruel jokes he played on her over the years. Seeing her alive and well awoke Fenicus to the fact that he actually loved his little sister. Pulling back from her, he took the small key he filched from the sleeping guard and began unlocking her shackles. Nervous energy filled his fingertips, making the simple task of manipulating the key unimaginably difficult.

Ariel watched his frantic effort and asked, "How did you escape?"

"Don't worry about that right now. We'll have plenty of time for stories later," Fenicus insisted, his eyes searching his surroundings as he worked the tumblers in the final lock. "We've got to get the others and get out of here."

"Tell me about it," Ariel whined. "I've been chained up here for days."

Fenicus's stalking gaze fell upon Darius. He sat slumped upon the floor, unstirred by the excitement of Fenicus's return. To his surprise, his old friend did not look like the same arrogant, honor-bound dragon that he once feared. This was a tired, broken dragon; a dragon that had no will to stand, let alone fight. Saddened by the pity he now felt for Darius, Fenicus snapped back to the task at hand as the last length of chain clanged against the floor.

Then, from a distant corner of the room, Talon's raspy voice called out. "Some of us have had it worse than others." It was a voice Fenicus felt great comfort in hearing. Craning his neck to see past his sister, he found Talon kneeling on the floor, still shackled to the wall. Numerous gaping wounds marked his body. The blood that dried over the gashes marked him like stripes on a tiger. Fenicus squinted at the sight of his friend's encrusted lesions. They made uncomfortable tingles ripple through him.

"Here." Fenicus turned back to his sister and handed her the key. "Take this and set the others free. And be quick about it."

Fenicus moved to Talon's side and tried not to focus on his unsettling appearance. "What happened to you?"

"It was that wizard," stated Talon scornfully while trying to stand, "Calidin. He's to blame for this. He's to blame for all of this." He fought through noticeable physical discomfort to right himself. His anger, however, did not provide enough motivation to master the pain. He began to stumble just as he was halfway to his feet. Fenicus rushed to his aid, catching him and helping him up the rest of the way. "If it wasn't for him, they'd never have invaded Berathor." He slammed his fist against the wall in frustration. "Arggg!" The entire chamber shuddered. Bits of stone and dirt rained down from above. "He's too powerful to stop."

Fenicus attempted to use the tip of his nail to unlock Talon's shackles and was surprised to find it a little easier than fumbling about with the key. "Well, if we don't get out of here soon, that wizard's going to be the least of our problems."

"What do you mean?" Talon asked. The sound of worry was unmistakable in his voice. "What's wrong?"

Fenicus nibbled on his bottom lip, searching for a way to break the news to the others.

The entire dungeon fell breathless, silent, awaiting his answer.

Looking at all his friends, Fenicus wondered if the truth would create a panic. Then again, perhaps a little panic was exactly what was needed to ignite the fire of rebellion in those overcome by self-pity. He drew in a deep breath to calm his nerves.

"Kell and his men intend on killing us all, tonight!" He then cursed himself for being honest as he watched everyone come unglued. Voices cried out from all over the dungeon, talking frantically above and beneath one another.

What do you mean? Why? What did he say? Tonight? Did he say tonight?

"Are you sure?" Talon asked amidst the din of noise and confusion.

Fenicus whirled about at the hysteria his news instigated. "Yes, I'm certain. I overheard a few of Kell's men in the passageways." The noise became so overpowering that he could no longer hear Talon. Lip reading was not one of his better skills. All the voices pounded relentlessly at his head as the crescendo of noise grew to an unbearable level. He tried to stop-up his ears with his fingers but it was no use.

"Shut up!" Talon bellowed above all the other voices. The ringing echo of his voice hung in the air. An eerie stillness followed. Only the muffled sobs from the dragonlings bubbled forth. Talon spoke again. "Why are they doing this? What did we ever do to them?"

"We didn't do anything," Fenicus replied. "It's our scales they want. They're planning on skinning us alive to make some sort of armor."

"That's a pleasant thought," Talon interjected sarcastically. He grew closer to Fenicus. "Is that all?"

"No." Fenicus's voice was cold, void of feeling. "They're

also planning to make our blood into some kind of invincibility potion."

"Oh," Darius blurted, "wonderful! How'd they figure that out?"

"Quiet!" Talon snapped at Darius. "It must've been Calidin. I'd be willing to bet my life on it. He seems to know things he shouldn't, things that no human should know. He's probably told Kell all there is to know about us." He fell silent, pondering this new knowledge. "But, if what you say is true, then we've indeed run out of time."

"What do we do?" Ariel squeaked, her voice sounded fearful and uncertain.

Fenicus noticed that everyone was now free of their bonds and standing in a large circle around him. "Like I said before, we've got to set our parents free. But there's something I must take care of first." Fenicus scanned the crowd for Darius who stood silently behind Dozer and Talon, hoping he wouldn't be seen. He crossed the floor toward him. Both Dozer and Talon parted to make way for Fenicus.

The entire chamber fell silent. Every pair of eyes followed him as he made his way through the crowd. Darius lifted his head to meet Fenicus as he approached. His features were somber, his shape languid. His words poured from his mouth quite strained and raspy, as though it took a mighty effort to speak. His remorse was unmistakable. "I'm sorry, Fenicus. I never meant for anything—"

Fenicus held up his hand to put an end to Darius's apology. "I forgave you a long time ago, long before I forgave myself. But I need my old friend back now, Darius, more than ever. I can't do this without you." He put out his open hand before Darius in a show of friendship. At that moment, Fenicus noticed a certain lightness of spirit push away the dark clouds looming over his friend.

Darius glanced from Fenicus's hand to the other young dragons, lingering on Dozer, Talon, and Laurel. They nodded in answer to his quiet inquiry. Darius grabbed hold of Fenicus's forearm and the two locked in a strong handshake.

"If you've a plan for getting us out of here, Fenicus," Darius asserted with the same vehemence Fenicus was used to hearing from him, "let's hear it. I'm sick of rotting in this prison. Whatever it takes, I'm with you."

"Glad to have you back, Darius. It's been too long."

Darius nodded. He then spoke to his peers. "What about the rest of you? Are you ready to fight?" his voice boomed.

An impassioned roar of unity against their oppressors filled the dungeon.

"All right! Let's do it." Turning to lead the assemblage of dragons out of the dungeon, Fenicus paused. He caught sight of both his sister and Laurel who looked like mothers on the nest. Both of them carried several tiny dragonlings along the length of their necks. Each of the little ones latched onto their spines as they would their own mothers. Unaware of the chaos that surrounded them, the dragonlings sought the warm touch of a female. Ariel and Laurel, though unlikely to mother any young for another fifty years or so, took to it without much resistance, as did their passengers. In fact, looking at it with more adult eyes,

Fenicus didn't think it looked so odd after all, though he couldn't help chuckle a bit. The thought of his sister having young of her own was at times a humorous if not frightful idea. Conversely, looking at Laurel, he felt that the motherly adornments made her glow.

Having assessed their cargo, Fenicus understood the importance of protecting them. "I want you two to stick by Darius and Clink. If anything should happen, they'll keep you safe." Coming about as he approached the doorway, he addressed the rest of them. "The rest of you, try to stick together and don't get lost."

Ariel leered at Remus and Narix who were slinking around behind her. They were still attached at the hip, seemingly trying to keep out of sight and avoid being chosen for anything really dangerous.

"That means you." Ariel shot daggers at them with her piercing glance.

Fenicus noticed Talon and Dozer standing by his side. "Can you two keep to the rear of the pack? If anyone tries to sneak up on us, it'll be up to you to fight them off until more help arrives."

The dragons quickly fell into place; all were at the ready for whatever might come their way. Caspar, another diminutive member of Julius' family, took it upon himself and rushed to the doorway to await Fenicus's command to throw the doors wide.

"Everybody, follow me," Fenicus commanded as he unfurled the stolen map that he held in his sweaty grasp. He twisted and turned it, trying to properly orient it to their position. He gasped an audible "Duh!" when he figured it out. Finally ready, Fenicus nodded to Caspar who flung open both doors and moved with vigor into the passageway to guard their escape.

As Fenicus passed through the doorway and into the passage, Caspar stepped in front of him. "What else can I do, Fenicus? I really want to help."

Fenicus watched as the procession began to move into the passageway and collect there. He tried keeping a headcount but lost track halfway through. "Just stay with everyone else," he huffed in frustration. "And make sure your brother doesn't get trampled."

"Hey," Caspar interjected with a firm tone, "I might be small, but I'm faster than everyone else. Talon and Dozer could use my help in a pinch."

Fenicus couldn't deny his speed. While he was almost half the size of other dragons his age, there wasn't a single dragon that could beat him in a race. The numerous medals he had won in aerial slalom and sky sprints during the Founder's Festival each year were proof of that. Being smaller clearly had its share of advantages. "All right."

Caspar was about to move through the crowd toward Talon and Dozer when Fenicus grabbed him by the arm and yanked him back.

"Wait a second! There's a man lying unconscious outside the dungeon. I clubbed him in the back of the head with a bottle. If anyone finds him like that they'll know something's up. Can you take care of it?"

"No problem," Caspar answered, saluting Fenicus like a member of the sentry. With a nod from Fenicus, he was out the door. Once in the passageway, he found Fenicus's human victim. Without wasting any time, Caspar grabbed the toppled stool and set it aright. He then moved to the unconscious man to do the same but stopped. He stared oddly at him. A brusque, unsure shrug of the shoulders and Caspar picked the man up off the ground rather roughly, and with equally less finesse, set him down upon the stool. Holding his tiny head in his large hand, Caspar laid it back against the wall.

Once Talon and Dozer moved into the passageway, Caspar blew out the torch burning overhead, casting the human in shadow. He then moved back to the doors to close them. Something crunched under his feet. Caspar looked down at numerous shards of broken glass glittering upon the floor. They had once been part of the liquor bottle Fenicus had smashed over the guard's head. While an impatient passerby might overlook the guard's injury, the broken bottle would definitely attract unwanted attention. Using his tail as a broom, Caspar swept the chunks of glass into the dungeon while Talon and Dozer stood sentinel over the rest of the dragons as they moved down the passage. Grabbing hold of the iron pull rings, Caspar drew the doors shut and rejoined Talon and Dozer.

To the rear of their position, a dim glow appeared from an adjacent tunnel that grew brighter with each moment. The faint sound of a man whistling likewise grew stronger. Caspar blew out the torch above the man and the three dragons rushed to catch up with the rest of the party.

At the front of the procession, a bit of confusion put a momentary halt to their progress.

"What's wrong, Fenicus?" Darius inquired.

Staring at the map, Fenicus could not discern which way he needed to lead them. Though the map seemed to be complete at first glance, he couldn't figure out for the life of him why the passageway only turned to the right when it should, in fact, terminate in a T with the left hand side leading to a ramp to the lowest level. Inspecting the map, Fenicus discovered that this passage had yet to be finished. The map contained broken lines representing where the ramp was intended. Examining the wall, he saw that Kell's men had begun digging the passageway, but a large boulder tangled up in a gnarled nest of roots had impeded their progress.

"Damn!" Fenicus cursed to himself. "The map's wrong. This tunnel was never finished."

"So what do we do now?" Darius asked, his patience wearing thin.

Just as Fenicus began to form an uncertain answer with his lips, a familiar voice caught his ear.

"Fenicus!" The high-pitched voice of a child emanated from the right hand passage.

Darius and the rest of the dragons within earshot of the voice leered down the passageway where a small human boy sprinted toward them. They cast looks of confusion at the boy and then at Fenicus.

"Malkolm!" Fenicus called out as his young friend drew near. Fenicus confided in Darius, "You asked me about a plan." He jerked his head in the direction of the approaching human. "He's it."

Audible gasps of disbelief filled the corridor behind Fenicus. Whispered voices slithered throughout the congested throng questioning everything from Fenicus's sanity to how soon they'd all be dead.

A look of deepened shock sprawled across Darius's face. "Your plan's a human? Are you kidding? You're trusting one of them?"

"Look, Darius," he said impatiently, "if you're going to trust me, you're going to have to trust my judgment too. Believe me, what we were taught about humans doesn't apply to all of 'em."

Fenicus placed his left hand upon Darius's right shoulder. "Have some faith, will you?"

"All right," Darius appeased his friend.

Fenicus turned his attention to Malkolm who now stood before him, breathing heavily. "How'd you find us?" Fenicus inquired of Malkolm.

"Oh, I've spent quite a few cold, snowy nights hiding down here. It's so big that no one ever discovered me."

The news seemed to bolster Fenicus's confidence in his little friend. "Well, that's good. We need your help." He held out his hand to Malkolm. In his open palm lay the frayed woolen fabric map.

"What's that?"

"It's a complete map of the keep," Fenicus explained. He scratched at an itchy patch of dry scales on the side of his neck. "Or so I thought. From what I can tell, either the map or the keep is incomplete. I can't tell which."

Malkolm carefully lifted the map from Fenicus, squatted down upon dirt floor, and laid it out before him. He positioned his finger on a small red box positioned a few inches off to the right of center. Glancing up, he seemed to be orienting himself with both the map and their position. "Well, as far as I can tell, this is where we are. On the second level."

Fenicus decidedly joined Malkolm at floor level while Darius watched them both. Fenicus then placed his index finger down upon another section of the map detailed in green. "I think this chamber is where our parents are being held. I wasn't too sure though. This writing doesn't make a whole lot of sense to me. Am I reading it wrong?"

Malkolm shrugged his shoulders.

"You mean you don't understand it either?" Fenicus asked snidely, forgetting himself and his company for the moment. "It's in your language isn't it?"

Malkolm nodded in the affirmative, but the reddish hue overcoming his face signaled a point of embarrassment for the boy.

"You mean you can't read?" Darius inquired dolefully.

A troubling scowl washed over Malkolm. "I never learned how. I didn't have anyone to teach me."

Looking upon Malkolm, Fenicus felt a fool at making his small friend feel such discomfort. "I'm sorry, Malkolm. I wasn't thinking."

Malkolm shrugged it off as though the insult made no difference to him. He grinned weakly to Fenicus, who now knew all sins were forgiven. The dragon rubbed Malkolm's head gently, mussing his hair. Malkolm laughed.

Malkolm then pointed out a narrow passageway embroidered on the map not too far from their current position. "While I can't read it, if this was the chamber they were in," Malkolm motioned with his head toward the gathering of dragons, "then they were right above your parents.

"And there's a ramp over here." Malkolm fingered the map again with a tapping motion. "That should do it. It won't be nearly as fast as this passageway would have been, but if we follow it down to the lowest level, it should get us where we need to go." He looked longingly at Fenicus, Darius, and the rest of the dragons whom now seemed to be hanging on his every word.

"All right, Malkolm." Fenicus nodded. "Since you're familiar with these tunnels and passageways, you're our guide. You're up front with me."

A thumbs up from the boy signaled his readiness.

"Good, let's go!" Fenicus insisted, taking a few steps down the tunnel.

Darius moved alongside Fenicus for a few steps and whispered quietly to him in their dragonian tongue. "I hope you're right about this kid. We can't afford any mistakes." Darius then fell back with everyone else.

The end of the procession cleared the passageway just as Sven rounded the corner behind them.

16

The community longhouse stood in the shadow of the hilltop tower, which overlooked the bailey. Inside, fifty-eight hearty men awaited the arrival of their mighty chieftain. Many of the men quarreled with one another over who would have the honor of sitting beside Kell when he arrived. Some offered to trade fine weapons, armor, and livestock for the rare opportunity. One even offered his wife to another man as payment. Regardless of their jockeying for position, the two chairs seated nearest Kell's remained vacant, awaiting Sven and Calidin.

A sudden hush fell over the gathered soldiers. Kell strolled through the main doorway, the hood of his jerkin draped over his face. When he drew it back, the entire building erupted into cheer. The great chieftain grinned and bowed to his men, acknowledging their praise of him. He motioned for them all to sit and they did so. Their cheers died out to silence.

At Kell's beckoning, a bright, cheerful woman strode over and took the burden of his furred jerkin from his shoulders. Her movements were serene, airy, like a cloud of fog passing along the ground. She retreated to a small stool where she sat, holding his covering in her lap.

Kell assumed his position at the head of the massive table. His eyes glanced in wonderment at the two seats beside him that still sat empty. It was awkward for both Sven and Calidin to be late, let alone absent from such revelry. Sven, he knew, wanted to check on their prisoners one last time before he settled down for a single moment of enjoyment. Calidin, on the other hand, rarely ate and always seemed to vanish at the most inopportune times. Kell passed off their nonattendance as a measure of their duties or idiosyncrasies and hoped they would soon take their places beside him.

Kell cupped the stem of the wooden goblet sitting on the table before him and lifted it up to eye level over the table. A trickle of the pungent smelling liquor spilled over the brim and ran down over his fingers. As if on cue, all of his men proudly replicated their superior's actions.

"Tonight," Kell announced, "we come together to celebrate the beginning of a new age—an age of prosperity unlike any ever witnessed before. It was my dream of uniting the clans, my vision that shaped our future, our destiny. But it was your work, your sacrifice that has brought us to this moment—to this precipice of greatness."

Kell paused. His men howled primitive war cries of success and triumph at his words. The floor of the chamber shook at their rumblings. When their words died down, he continued his praise.

"And let us not forget the sacrifices of our fallen brethren, of those who forfeited their lives so that all of our hopes and dreams might come to fruition. May Odin welcome them into the halls of Valhalla and feast to our triumph!" Kell's voice grew to a crescendo as he bellowed out his final words. He thrust his goblet into the air, spilling more of the liquor on the table. His men once more mimicked his actions from one end of the longhouse to the other and began to chant his name.

Kell waved his hands toward his men in a quieting manner and their murmurs withdrew. He finished his speech. "Everything we set out to do has come to pass. We've captured the dragons. We'll soon have filched them of their gold. All that remains is the unification of our people and the vanquishing of all those who oppose us. Tonight we feast to victory!" He thrust his chalice one last time into the air and then downed what remained of its contents. All the men seated at the table drank their goblets dry in singular, chugging swigs and slammed the empty vessels upon the table. With a rhythmic pace, the men began chanting "Kell" and banged their goblets upon the table, adding power to his name.

A score of beefy wenches emerged from behind a woolen curtain at the far end of the longhouse. In their hands they carried wooden serving trays. Upon those trays rested a bounty of the most succulent roast pigs, venison shanks, beef flanks, whole chickens, loaves of hearty breads, dried fish, and innumerable other foods. They carried the platters to the table with grace and care. But once placed thereon, the men tore at the smorgasbord like ravenous animals.

Kell sat and gauged the spirit of his men, observing their gay, carefree nature. He smiled wide, relishing all that he accomplished while trying not to brood over what had yet to be done. He knew well how important it would be in the days and weeks to come to maintain a high level of morale in his men. From here, the days would only grow darker until total success was achieved. Kell, confident in the temperament of his men, took his first mouthwatering bite of meat. His mind settled on the moment, and he paid no more attention to the absence of Calidin and Sven.

*　*　*

"Blasted oaf," Sven grumbled impatiently at the sight of the lump of a man sitting asleep on the wooden stool. *Another distraction keeping me from dinner*, he thought. "Wake up, Harold!" He spat at the man.

The man did not stir at the harsh sound of Sven's voice. In fact, he neither snored nor made any other sort of sound. It was difficult for Sven to see the man in the dimly lit halls beneath the tower, especially since the torch that hung overhead had been snuffed-out.

With an agitated grunt, Sven cuffed Harold across the top of the head to rouse him from his slumber. Instead of snapping awake from the force of the blow, his motionless form tumbled from the stool and fell with a thud. Sven stared in uncertainty at the sprawled-out form lying on the floor. Though he knew Harold to be a hearty drinker, there was no spirit potent enough to dull the impact of such a blow. Sven knelt down to examine him. His breaths were shallow. He examined him from head to toe. Behind Harold's right ear, Sven discovered a dark substance that glistened in the pale torchlight. He narrowed his eyes to get a better look at it, but he couldn't see.

Sven stood with a huff and walked several paces down the tunnel where he liberated a torch from its bracket. The roar of the lapping flames whispered in his ear as he carried it back toward Harold. With an aura of warm light now filling the area, Sven did not need to examine the area too closely to discover the root of the mystery. The glistening substance was in fact blood seeping from a deep gash along the side of his head. The red plasma that bubbled from the wound took small fragments of skull with it as it flowed.

Sven then became keenly aware of an eerie quiet that overcame his senses—a quiet so consuming that all he heard was a dull ringing in his ears as one might hear while sitting alone in the dark at night. Not a single sound mingled its way through the rough-cut planks of oak that comprised the doors to the inner dungeon. There were no whispering dragons, no clanging chains. Nothing whatsoever.

He panicked. Moving with deliberate steps, he thrust the burning torch in his hand toward the flameless one in the bracket above his felled subordinate. With it lit, he moved to the closed dungeon doors. With his free hand braced against the right-hand door, Sven shoved against it with all his weight. The door groaned wearily upon its hinges. Slowly, Sven swung the door ajar. After only a handful of steps, a loud snap echoed from underfoot.

Something hard had cracked beneath his step. Sven stepped back to look upon the floor. There, lying in splintered shards upon the ground, were the broken remains of a glass bottle. Glancing back at Harold and his wound for a moment, the shattered glass took on an ominous meaning. Anger welled within him like a river. *Have we been betrayed?*

Sven rammed his shoulder against the door. It swung wide. Unfolding before him, the landscape of the inner dungeon made his heart sink in his chest. He drew in a short, dreadful breath, aghast at the alarming reality within. As fast as his legs could carry him, Sven raced back up the tunnel toward the tower with one desperate thought in mind—*the bell!*

*   *   *

Shouting voices outside the dungeon awoke many of the adult dragons from a state of weary slumber. The voices sounded fearful, alarmed by something unexpected. Metallic noises ensued like weapons being unsheathed and struck against an opposing force. The adult dragons sat in hushed silence. Many of them struck odd glances at one another. When anyone tried to speak, another quickly hushed them. The tinges of battle soon subsided along with the strained voices. Whatever happened beyond the door had come to an end.

Clink!

The hinges of the double-doors whined as they swung open. The dragons squinted at the sound.

Through the doorway slipped whispering voices. But these were not the same ones; these were familiar voices speaking in familiar tongues. Their words grew louder in volume. Finally, from the inky darkness of the passageway poured a host of young dragons led by Fenicus. On his back sat Malkolm. At the sight of them, the adult dragons broke out into both cheers and sobs of joy. Many of the youngest dragons sprinted to their fettered parents to hug them. Ariel and Laurel wasted no time in reuniting the infants they carried to their parents.

Malkolm leapt down from Fenicus and rushed toward the nearest dragon. The limp, beaten frame of Azriel leaned feebly against the dungeon wall. He watched as the small human approached. With no visible fear or apprehension whatsoever, the young boy grabbed hold of the chains anchoring Azriel to the dungeon wall. He began to work the stolen key in the lock until a barely audible *clank* rang out from the inner mechanism. Pulling the locks open, the chains rolled noisily through their anchors and fell into a heap upon the floor.

No longer buoyed by the strength of the chains, Azriel fell to the ground. He continued to watch the small human work to free his wrists and wings from their bonds.

"Why are you helping us?" Azriel rasped like a giant snake.

Malkolm looked upon the sickly dragon for a moment. "Because Fenicus is my friend, and what my kind's doing to you is wrong."

Azriel nodded and exhaled, "Thank you."

Malkolm just smiled at the dragon and departed from him to help the others.

Meanwhile, Fenicus heard his father's faint voice calling

out to him amidst the rumble of other voices. The flood of sound made it difficult for the young dragon to find his father. He moved his head from side to side, up and down, in search of him. Fenicus called out for his father while he maneuvered through the congested throng. Standing behind a blockade of dragons, Fenicus felt a surge of frustration build up inside. He ground his teeth to keep from lashing out at those struggling all around him to free themselves. Then, from behind, a heavy hand fell with a thud upon his back. Whirling about, Fenicus locked eyes with his father, pulled him close, and gave him a strong hug. He felt the air escape his lungs under his father's vise-like grip.

"We thought we lost you forever," Farimus spoke solemnly in his son's ear. He pulled back and looked him over. "What in the world happened to you? Everyone thought you were dead."

"It's a long story, Dad. A story for another time." Fenicus looked longingly at the other dragons surrounding his father. "Dad, where's Ma?"

Farimus motioned with his head for his son to turn around. There, waiting with open arms, stood his mother. Fenicus ran to her. He held her for a moment and pulled away to tell his mother and father what he'd learned.

"Mom, Dad," Fenicus urged, "we've got to get everyone out of here before it's too late. It won't take long before they realize what's happened."

His father huffed. "It's no wonder this room isn't crawling with Kell's men already."

At first, Fenicus did not understand his father's

comments. Then he realized that his father's gaze followed Malkolm around the dungeon. He knew exactly what had drawn his ire. Fenicus shook his head. Their moment of warmth was over.

"I know what you're thinking, Dad, and you're wrong."

"Am I?" He leered back at his son. "How could you trust one of *them*?" His voice rose over all others in the chamber. "They're the reason we're here! They're the reason our race was nearly wiped out! They're all the same, Fenicus." Farimus paused to catch his breath. "Did all our teachings escape you?"

"No," Fenicus barked at his father, his voice even louder in volume. "I remember all my lessons. But Malkolm's different. He's not like the others."

"Bah!" Farimus snapped back. "You're just a child, what do you know?"

"What do *I* know?" Fenicus questioned.

A haunting silence fell over the dungeon. Fenicus and Farimus stood at the center of attention.

Mariel forced her way between them. "Hey!" Mariel whispered in a not-so-quiet whisper. "Stop it, you two!"

"I've been out there, Dad." Fenicus swung a finger toward a random wall. "What have you done but sit in a dungeon and rot? I know more about this world we've been hiding from than most of you." Fenicus glared at the audience that surrounded them.

"Quiet down," Mariel pleaded a little more forcefully this time.

"Oh, I see! A few days out there on your own and you're an expert. I guarantee you that boy will turn on us the first chance he gets. You're a fool to trust him."

"Enough!" Mariel screamed.

Fenicus and Farimus held their tongues. Fenicus grew painfully aware of the spectacle that they had made of themselves. Farimus looked down where Malkolm stood at the feet of his son, looking up at them both. Farimus and Fenicus stared at one another. Fenicus knew that the only thing left to do was apologize.

Before either of them could play the part of the adult and apologize, a somber sound filled the air. Three airy tones rang aloud at perfect intervals. Several seconds waned and then the tones began again. Though the sound was pleasing to the ear, it portended doom. Their rebellion was no longer a secret. Time had officially run out.

17

Ding! Ding! Ding!

The alarm bell rang atop the stone tower. An eerie hush fell over the entire village. Again the tones sprang forth from the bell.

Ding! Ding! Ding!

Everyone in the village snapped to action. Shutters slammed closed. Bracer bars shimmied behind doors. Mothers beckoned their children home.

The gathering within the longhouse came to an abrupt end. Each man sprang from his chair and made for the nearest exit, fighting one another to escape the enclosed walls and reach their duty stations. Several men sprinted across the courtyard toward the main gate. There they worked their hands raw upon a wooden hand crank, lowering the portcullis into the down and locked position to seal the palisade from any unwanted guests. With one loud *clank* the gate slammed shut. The din of crisis ripped through the village.

Kell strolled forth from the longhouse into the darkened courtyard. He seemed immune to the chaos reigning around him. Gazing up at his tower, only one thought concerned the stoic chieftain—*why has the alarm been sounded?* From that lofty perch above, all lands within the realm were visible to the naked eye. Unaware as to whether the village was under siege by another clan bent on pillaging their storehouses or a greater, underground terror that found its way to freedom, Kell launched himself into a sprint up the wood stairway that led aloft. He had to speak to whoever had sounded the alarm. Hurtling two and three steps at a time, Kell pushed himself to the brink. His heart pounded against the walls of his chest, his breath grew short and shallow. Beads of sweat collected on his brow, causing strands of hair to stick to his face. Though his will powered him onwards, the blazing pace he began at the foot of the stairway started to take its toll. While each pounding step brought him closer to the stone fortress, the throbbing in his calves and quadriceps screamed at him to rest. A deep, burning sensation chewed at his legs. Unable to keep his leaping gait intact, Kell slowed to a one-step-at-a-time ascent.

Nearly out of breath and on the verge of collapse, Kell saw the doorway to the stone tower slowly come into view. As he approached the top step, a new sound assaulted his senses—an explosion born of anger and forged in the fires of rebellion. Kell spun his body around like a top to see its cause.

To his stunned horror, he stood witness to his men screaming and hollering for help at the base of the walkway, their bodies engulfed in flame. Most of those who raced to the scene to lend assistance ran away in fear. With a sudden heart-crushing force, the reality of the situation hit Kell. *The dragons broke free!* Finding strength reserves deep within, Kell rose from the stairs on unsteady legs. He made his way clumsily back down the stairway.

Just as Kell felt some of his energy coming back, the sound of rushing wind and a great flash of light engulfed the courtyard below. The gnashing teeth of a mighty conflagration grabbed hold of the breakaway section of the stairway and tore into it with reckless abandon. The dry timber lit up as if it were drenched in oil.

"No!" Kell screamed. The men who manned the lifting mechanism floundered about the ground in a blanket of agonizing flame that would not relinquish their flesh. Their painful wails sent chills down Kell's spine. The backsides and hindquarters of the oxen caught the full fury of the dragon flame that poured forth from under the lowered stairway. They moaned painful cries as they bucked at the walls of their pens, unable to shake free of the deeply set claws of the fire. Both of the poor animals busted through their pens and ran about the courtyard before collapsing beside their masters in a steaming heap of charred, tortured flesh.

A new, horrifying image grabbed hold of Kell and pulled his attention away from the gruesome depictions below; a raging fire now raced up the stairway toward him. Kell turned back up the stairs and ran as fast as his weary legs could carry him. Step after step, he felt the surge of heat welling up behind him as the rush of flame ascending the walkway closed in. He felt his heels and back begin to burn with the intense heat that reached out toward him with rending nails. With a desperate leap, Kell thrust himself forward into the air a few steps from the top of the walkway. His body struck the ground hard, causing him to skid along before coming to rest on his back. He patted himself down in a blind rage to put out any fire that may have latched onto him. Clamoring to his feet, he stood helpless as the dragon fire engulfed the palisade that protected the tower.

All around him, cries rang out. He felt utterly powerless against the events unfolding around him. Even the men that kept a relentless vigil atop the palisade catwalk were overcome with hopelessness and flung themselves from the twenty-foot high wall to the ground below in order to escape the angry flames. The crunching of broken, splintered bones preceded a new set of desperate screams of pain.

Knowing he must do something to stem the losses, Kell made his way into the tower.

*   *   *

"Get out of here!" Azriel shouted between breaths of fire. The flickering flames that lapped along the underside of the wooden stairway cast a warm light upon the faces of all the dragons looking on. They all stared at Azriel in disbelief. "I'll hold them off while you get to safety."

Laurel pushed her way between the throng of dragons

and ran to his side, grabbing hold of him. "You can't do this, Azriel," she said through sobs, looking up sorrowfully at her older brother. "You promised Ma when she died that you'd look after me. You promised! Don't you leave me!" She began hammering on him with her fists.

Azriel reached out and held her flailing arms. When she no longer struggled against his grasp, he let her arms fall free. He took her head in his hands and spoke to her consolingly. "Kiddo, we both know there isn't anything that can save me now." He offered forth a confident, courageous front. "If I can ensure your survival and the survival of everyone by sacrificing what's left of my life, I'll do so without a second thought. Besides, I'll still keep a close eye on you, even if you can't see me."

Laurel's cries grew louder. She hugged her brother tighter than before. "But who will take care of me? I can't do this without you. You're the only family I have left." Another hand fell softly atop her head.

"Don't worry about her, Azriel," Galadorn spoke. "We'll take good care of her." He extended his other hand toward the brave sentry captain. "You'd have made your parents proud."

Malkolm looked up at the tender exchange that took place. A sad and thoughtful expression hung heavily on his small frame.

Azriel's hand met Galadorn's. "Thank you, sir. There's no better way for a warrior to die than in battle." Releasing his grip on the elder dragon's hand, he wrapped both his arms around Laurel. "I love you so much, Sis."

"I love you too, Az."

Azriel whispered in her ear. "Promise me something?"

"Anything!"

"Live your life," he uttered with a tear in his eye. "Live your life and be free. Find that which makes you happy and hold on with everything you've got. But you can't be afraid to tell him how you feel." His eyes wandered to Fenicus. "You two have a chance if you stick together. You're the last of the Veilstars, Laurel. Make sure our family doesn't die out forever."

"I will," Laurel squeaked. "I will."

Azriel tried to pull himself free of his grief-stricken sister, but she wouldn't let go. "I must go!" he pleaded with her. "Please let go, Laurel. You aren't making this any easier on me."

Galadorn took hold of Laurel and pulled her free of her brother. With outstretched arms she wailed for him to come back, fighting to break free of Galadorn's grip. He nodded to the doomed captain of the sentry. Azriel slapped his tail against the ground and turned to face his destiny. From his jaws erupted a suppressing fire. His wings beat steadily, feeding the flames. Everything around them burned and crackled. It was time to fly.

Fenicus realized that amidst the tumult of activity, Malkolm might be easily overlooked and crushed underfoot. He knelt down before his friend. "It's getting too dangerous for you around here," he stressed. The eerie sound of Azriel's fiery breath singeing the air around them and the screams of his victims echoed in the passageway. "There's nothing more you can do here, Malkolm."

"But—" Malkolm protested.

"No buts. I can't do what I have to if I'm worrying about you." Pulling the amulet from around his neck he presented it to Malkolm. "If something happens to me, I want you to keep this. A way to remember me." A somber grin pursed Fenicus's lips.

Malkolm shook his head in vehement disagreement.

"Look, if I make it out of here alive, I'll come find you, Malkolm. I promise. But I need to know the amulet is in safe hands and I need to know you're safe." Fenicus looked him in the eyes. "Now please, go, before it's too late."

Bowing his head, Malkolm accepted the amulet from Fenicus. As he lowered the chain over his neck, a flash of blue light overcame the amulet and it shrunk to fit its new master. Malkolm tucked it beneath his tattered shirt and ran off into the bowels of the keep.

Meanwhile, the dragons continued to take flight from under the cover of Azriel's flame. All the women and children sped to the front of the teeming mass of dragons at Galadorn's urging. In order to protect the others while they took flight, Galadorn kept vigil over the exit. He spewed forth a layer of cover fire all around Azriel, which incinerated crossbow bolts and arrows hissing toward the valiant, dying dragon. Balthazar stood close by, shaping the fire into demonic apparitions with his sorcerer's powers. Godlike titans grew from the swirling flames, hurling balls of fire and blasts of intense heat at their human combatants. Their screams of terror could be heard all across Gotland.

Fenicus and Farimus started moving toward the back of the procession to protect their escape effort from a rear assault. Mariel followed them the entire way. Father and son had not spoken a single word to one another since they left the dungeon.

"What is the matter with you?" she demanded as they worked their way through the mass. "Can't you two put your differences aside until we're out of this godforsaken place?"

Having reached the end of the line, both Farimus and Fenicus took up guarded, defensive positions, leering down into the depths of the underground keep. But neither of them answered Mariel. They took slow, backward paces toward the exit as each dragon escaped and the line grew shorter. Both Farimus and Fenicus kept their eyes trained on the passageway, never looking at each other or Mariel for that matter. They were so very much father and son.

Their silence was then interrupted by an alarming sound that meant their emancipation was at risk. The rhythmic puffing sound of rushing air no longer bounced along the passageway. Instead, Fenicus heard the growing whisper of human voices snaking around the depths of the underground tunnels and in the courtyard beyond the enflamed walkway.

Balthazar forced his way through the few remaining dragons preparing to take flight, dragging his niece with him by the wrist. "Azriel's dead. The humans are breaking through the walkway outside. We've got to go."

Farimus looked to the exit. "Where's Galadorn?" he asked his brother-in-law.

"He took off with Laurel once all the little ones and their mothers were safely away."

"Damn it!" Farimus hissed. "Get Ariel and the others out

of here," he demanded. "And take Fenicus with you too."

"I'm not leaving without you," Fenicus demanded steadfastly.

The anger on Mariel's face was undeniable. "Stop trying to play hero, you two. You don't need to prove anything."

Down a nearby, adjacent passageway, the faint glow of torchlight appeared and grew stronger with each moment, as did the sound of marching feet. Fenicus and Farimus turned away from the direction of the oncoming threat and began pushing and shoving the others out the door.

"Mariel," Farimus urged, "get Ariel and get out of here now!"

"But," Mariel started to argue but was cut off before she could form another word.

Farimus turned and screamed at her. "Go! We'll hold them off."

With trembling hands, Mariel took Ariel's hand and lifted off into the sky. Balthazar took off directly behind her. There the two dragons stood as a host of armed men lead by Calidin turned the corner and fell upon them. Farimus immediately breathed a blast of fire in their direction. The flame clung to the floor, walls, and ceiling, forming a complete circuit that stopped the humans dead in their tracks. Farimus then fired a second volley at the humans as they began to fight their way through the wall of fire. He stepped in front of his son and pushed him back toward the exit. "Take off, Fenicus! I can't hold them off much longer."

"Either we both fly out of here together or not at all."

"Damn you, boy," Farimus growled. "For once in your life, do as I say without arguing with me!" From his toothy jaw another superheated exhale erupted forth, setting the very air on fire and sending the humans sprawling on the floor and against the walls. But through those flames strode Calidin, totally unaffected as if some protective bubble encircled him.

Fenicus felt a change coming over him that he had never felt before. Watching the human wizard pass through his father's deadly flames without so much as a singed hair made the small spark lingering in his chest burst into a flame. He felt every emotion he carried with him since his departure from Berathor catalyze into a swirl of power. He watched his father make another attempt at incinerating the mystical human. The flames poured forth in a tight spire straight at Calidin, but instead of cowering away the wizard pressed his hand out against the oncoming onslaught of flame. Even though the heat of a dragon's breath could burn through any known substance, this man stopped it cold with no more than a fleshy hand. He should have been turned to cinders, but he stood unaffected by Farimus's best efforts.

Calidin then snapped his outstretched hand downward and extended his index finger toward Farimus. The spire of fire recoiled back into Farimus's mouth. The force of the recoil threw the dragon back against the door, shattering it into splinters. His limp body spun hard, bouncing off the doorframe before crashing upon the ground outside. There he fell beside Azriel's arrow-ridden body. Fenicus stared slack-jawed at the wizard. Then he realized what he must do.

Fenicus wheeled his head back, felt the surge of fire

building up within his chest, and then brought his head to bear at Calidin. Through narrowed eyelids, Fenicus glimpsed the wizard thrusting his hands at him in a desperate, choking gesture. It was as though Calidin controlled the very air around them. Fenicus felt two hands, much in the same fashion that the wizard held his hands, squeezing his throat. He began to choke from the flame backing up in his chest. An odd sensation washed over him. The last thing Fenicus remembered was feeling the fleeting warmth of his flame getting snuffed out like a candle. Then everything went black.

18

Kell paused before reentering the community longhouse. His heart was heavy with despair and responsibility. Less than hour had passed since they celebrated their triumphs. Less than an hour ago, all his men sat with him at a feast unlike any they had ever known. Less than an hour ago, life was perfect.

Walking through the entryway, he saw the tragic end brought about by his actions and inaction. Those he commanded lay injured and dying upon the room-length table, along the bloodstained floor, and propped up in chairs. The longhouse, once filled with laughter, now stood as a makeshift infirmary filled only with the sounds of agony and pain. The air itself reeked of death. Those men and women who were wise in the ways of healing and herbs worked diligently to save those they could. For those they could not save, they did the best to ease their suffering with potent painkilling concoctions and liquor.

The entire scene felt so surreal to Kell. It seemed as though it was born of some nightmarish dream from which he could not awaken. The stench permeated everything including the lapel of Kell's jerkin, which he held over his nose and mouth. He did his best not to succumb to the pangs of nausea churning in his stomach. One step at a time, he made his way through the longhouse, looking over every one of his fallen men: the young, the old, the injured, the dying, and the dead. So many faces he knew, so many he didn't, yet every one of these men sacrificed themselves in order to see Kell's dream come to fruition. Kell could not help but wonder what they did to deserve such an end. Yet, the one person he should blame, the one person who was most at fault, escaped culpability since no one could lay blame upon the proud chieftain without paying the price for making such accusations. So Kell blamed the dragons because, in his eyes, their desire to be free brought this agony upon his men.

Angus Valkyr approached with brisk steps from the other end of the longhouse. Kell paid no notice to him as he drew near, only to the anguish his eyes bore witness to.

"M'lord?" Angus inquired softly amidst the shadow of death, as if not to draw its attention to him. Kell lifted his head and stared at Angus. His bloodshot eyes seemed to burn right though Angus. "One of the guards who was burned in the fire wishes to speak with you." Kell's attention still seemed displaced. "Sir, he's dying." His eyes, which before seemed to be looking at everyone and everything but Angus, locked on him as if the chieftain awoke suddenly from a deep slumber.

"Who is it, Angus?" Kell asked with a lump in his throat. He shook his head a bit to shake off his somber mindset. The composure he lacked since entering the longhouse began to return.

Angus looked to his right, down the length of the longhouse and then back to Kell. "He's one of the walkway guards, sir. He keeps rambling on and on about a spy, someone who he thinks aided the dragons."

Kell clenched his jaw. "Take me to him."

Angus led Kell to the other end of the longhouse, past other fallen men who reached out for him, who called out to him for mercy as he passed by. But their pleading tones fell on deaf ears. Having reached the other end, Angus brought Kell over to the fallen guard who lay upon a pile of bloody rags. The chieftain barely recognized the man as Magnus Anduir. His skin was so badly burned that it was riddled with blisters and deep, bleeding cracks. A small patch of skin on his face remained unscathed. Upon laying eyes on Kell, Magnus's face became alive despite his condition. His scorched hand reached out for the chieftain as he drew near. The smell of burnt flesh overpowered Kell for a moment. He turned away from Magnus, swallowing hard against the overpowering nausea. Feeling it subside, Kell turned back to Magnus and knelt down beside him. The fallen guard immediately grabbed the lapel of Kell's jerkin, pulling him closer.

"Rest easy now, Magnus," Kell calmly uttered. He placed

his left hand upon an exposed portion of the guard's chest where the skin was not burnt. Gently, he urged him to lie back down. Magnus relaxed back into his bloody bed, gasping in anguish as his back pressed into the ground. The guard's charred hand fell from Kell's jerkin to his knee. "There was something you wanted to tell me?" Kell felt Magnus's fingernails dig sharply into his knee. His eyes lolled about in their sockets until they locked on Kell.

"A traitor!" Magnus hissed through a pained grimace. "A child stole—" he groaned. His breathing grew shallower with each passing breath.

"Yes, what about this child? What did it do?" Kell implored.

"He...he..." the guard struggled to form his words. He fell further and further into death's shadow.

"You can do it, Magnus, tell me what happened so I may avenge you."

Magnus took a deep breath. "He stole my purse... drew my attention away...away from the keep after Calidin...came back with the dragons."

"What happened to this child?" Kell pleaded.

"He escaped, m'lord." Magnus's eyes then grew wide as if overcome with surprise. He arched his back and gasped. Each word leaked from his mouth. "He ran off... into...the...night." Magnus's eyes opened wide as the last word pursed his lips. His breath escaped him in a long, wheezing exhale. He slumped back lifelessly upon the floor.

Kell placed his hands over Magnus's forehead. He slowly lowered his hand down over the guard's pale face, closing his eyelids and laying a brief warrior's prayer upon him.

"May you find your way to the Valrgind and to the great Einherjar. May Odin welcome you into Valhalla and may you find peace in the halls of eternal glory."

Rising to his feet, Kell called to Angus who had stepped aside for a moment to provide care to others in need. Angus pulled a woolen blanket over the head of another of the deceased and returned to his chieftain's side with hurried steps.

"Yes, m'lord?" Streaks of blood stained his hands and face.

"Find Calidin immediately. Bring him here."

A startled look flashed across Angus's face. His eyes, wide with amazement, focused on something directly behind Kell. Noticing his change in demeanor, Kell turned about to find the hooded wizard standing behind him. He stumbled back, clutching at his chest. His pulse raced at the unexpected sight of his servile wizard.

"Damn you, Calidin!" Kell ground his teeth and clenched his fists. Of all the wizard's peculiar behaviors, his ability to materialize anywhere at will gave his master fits of grief. Kell stood on the precipice of strangling his most valued emissary.

Calidin cocked an eyebrow at the display of anger. A muffled chuckle of laughter bounced around in the wizard's throat. "How may I be of assistance?" Though the words were proper and respectful, the tone he took in saying them was anything but. He looked at the carnage that surrounded them and shook his head.

"We succeeded in killing one of the dragons, have we not?" Kell inquired.

"We did indeed, m'lord."

"Excellent." An evil gleam flickered in Kell's cold eyes. He drew uncomfortably close to the wizard, leaving a few sparse inches of space between them. "I want you to take your best men and a score of our smiths and set them to work descaling the dragon to make new armor for my forces."

The wizard craned his head hard to the left, making his vertebrae pop. He then nodded with a reluctant scowl.

"And, I want you to squeeze every drop of blood from its wretched carcass and brew the invulnerability potion. There should be more than enough lurking beneath its flesh to provide each of my men with one vial." Kell saw the shiftiness lurking in the wizard's infirm posture. For the first time, he found something that got under the wizard's skin. *Is it possible he might betray me?* Kell wondered. "Is there a problem?"

The look upon the wizard's face did not match his response. His voice sounded defeated in response. "No, there's no problem. It shall be done."

Just as he entered, Calidin vanished into thin air. Kell swore under his breath before returning his attention to the scores of the dead and dying.

19

Mariel and Ariel Flint landed just beyond the entryway tunnel to their warren. The elder Flint female watched all around her as other families, whole families made their way back to Berathor. Approaching the entryway, Mariel's hand came to rest on the arch. Her head dropped, her eyes closed, and she punched the outer wall. A howl of anguish filled the air. The feel of Ariel's small hand stroking Mariel along her backside brought her back from the edge of despair. She gently lay her head beside her daughter's for a moment, trying to remember that not everything that mattered to her was lost.

On leaden feet, the two Flint dragonesses made their way along the tunnel and stepped just inside the inner archway. Her eyes fell upon what remained of their home.

It lay in complete shambles, their belongings cast to the wind. Unlike the other families who suffered material losses, the loss for the Flint family was much dearer as it was one of flesh and blood, and nothing could fill the emptiness left behind by the missing kin.

Mariel knew that no warren, no homeland, no matter how fancy or warm or comfortable, could ever be called home without Fenicus and Farimus. Being completely unsure of what had become of them, all she could do was cling to Ariel for comfort.

Ariel leaned her small body against her mother for support and cried. Mariel unfurled her wing and wrapped it around her daughter, pulling her close to try and soothe the hurt away. She placed a comforting kiss upon her cheek. Ariel nestled closer into her mother's body. Mariel then felt her daughter's limbs go slack and reached out to catch her. She settled them both upon the cold stone floor.

Ariel turned her tear-streaked face toward her mother. "Will we ever see them again, Ma?" Almost imperceptible convulsions moved through her as she sobbed.

Mariel placed her hands along the sides of Ariel's face, wiping away the tears with her thumbs. "I don't know, sweetie," answered Mariel, shaking her head. "I just don't know." A heartsick grimace spilled across her face. In her heart of hearts, she feared the worst. No matter how hard she willed herself to believe that Fenicus and Farimus had found a way to escape Kell's clutches, she kept coming back to the same realization—without help, her son and husband were never coming home. The power Kell's wizard wielded over them was too great, too strong to resist. Without assistance, they would likely live out their last days as prisoners. She could not live with that thought for a single moment longer than it took to conceive. A determination stirred within her. Mariel had to find a way to save her family.

"Sweetie," she paused to lock eyes with her daughter, trying to convince Ariel and herself that the words she was about to speak were the truth. "They're coming home. I don't know how, but one way or another, we'll see them again—I promise!" Mariel's grimace turned to a confident, determined smile.

Looking past her mother and through an open window, Ariel's eyes met the peaks of the Tatra Mountains. Her face brightened and her head perked up. She looked to her mother with eagerness. "Ma?"

"Yes, dear?"

"What about the Elders? Couldn't they send out someone to go find them? They did last year when Julius got lost in the mountains."

"That's right!" Mariel gasped. "They'd surely help out! After all, it was Fenicus and your father who helped everyone escape. I'd even say the council owes it to them." Mariel patted her daughter on her rump, urging her to get up. The two of them rose to their feet.

As Mariel was about to say something, the sounds of feet padding against the ground outside the entryway distracted her. She turned about to see her brother squeeze through the doorway with a small sack slung over his shoulder. His profound hindquarters barely fit. Mariel rushed toward Balthazar and hugged him. Ariel followed suit. He opened his arms and held them close.

"Thank heavens!" Mariel exclaimed, overjoyed by her brother's survival. She pulled back from Balthazar to look upon him. Ariel took her mother's hand and stood next to her. "I heard rumors that you didn't make it, that you were captured too."

"I'm fine sis, really." Balthazar looked around the house. His gaze fell upon Mariel and Ariel. "They didn't come back?"

Ariel began to weep again. Mariel glanced at her briefly, placed her arm around her shoulders and pulled her close. "No. We got separated during the escape. By the time I realized they were missing, it was too late to turn back. I tried asking around but everyone seems to have a different answer. All I know for sure is that something's got to be done, someone has to go out after them."

"I agree, but who?" He shrugged. "The Council has already ordered everyone to abandon Berathor and make for the Golden Vale, including the sentry. There's no one left to go out, no one crazy enough that is."

Mariel sagged at his words. She could not look at her brother as she felt all hope slipping away.

"I didn't mean it like—" Balthazar apologized. Before he could finish his sentence, his sister cut him off.

"Well they're gonna listen. I'll make them listen. I'm not going to stand *here* and just forget about my life, about everything I've ever known because someone's afraid for their own hide. If no one else will go after them, I will. But I'm gonna do my damnedest to convince the Council otherwise."

"Then I'm going with you."

For a moment she was glad to have her brother's help, but she thought better of it. Mariel smiled lovingly to her brother. "No, I can't ask you to come with me. This is my fight now. Besides, someone's got to look after Ariel if I don't come back."

A look of fear fell over Balthazar. "Don't say that! You're coming back."

Mariel placed a quieting finger upon his lips, silencing him.

Balthazar shook his head. "Please don't do this. There's got to be another way."

Mariel brushed a loving hand across his cheek. "Everything will be okay, I promise." Turning about on her heels, Mariel gazed at her beautiful daughter who looked so unsure and scared. "I want you to go get your stuff together and go with your uncle. He's going to look after you until I come back." She leaned in to wrap her arms around Ariel. Mariel squeezed her like she was saying her final goodbyes. She knew that she might well be flying to her own demise. Before she pulled back, Mariel whispered a few final words to Ariel. "Take care of your uncle. Look after him. He needs you as much as you need him right now."

Ariel asked her mother one final question. "When will you be back?"

Mariel looked up to her brother. A hopeful smile pursed his lips and he nodded gently. He lowered his hand to her shoulder. Mariel turned back to Ariel and gave her the only answer that mattered. "As soon as I've found your brother and father, we'll all be back." She leaned forward and placed one final, tender kiss upon Ariel's brow.

Standing up to face her brother, Mariel hugged him goodbye. "See you soon, twerp. Take care of Ariel."

"I will."

*   *   *

The two large stone doors that led to the Elder Council Chamber loomed at the end of a long passageway. Brilliant luminescence seeped from the narrow gap that surrounded each door. The hallway was generally unremarkable. Every twenty paces or so, small sculptured torches in the shape of upturned dragonheads jutted from the walls. They provided ample illumination. The walls were smooth; not a single bump or rough patch marked the surface. The floor, on the other hand, was noticeably different. Hundreds of rectangular, sandstone tiles comprised the floor. Carved into the face of each were detailed pictograms that told the complete history of their species.

With each step Mariel took toward the chamber doors, she read about the struggles of her species against mankind. Their story seemed to repeat itself over and over again. Every time, the human race advanced into their lands, the dragons withdrew without much of a struggle. The pattern sickened Mariel. She thought of all the families that were scrambling to gather up their belongings before abandoning Berathor Valley. It was like every time before this one. No one questioned the wisdom of the decision. None of them fought to stay and fight; they simply obeyed the orders of the Elders without complaint. Where was their desire to fight, to hold their ground? The reality of what became of her people struck Mariel to her core. Perhaps all their time in isolation had made them soft. The instinct to defend their homes left them as they became too civilized. Fear of extinction drove them into exile, and now, when they needed it most, their courage was gone. Someone had to take a stand.

Approaching the last stone that contained any markings, Mariel felt sick to her stomach. It read, "To preserve our race, the migration to the Golden Vale began without delay." They were so sure of their decision, so willing to retreat once more, that the last stone had already been carved and placed. It was as if the decision had been made long before any invasion. Perhaps, she thought, it was time for the dragons of Berathor to rise up and become the legendary monsters mankind feared for so long. She sneered at the two heavy doors ahead of her, determined to not leave until she convinced the Elder Council that she was right. Inside her, a monster began scratching and clawing its way out.

Her hands gripped the cold stone handles and pulled the doors open. The flood of white light that poured from within momentarily blinded Mariel. Once her eyes adjusted, the first thing she saw were the four Elders seated in a semi-circle upon a raised sandstone platform amidst a heated discussion.

The half-moon shaped room had been crafted out of the mountainside along with the rest of the outer hall. It was lit by more of the same dragonhead torches that lined the outer hallway. These torches, however, did not burn with any ordinary flame. They burned white, gave off no warmth, and produced a level of light unattainable by fire born of flint and tinder. To her left and right stood two unlit archways. Oddly, none of the blinding light bled into those areas. The rest of the walls were plain. No carvings, no paintings, no tapestries.

Mariel watched them for a moment. The Elders cast accusing fingers at one another. Sharp words and assertions of innocence and guilt dominated their discourse. The first to recognize her presence was Galadorn, the eldest and most respected member of the council. With a simple gesture of his hand, the other Elders fell silent. They all looked upon her humble frame.

Mariel stood with her head bowed, her hands clasped over her heart. She gulped hard to clear her throat. "I apologize for my intrusion," she said hesitantly. Her face rose to meet their gaze. "There's a matter of the utmost urgency I must discuss with you."

Matthias, the youngest of the four elder council members, was a rather plump dragon. He wrapped his thick-knuckled fingers around the edge of the platform, every bone cracking as his hands tightened; his eyes focused on her with disdain. "What matter could be more urgent than the evacuation of Berathor?" he questioned her, barking out every word like an angry dog.

Bolting to an upright position, Mariel looked to the contemptuous elder. "It's an urgent matter to me, councilor." She took a wary step in the direction of Matthias to address him pointedly. "It's about my family, my—"

Another voice interrupted her. "We're well aware of your situation."

She glanced in the direction from which the words were issued. There she saw Thorn, the third oldest of the group and imminent heir to the Master Councilor's post. He looked upon her with concern.

Thorn leaned forward. "Wouldn't your time be better spent taking care of your daughter and packing up your home?"

It took every ounce of effort Mariel could muster to not gnaw her bottom lip off. Her teeth clenched down hard while she fought the urge to release all her anger, all her hurt upon the Elders at that moment. She collected herself and spoke in a calm, even tone. "Excuse my ignorance and rudeness, but what good will packing up my home be? My son, my husband, they're both out there somewhere. They're my home, my life. Aren't you going to send someone out after them?" Her voice grew sharp and desperate as the last word escaped her lips.

Matthias snapped at her. "What would you have us do?" He rose from the platform, as did the volume and vehemence of his voice. "Should we risk more lives to save your family? May I remind you that you carry little weight within this chamber? Your loss, as great as it may be, does not constitute the need for action on our behalf." Suddenly, his tone grew haughty. "Besides, we did not ask them to sacrifice their lives to save the rest of us." He turned about, slumping back across the platform like a luxuriating king.

His words seethed in Mariel's mind. But beyond the words, it was the insinuation they carried that caused the kettle to boil over. Infuriated, she no longer found the strength or the desire to check herself in the presence of the Elders. "If it wasn't for Fenicus and Farimus, none of us would've escaped that damned place. We all owe them our lives for the sacrifice they made."

"It's a risk we can't afford," Matthias snapped. "We need every warm body we've got to make this move happen. Sending anyone out to attempt a rescue would not only leave us shorthanded but also expose us to another attack. Their lives are just not worth the risk."

Mariel gasped audibly at his heartless assertion. She then took a few powerful strides toward Matthias and stared him down. "How dare you?" She spat at him. "How dare you pretend to be so bold, sitting here all high and mighty? You sit there in judgment of me and my family when you have no understanding of what it's like to be in my position. You've no family of your own. You self-righteous, unfeeling son-of-a—"

The sound of a slamming fist against stone silenced Mariel mid-sentence. In a fit of anger, Matthias rose to his feet. The spines along his back glowed warmly. "How dare you talk to me in that tone!" Wisps of smoke billowed from his nostrils.

Before Matthias was able to make another movement toward Mariel, a stern, quieting hand fell upon his chest. Galadorn stepped between the two of them. Matthias, poised to strike, looked upon the barring hand with displeasure. His flaming eyes rolled upwards to meet Galadorn. Matthias took the Master Councilor's gentle suggestion and returned to his resting place with an audible huff.

With a hand over his heart, Galadorn attended to Mariel. "Please excuse Matthias's remarks, Mariel. We're all under a lot of pressure." He motioned to Mariel to settle herself upon a lower standing platform to her left. Mariel looked at it and back to him, visibly angry and too worked-up to take a seat. "Please!" he urged her. She settled her weight down upon the stone without further resistance. Galadorn stepped down from the elevated platform. He knelt beside her.

"Mariel," his voice soft and caring, "we all understand the hurt you must be going through. Believe me, none of us are marginalizing the sacrifice of your son and husband by any means. We cannot possibly put into words how much it means to us, to all the dragons of Berathor. And you're right, we do owe them, we owe them our lives if not more for their sacrifice. But you've got to look at it from our perspective. The loss of Fenicus and Farimus is more than any of us was willing to accept, let alone losing a valuable warrior such as Azriel. But it's a reality we all must deal with. The humans are too many in number, too strong. To send anyone out on a rescue mission would only result in the loss of more lives, and we just can't afford to take that risk as a species trying to survive." He placed his hand over her own as she fought to smother her emotions. His words came forth slowly, conciliatorily. "We must honor their sacrifice and move on. If they had their say, Mariel, they'd say the same thing. Search your heart. You know it's true. They gave of themselves so we'd survive. To risk more lives would dishonor their sacrifice and undo everything they..." he paused for a moment. "Everything they gave so our species could live to fight another day."

Live to fight another day? Mariel's blood boiled. Her tears evaporated and rage took their place. Just how many times had they retreated so that they could *live to fight another day*? When did they finally plan to fight back? When was enough, enough? She then knew that they were not afraid of weakening Berathor, nor were they afraid of not having enough manual labor to assist in the move to the Golden Vale. They simply were afraid.

Centuries passed without a serious threat to the tranquility of Berathor Valley. While a few dragons maintained their razor sharp instincts for warfare, the majority of them became complacent, docile; the equivalent of a four-ton domesticated dog. Mariel felt uncomfortable in her own skin. This lowly state was not what Weylark had in mind when he led them into exile. He hoped that their numbers would swell so that they might one day reclaim Earth as their own. If he were alive to see what had become of their once proud, dominant race, Mariel assured herself, he would be ashamed to be a dragon.

Mariel glared at Galadorn with daggers. He rose from his kneeling position and warily backed away from her. She too rose from her seat to face the Elders.

"So that's it!" Mariel erupted. "That's your plan? Tuck our tails and run, huh? And hope, hope that they don't find us again, hope that Fenicus and Farimus don't lead them right back to us. You know how powerful Calidin is!" Mariel moved closer to the four silent Elders. Her tone grew pained, pleading. "We've lost so much because of them already, abandoned our homes, changed our lives to suit their dominance. When do we stand and fight? When do we stop running away from them? That's what you said my men sacrificed themselves for—to live and fight another day. If we don't stand and fight right now, then we may never live to see another day."

"Mariel," Methuselah interjected. Unlike Matthias, he was widely known as a quiet leader. Many thought it was because he valued deep contemplation over wasting breath speaking half-measured words that one might later regret. Those who knew him understood that his quiet nature resulted from the strong lisp with which he spoke. A long, swirling scar that stretched from his gums to his snout was the likely culprit, some injury from his youth. "Your point ish well taken. And that'sh exactly why we musht flee. There will be a time, a right time to shtand our ground and fight for our very exishtensh if needsh be. But now ish not that time. We need to be at our shrongesht if we are to make a shtand, not in a time of weaknessh like we're fashed with now. I deeply regret your lossh. Your shon and hushband were both fine dragonsh, modelsh of bravery and courage we'll all remember, eshpeshially young Fenicush. But the deshishion of the counshil musht shtand. We musht do what'sh in everyone'sh besht interestsh, regardlessh of the prishe we might pay. I can only hope that the ancient onesh shee your loved onesh shafely acrossh the void."

Mariel shook her head despondently. "Then I'm going after them! If you're too afraid to make that decision then I'll go by myself."

"No, Mariel," Galadorn demanded. He grabbed her arm. "You can't go after them. We need you here, not out chasing ghosts."

"To Hell with you!" Wrenching her arm free of

Galadorn's grip, Mariel turned away to take her leave of them. She took only one step before two awkwardly dressed dragons emerged from the shadowed archways and blocked her path. Their likeness was completely unfamiliar to her. More so, their accoutrements bore a menacing nature. Both dragons wore long, black capes that covered their wings. Plates of red, metallic armor covered the most vulnerable portions of their legs, arms, and torso; golden spines accented their vertices. In their hands they held bladed polearms that they pointed aggressively in her direction. They were the legendary Elder Guardians, the elite bodyguards of the Elder Council. Raised from birth, they lived and breathed a singular, lifelong purpose—to selflessly give their lives to protect their revered leaders. Now that they blocked her pathway, she leered back at the Council.

"Am I now a prisoner?" she asked venomously.

"It's for your own good," Thorn insisted. "One day you'll understand and be thankful for what we've done."

Mariel thought otherwise. Her deadly stare morphed into a grim smile.

Galadorn, who stood closest to her, dashed away from her just in time to avoid her wrath.

Whirling about to face the two dragons blocking the door, Mariel moved to her left and sped straight toward the leftmost guardian. Reacting to her movement, he brought his weapon around, slashing it horizontally at her midsection. The speed of his strike took her by surprise. Unable to adjust her whole body in time to avoid the attack, she lowered her elbow and blocked the blow with her forearm. The shaft shattered into splintered pieces of wood;

the iron tip and counterweight base of the weapon fell to the floor. The guardian staggered from the loss of balance caused by her defensive maneuver.

Turning her back to him, Mariel ducked her head and whipped her tail about in a sweeping parabola. Her whirling counterattack found its mark. The spiny tip of her arching tail connected with a thud against the guardian's cheekbone. He reeled from the impact and collided with the far wall.

She sat crouched for a moment, her right hand clutched at the pain that seared through her left arm. Her hand discovered several large splinters of wood lodged painfully between her scales and the raw flesh beneath. She growled and winced as she pulled the chunks of wood free and cast them across the floor.

Before she could stand and come around on her other opponent, Mariel felt two strong hands clasp around her wrists and pull her off balance. She stumbled backwards, nearly tumbling to the ground. Slamming her tail against the floor, though, she stabilized herself. In that split-second, Mariel regained her footing and pulled against the force tugging at her limbs. Looking over her shoulder, she saw that the guardian whom had a hold of her had a gash on his cheek. He recovered fast, she thought. She felt his foothold on the ground giving way. The guardian's feet skidded and bumped across the floor. For a brief moment, she felt as though she had gained the advantage. A sudden rush of pressure from behind caught her off guard. She knew she made a terrible miscalculation.

The council guardian thrust his weight in the direction she was pulling. She stumbled forward from the surprising tactic and fell face first against the ground. Before she could wrestle herself free from his grip, she felt her arms being drawn upwards and behind her, immobilizing them.

Not ready to surrender, Mariel brought her tail around and blindsided the other guardian who closed in on her from the left, his polearm poised to strike. The bony tip of her tail hit him in the back of the head. A loud clang from his fallen weapon echoed through the chamber. She then swung her tail back toward the guardian standing astride her back. He let her hands go and dove out of the way.

Mariel leapt to all fours and turned about to face her remaining opponent as he too rose from the floor. The two circled around one another, looking for an opening to exploit. Mariel moved first, rushing at him bearing teeth and talons. He countered by sliding beneath her. With a swift front kick from both legs, he hit her squarely in the chest. She grabbed at her ribs and fell on her back.

Scrambling to his feet, the guardian took advantage of her prone, injured position. He moved over her, removed a set of bindings from within his cape, and sat astride her body. Grabbing her left wrist and wrenching it up, he secured one of the shackles. Then he took hold of her other arm and attempted to secure the other end.

In a flash, the pain in her chest subsided, only to be replaced by a horrifyingly familiar feeling that swept through her like a raging river. When the cold iron bindings closing down around her wrists, they brought back all those terrible moments of captivity and the feelings of helplessness. It was a feeling she never wanted to experience again and one that made her forsake all reason and remorse.

The guardian, still straddling Mariel's torso, found himself suddenly enveloped in a conflagration of intense flame. Desperately, he dove to his left and grabbed the polearm that fell from his comrade's hand. Scrambling back to his feet, the guardian swung the weapon over his head and prepared to bring it down upon her with all his strength.

"Enough!" a booming voice filled the council chamber. The council guardian froze in place, his chest heaving. Mariel, lying on her back with her eyes closed in anticipation of the impending deathblow, looked to see who put a stop to their fray. Just when her eyes moved from their target, the council guardian drew his weapon back as if to strike her regardless of his orders. The voice boomed out again.

"I said enough, Kistra!"

Mariel's eyes whipped to the council guardian poised to attack her. The dragon guardian halted, withdrew his weapon for good, and went to the aid of his fallen comrade. Mariel relaxed against the floor, closing her eyes as she concentrated on catching her breath. When they reopened, she saw Galadorn standing above her, his hand extended. It was his voice that prevented the council guardian from striking her down. With a measure of distrust, she took his hand and erected herself. Galadorn immediately removed the shackles from her wrist.

"What are you doing?" Matthias hissed.

Galadorn glanced back at his fellow council member. "I'm letting her go."

"You can't be serious," the same grating voice eked out. "After what she's done, after everything that has come to pass." Matthias stood and pointed a bony finger in her direction. "She must be held accountable for her actions!"

The venerable old dragon excused himself from Mariel for a moment and came about to face the fiery council member. Galadorn moved in close, his breath bearing down on Matthias, his wings flailing in anger. "I've listened to you long enough, Matthias. Silence yourself or I'll silence you!" He bellowed those final few words at an ear shattering volume. Wisps of flame sparked from his mouth when he screamed. The hotheaded Matthias slunk back upon the platform and looked aside in fear. Galadorn's posture relaxed, his wings closed back on themselves. He turned back to address Mariel.

"Though I don't agree with what you're doing, Mariel, I understand. If it was my family was out there, I couldn't let them go either. After all, what good is life if we don't have the ones we love around us to enjoy it?" Galadorn smiled. He extended his hand to her in friendship.

Mariel found it very difficult to contain her emotions. She chewed at her bottom lip. Her stare bounced around the chamber fitfully. It took all her strength to resist breaking down at that moment. Looking upon Galadorn's gracious, forgiving gesture would be just enough to break the dike. Her eyes finally locked on Galadorn as she took his hand.

Galadorn took a hold of her hand and pulled her close for a friendly, consoling embrace. After a few moments she pulled back from him and wiped the tears from her eyes. A subtle giggle composed of despair and happiness escaped her mouth.

Galadorn cupped his hands around Mariel's broad shoulders and spoke to her. "Now get out of here and go save your family. And make sure you don't forget to come back with them. I don't think I could live with letting you go out there if we lost you too."

Mariel nodded back. "Don't worry about me. If I make it, we'll rendezvous with the rest of you in a few days. I promise. Just make sure you get everyone to safety."

Mariel took her leave of Galadorn and the rest of the council. With her head held high, she passed by the fallen guardian and his comrade and took hold of the door, pushing it open. A split-second before she shut the door, she heard Galadorn call her name. She peered back through the door, which stood slightly ajar.

"Good luck, Mariel." The great dragon bowed his head. When he raised his head, she was gone.

20

Soaring high above the countryside, Mariel Flint was on the hunt. Her big, green eyes perused the land, looking for the one human she knew could help her find her son and beloved husband. Though the land was wide and covered with many small forests and rolling fields, her acute eyesight could pick out the smallest field mouse scurrying through the tallest grass. And at such heights, she knew that she appeared as nothing more than a bird of prey circling overhead.

Her search covered a great deal of land from the southernmost tip of Gotland to the city of Valstena, the place where the fair-skinned humans held the dragons hostage. As Mariel followed the windy roadway northward, wispy, shadowy memories of having travelled its muddy length in shackles leapt into her consciousness. The recollections made her cringe in discomfort.

For some time she flew, hoping to catch a glimpse of Malkolm's blond hair shinning in the sunlight. Here and there she saw small handcarts being pulled by peasants, but she never saw her son's human friend—a friend whose bond she doubted. Mariel could not shake from her mind the possibility that the boy that Fenicus had befriended was nothing more than a dishonorable rogue. She understood, though, that her son was generally a good judge of character and would never trust anyone who wasn't worthy of such faith. Why would now be any different?

Quickly, night drew in on her. Her massive size left her with only a few places to retire to. For a short while she considered maintaining her vigilant search in the nighttime hours where she could fly low without the fear of being seen. However, her body grew weary from the countless hours of flight. Though they were born to fly, dragons had arms and legs for a reason. Mariel decided to catch a few hours of sleep before resuming her search just before dawn.

Descending through the cool evening air, she set down near the base of a small mountain chain that cut into the countryside. There she found shelter in a hillside cavern that appeared to be just big enough to hide her bulky form. Careful not to be seen, Mariel scanned her surroundings for anyone near enough to see what she was up to. She then ducked her snout into the entrance of the cave and let forth a burst of flame. The fireball illuminated the inside of the cave so well that she got a clear view of the layout within. To her surprise, the cavern was rather roomy inside. Free of any other inhabitants, she decided that it was her best option for the night. Mariel crawled inside and curled up in a ball, falling asleep quickly. Grisly, worrisome images haunted her dreams that night.

*   *   *

A singular beam of sunlight poked its way into the cavern to fall directly on Mariel's eyelid. Morning had come! Her head snapped up. She gasped, knowing all too well that she had slept too far into the day. Her chances of searching during the pre-dawn hours were now gone.

As she approached the entrance to the cave, her eyes struggled to adjust to the bright sunlight. Within the darkened veil of the cavern she stood, monitoring any movement her eyes could pick up in the countryside. Knowing no one could see her as long as she remained obscured in the darkness, she took her time evaluating the situation at hand.

A short time later, Mariel emerged from the protection of the cave. With a few lumbering steps, Mariel generated enough speed for takeoff. She beat her elegant wings and lifted off into the morning sky. Higher and higher she flew until she reached a height safe enough for soaring. With her wings fully extended, she glided on a soft cushion of air. Scanning the landscape below, she once again began to follow the lonely roadway she had spent tracing the day before. For a moment she thought her eyes were deceiving her with the leftovers of an overworked mind. Then her heart filled with joy and anger—joy that she could possibly have found the proverbial needle in the haystack and anger that she may have also found her son's betrayer. If she had indeed found who she was looking for, a reckoning would soon be at hand.

With a sudden jerk of her rudder-like tail to the right, her body veered in that direction, turning sharply down toward the road. Then she drew her wings back slightly like two shallow parachutes to slow her descent toward the ground. Like a dive-bomber, she homed in on her target. The boy grew nearer by the moment.

Malkolm walked along the dusty road, head hung low, kicking a small rock about with each step. Without warning, an odd shadow overcame him like a towering tree blotting out the light of the sun. He looked down at it. The shadow was getting larger. Stopping dead in his tracks, he looked up. His jaw fell agape.

Mariel hurtled toward him from above and crashed down onto the road with her talons drawn, blocking his path. The gust of wind from her landing threw Malkolm back several feet and onto his back. She loomed above him. Mariel lowered her long neck in his direction, bringing her eye-to-eye with the young boy. Malkolm cowered into a ball, his legs tucked beneath him, his arms crossed in front of his face protectively.

"Don't eat me!"

Mariel tilted her head curiously, retracted her wings, and then withdrew to a less threatening posture. She extended her hand to Malkolm. "I don't want to eat you." She smiled. Her razor sharp teeth gleamed in the sunlight. "You'd barely be a snack."

Malkolm gathered himself and rose to his feet, dusting himself off. Placing his hands on his hips, he stared at her quizzically.

Mariel settled on her haunches. "You don't remember me, do you?"

"I only know one dragon by name, ma'am." He scratched his head and looked her up and down. "You're a ma'am, right?"

"Yes. You're very perceptive."

"What does that mean?"

"You see things clearly. Not every human knows the difference between a male and female dragon. And you're so young. It's no wonder my son took a liking to you."

His face lit up. She never saw many humans in her life, but the boy's emotional display was unmistakably that of someone filled with joy.

"You're Fenicus's mother?"

"Yes. My name's Mariel. Yours is Malkolm, is it not?"

Malkolm walked closer to her. "Yes, ma'am." He then frowned with great sadness. "I'm so sorry, Mrs. Flint, it's my fault," he pleaded. "I ran when I should've fought. If I hadn't listened to Fenicus this never would've happened." The dirt that was caked on his face began to wash away with the flood of tears that streaked down his cheeks.

Mariel shook her head, fighting off Malkolm's wrongful self-accusation. "There was nothing more you could have done to save them."

"My life doesn't mean anything. I'm just a worthless orphan. At least if I died trying no one would miss me. At least I could die knowing Fenicus was free."

Mariel could not believe that Malkolm thought his life was so meaningless. She knew better. All lives, regardless of their station in the order of nature, had been granted the gift of life for a reason. Even this boy served a purpose, a greater purpose than anyone could forsee. And from Malkolm's unsolicited confession, she saw in him what her son did. There was no veil of deceit to this small human. Though he was tainted by the cruel world of neglect around him, there was an honesty to him that went beyond all known notions of humans. His heart was pure. The part of her that wanted to interrogate the boy ebbed away like a tide. All she felt was compassion. Her hand reached out and gently patted his head.

"Malkolm," she said in a soft, motherly tone, "you're not worthless. You did what you thought you had to do to survive." Her long finger moved beneath his chin and lifted his face so they were eye to eye. "There was nothing more you could've done to save him or my husband. They did what they did by choice."

Malkolm hunched his shoulders and frowned.

"Malkolm, I have an idea of how to set them free, but I need your help. Will you help me?"

Malkolm seemed instantly filled with exuberance. He surprised Mariel by rushing toward her and ineffectively hugging the calf of her left leg. He looked up to her. "Of course I'll help. I won't let you down, I promise."

She patted his back. "I know you won't."

"What do I have to do?"

Mariel scooped him up into her hands and held him up close to her face. "Do you still have the key to the shackles?"

Malkolm furrowed his brow. His hand disappeared underneath his tattered shirt. From beneath it he drew forth a large ring with one newly crafted bronze key. "Do you mean this?" A huge smile washed over his face as he held it up to her.

Her eyes lit up at the sight of it. The key's shiny surface glittered in the sunlight. "Yes, my dear boy, that key." She hugged him tight, nearly pressing all the life out of him. A few coughs cracked from his lungs before she realized his discomfort. Mariel pulled away from him and set the boy back down on the ground.

He scratched at his head thoughtfully. Then a panicky, worrisome grimace possessed him abruptly. "Oh no! Mrs. Flint," his voice cracked with nervousness, "they're going after the rest of the dragons! They're going to attack Berathor!"

"What?"

"I remember now, I heard some people talking about how Kell was taking Fenicus and Farimus back to Berathor to wipe you out."

Mariel closed her eyes, knowing this day would come. She only hoped that the rest of her kind cleared Berathor just in case her rescue attempt failed. At least then the rest would live on, at least for a while.

"They haven't left yet, have they?" she asked hopefully.

"No, ma'am. They're planning to set sail under the cover of darkness, tomorrow morning I believe."

A plan quickly started coming together in her mind. An attack at sea would limit her enemy's maneuverability, making them more susceptible to attack. Besides, she knew they crafted their sailing vessels out of wood, and wood and fire were a bad combination.

"I have to warn you, Malkolm, this is going to be very dangerous."

"I know, I know. I don't care about the danger. Whatever it is you need me to do, I'll do it!"

Mariel looked the boy up and down trying to assess his physical abilities. "Can you swim?" she asked.

He shrugged. "I'm pretty sure I can," he replied a bit hesitantly.

Mariel, though uncomfortable with his less than confident answer, knew there wasn't any other way to go. "Excellent. Here's the plan."

21

The sun had not yet risen above the horizon. Kell's forces were on the move southward along an empty highway. Hundreds of torches lit the way through the darkness like a swarm of brilliantly glowing fireflies. At the center of the marching mass were two dragons, chained, bound, and under the watchful eye of Calidin. The enchanted chains around their necks kept their scorching breath from surging forth. On their backs, restraining shackles held their wings in check, preventing them from lifting off the ground. All around them, cruel men with whips and bladed polearms struck at the dragons whenever they lagged behind. The southern docks came into view over the horizon as they marched.

Fenicus exhaled a long, shuddering breath. His

shoulders slumped. "I guess this is the end," his voice trembled. Fenicus craned his head in his father's direction. His face seemed worrisome, fearful.

Farimus saw how hopeless his son had become since they departed from the dungeons of Valstena. He knew the strength and courage it must have taken for his son to accomplish so much on his own; to leave Berathor, to track them down, to lead such a daring escape, all the while befriending someone a lifetime of teaching told him was a bitter enemy. In his son he saw a better dragon than he ever hoped he could be. The last thing he wanted to see was that shy, awkward child that Fenicus had left behind in Berathor return when courage was needed. While Farimus knew that his son had grown in leaps and bounds along his journey, he was still a boy at heart. Some of the realities of adulthood were just too much for such a young, untainted mind to cope with. Farimus loved Fenicus, and because of that love he realized he had to have enough strength for the both of them in the face of certain doom.

"Don't despair, son. We're not finished yet. If I can find a way to get us out of here, I'll do everything I can to make it happen, even if it means sacrificing myself so that you can get away."

Fenicus shook his head sternly. "No, Dad. Either we both make it out alive or neither of us does. We're in this together."

Farimus nodded honorably to his son, even more proud of him for the decision he made. Just then a painful reality struck Farimus. In the glint of the surrounding torchlight, he noticed that the scales along the back of his son's neck were beginning to shed and crumble off. A patch of tender flesh sat exposed to the air. While he was proud to die in battle along side Fenicus, he hated the thought that even if they escape Kell, he may still lose his son to that dreaded disease. Having seen what it did to his sister-in-law and now Azriel up close, he could not bear to see his own son succumb to its effects.

"When was the last time you took your molting draught?" Farimus questioned his son in the most nonchalant tone he could conjure, despite the worry swelling within.

The young dragon appeared to puzzle over the question for a brief moment. "I don't know. It's been a few days. Why?"

"I just that you're shedding a bit," Farimus answered, downplaying Fenicus's condition. "If and when we get out of here, you've got some catching up to do."

"I know, I know." Fenicus shook his head and snorted with displeasure, responding like he always did when Farimus and Mariel nagged him about it. "I wondered why my back was itching."

Their southbound hike came to a sudden halt. They now stood at the south dock and an array of sailing vessels anchored there. Like wisps from a forgotten dream, a flow of disjointed images overcame Farimus; shackles that bound him and the rest of his kind to the hull, of green blood pooling upon the deck, and the sting of sword blades and whips. He did not wish to venture upon any of those ships again, especially not in the role of a prisoner. All he wanted was to lay waste to each ship, engulfing them in flames and watching them sink into the sea with their masters aboard. But he wasn't in a position to take such action.

Calidin, standing just off to the left and about twenty paces ahead, thrust his staff into the air and waved its end around in tightly formed circles. A greenish-yellow light spewed from the staff's tip, accompanied by an ear-piercing whistling sound. A section the sailing vessel's stern swung backwards and down toward the dock upon a massive hinge. It made no sound the entire way. The hinged section of the stern settled with a clunk upon the wooden planks of the dock, forming a ramp for loading cargo, dragon cargo. The wizard lowered his staff, now asleep in his hand, and pointed it in the direction of the vessel. The thrust of a pointed weapon into each of their hindquarters urged the dragons forward and up the ramp.

Kell waited for them upon the command deck. He wasted no time in coming over to greet his guests. With his arms crossed in an arrogant posture, Kell examined his prisoners while a number of his men shackled Fenicus and Farimus securely to the deck. Then the chieftain turned and faced the east. A subtle blue glow filled the sky from just below the horizon. It slowly overtook more and more of the sky, eventually mingling with brilliant hues of pink and orange like paints being mixed upon an artist's palette. Finally, the sun climbed over the horizon, bathing the land in its warm rays. Kell closed his eyes as the light washed over him.

"The sun rises to honor me today, dragons. And when it sets below the horizon, it sets on your species. You're a plague upon the Earth, and it is my duty to cleanse it of your scourge. Bask in its warmth, in its beauty, for this is the last sunrise you'll ever see."

"What did we ever do to you?" Farimus asked scornfully. "What does exterminating our race accomplish?"

"Mankind is meant to rule Earth," the chieftain shot back. "If it wasn't for your species running and hiding four hundred years ago, you'd be long since extinct and nothing more than a memory."

Farimus could not believe the hypocrisy in Kell's words. "All we ever wanted was to disappear, to live in peace and solitude out of your way. We're not at war with you. We've done nothing to deserve this. Why couldn't you just leave us alone?"

Kell stepped closer to the Farimus, yanking down hard upon a chain attached to the dragon's neck. The two were eye to eye. "I was born to bring peace to my people, to unite the clans of the north under one banner and lead us out of darkness."

"How does slaughtering dragons and stealing our gold accomplish that?"

"Gold will bring me the allegiance of those who would otherwise stand in opposition to me. Most men can be bought. Your precious gold would serve that purpose."

Farimus searched for holes in the human's reasoning, digging wherever he saw a crack. "You said *most* men can be bought."

An evil cackle burst from Kell's mouth. "Well, that's where you come in, my friend."

"You mean our blood, our scales," Fenicus interjected.

Kell shot a curious glare at Fenicus. "How do you know

about that?"

"Oh, you'll find I'm full of surprises," Fenicus replied wryly.

"So that's it!" Farimus exclaimed, having pieced the puzzle together. "You never planned on letting us go. You planned to wipe us out from the very beginning." A vortex of rage surged in Farimus and left his body as a scream. "Is every word that escapes your lips a lie?"

Kell released Farimus's chain and walked a few paces away from the two dragons, facing the bow of the ship. "No, not every word. The truth is that it took me many years to sort it out, to weed out fact from fiction, legend from history. Finally, I put it all together. Your gold was but the first step in the process. With it, I could I buy the loyalty of the other chieftains. But to overcome the few who might yet oppose me, I needed an army that none could stand against. An army that if I so chose I could march into Rome itself and conquer the greatest empire on Earth without losing a single warrior. That's where your blood comes in."

"An invincibility potion?" Farimus prodded with a hint of concern in his voice. "Is that what you did with poor Azriel? Sucked him dry as he lay there dying?"

"The blood of your fallen comrade? Yes!" Kell pulled forth from his belt a small glass bottle filled with a purple liquid and topped with a cork stopper. He held it up in the air, letting the rays of the sun play with its contents. "It is indeed. I drew it from his body with my own hands." Kell tucked the vial back into his belt.

"How much of it did you make?"

Kell's lips turned into a devious grin. "Oh, there's more

than enough to make every one of my warriors invincible. Does that worry you?"

"It does," Farimus replied. "But we'd rather die fighting than give in to you. So if you think keeping my son and me hostage will make them lie down and beg for mercy, that's where you're mistaken. They'll fight to the death."

Kell shrugged at the suggestion. "It matters not. With the blood of your kind protecting my army and the power that my wizard wields, we'll stand before the rest of your kind knowing they have no hope of stopping us. And when we have finished draining every last dragon of every last ounce of blood, we'll conquer all of Europe and my people will finally know what it means to live in peace and happiness." Kell paused and inspected his nails, picking dirt from under them. "Unfortunately, the legends about fashioning your scales into impenetrable armor proved to be false. The scales of your dead friend couldn't stop an arrow at fifty meters. No matter. By nightfall, your race will be no more than a memory." He smiled at Farimus. "To tell you the truth, your kind does not die proudly. This Azriel whined and moaned like a pitiful child, begging for the torture to end. He was weak, just like the rest of you. And weakness always crumbles before true strength, which I possess."

Farimus lurched forward against his chains, snapping his jaws at Kell. "If I get out of these chains, I'm going to rip you apart."

Kell snapped his fingers in the direction of Calidin who was overseeing the final preparations before the ships set sail. The wizard looked with distaste at his master.

"Yes, m'lord?"

"I grow tired of the noise these two make." Kell turned about, flailing his cloak in a sweeping arc, and walked toward the bow of the ship. "Silence them!"

Calidin moved his hand across the faces of Fenicus and Farimus. The dragon's bulky forms collapsed into an unconscious heap upon the deck. The wizard made his way to the bow of the ship to join Kell.

"What do you want now?" Kell inquired, noticeably irritated.

The wizard's voice sounded mechanical—his tone matter of fact. "You have done nothing, then, to change your path? The fate written for you since birth is coming to its end. If you take these ships out of port, none will survive."

The chieftain shook his head. "All ships, prepare for launch," commanded Kell.

The chieftain's words repeated over and over again, being passed on from one crewmember to the next, one ship to the next until the message had reached every vessel and its captain. Each mainsail rose upon its mast, the wind filling them to capacity. Free of their moorings, all seven ships sailed free of the dock and headed out to sea.

Kell turned to Calidin. "Today, I'm going to prove you wrong."

22

Malkolm sat curled up in Mariel's clenched hand, his eyelids squeezed shut. His sweaty hands clutched at the bony knuckle of her curled index finger, which wrapped around him. The flesh of his fingers had become bloodless and pasty. Unaccustomed to flight or moving at such speeds, Malkolm found the entire experience to be rather terrifying. He groaned uncomfortably as she twisted and turned along her flight path in search of the fleet.

The ride eventually steadied. Malkolm slowly peeled back his eyelids, revealing the world to him in a manner that neither he nor any other of his race had ever experienced. He gasped aloud at the beauty of the sea—its white capped, rolling waves, the way it melded into the sky and reflected the puffy clouds, and the exhilarating freedom of flight itself. Completely releasing his grip of Mariel's finger, Malkolm spread his arms wide and pretended as though it was his wings keeping him aloft and that he could fly.

"Whooooohoooooo!" Malkolm howled.

"Glad to see you're finally enjoying the ride," Mariel commented as she curled her neck and looked at him. "I was beginning to think you'd gone into shock."

Malkolm shook his head and smiled. "No. This is amazing." After Mariel unfurled her neck to resume her inspection of the waterscape, an oddity to the west caught Malkolm's eye. A pair of creatures bobbed in and out of the water. Tall plumes of water sprayed into the air as each crested the surface. They appeared to be moving at a leisurely pace, heading westward, while Malkolm and Mariel flew southwards.

"Mariel," Malkolm called out to her.

"What is it?" Mariel craned her neck to look at him again, her tone impatient.

Malkolm pointed due east. "What are those?"

She looked out over the sea in the direction Malkolm pointed. "I think they're whales."

"Whales?"

"The largest and gentlest creatures in the world."

Curiosity caught the better of Malkolm. "Can we get a better look?"

"Sure," she replied.

Tilting the tips of her wings downward, Mariel began a gentle descent toward the water. She then contorted her neck and tail so that her flight path guided them directly over the whales. As they drew within a few hundred feet of the whales, however, an odd light glimmered along the southern horizon. Mariel whipped her head in its direction.

"Hang on!" shouted Mariel. She violently curled her tail around to the left and tilted her body in the same direction. Mariel turned aside from the whales in a swift, sweeping turn.

Malkolm wrapped both arms around her giant finger. "What's wrong?"

*   *   *

The two whales drew to a halt when the dragons passed overhead. One whale, slightly larger than its companion and marked by a crescent moon-shaped patch of white across its dorsal fin, took particular interest in the winged creature as it flew southward.

"Beastie!" Seamus yelled. His calls were not heard. He stared off in the direction that the dragon flew. *Did he save them?* Seamus wondered of Fenicus and his quest. He had heard the creaking planks and the muted human voices echo through the water to the south. Now having seen a dragon fly off aggressively in that direction, he wondered if he could be of any help.

"What is it, Seamus?" the other whale asked curiously.

"C'mon, Elisa." Seamus motioned southward with his flipper. "I've gotta debt ta repay."

*   *   *

Mariel flapped her wings rapidly as she flew only feet from the surface of the water. With each flexing thrust, their bony tips nipped at the water, making small splashes along the way. Her body flew straight as an arrow as she closed on the fleet. She pulled her arms and legs in closer to her underbelly, increasing her speed. The ships grew closer.

"Are you ready?" asked Mariel of her small passenger.

His voice quivered with nervousness. Taking a deep breath, he shouted, "Yes!" His hand grabbed tightly at the key ring encircling his forearm.

Mariel banked right sharply and loosed her grip on Malkolm. Pinching his nose shut and tucking his knees up into his chest, Malkolm hit the water with a splash. The water washed over him and he sank into the depths. After a few seconds, Malkolm gained his bearings and kicked his legs, pushing him upward. With a gasp, Malkolm surfaced and splashed about awkwardly in the waves, looking for the flagship.

His eyes immediately locked on Mariel as she flew overhead. Coming around hard to her left, she flew just below the gunwale of one of the ships and unleashed a deadly spire of fire upon it. Its timbers burst into flame, which spread until it had become a great conflagration. Some of the crew fired volleys of arrows at her when she passed by. Others fought to extinguish the flames. A few unlucky souls that caught the full force of her assault smoldered in piles of charred flesh upon the deck of the ship. In response, other ships were closing in to lend assistance.

Having seen how well her attack was occupying their attention, Malkolm knew it was his turn. Scanning left and right, he found that he was only a short distance from the flagship. He also noticed a rope that dangled down along its starboard side. Not being that great of a swimmer, Malkolm did his best to cut the distance between himself and the ship. Waves smacked him in the face repeatedly. After a few more mouthfuls of seawater, Malkolm finally reached the ship.

The rope dangled just out of his reach. Malkolm stretched his arms and barely grabbed on to the rope with his fingertips. Pulling himself up, he strengthened his grip on the rope and began his ascent. Hand over hand he climbed, unable to use his feet as they couldn't maintain solid traction against the algae-covered hull.

Some twenty feet from the bulwark, Malkolm heard a fierce rush of air approaching. Overhead he caught a flash of gold zoom by as Mariel flew overhead, extended her arms, and tore the mainsail to shreds with her talons. Malkolm cheered inside when he heard the shouts of frightened soldiers trying to fend off Mariel's seemingly unstoppable assault.

The captain barked out, "Hard to port, hard to port!" The ship came about. The hull creaked from the strain of the abrupt maneuver. Malkolm's cheers fell silent as the inertia of the turn sent him flailing out away from the hull. He lost complete grip of the rope with his left hand and tried to hold on as best he could with his right. Malkolm then felt the key ring slip loose from his arm. He looked down in horror. The key ring twisted through the air, splashed into the sea, and descended into the darkness. Taking in a big gulp of air, Malkolm dove headfirst into the water.

23

Mariel's onslaught had set three of Kell's ships ablaze; their crews had abandoned ship. The four other ships that remained seaworthy focused their attacks on the ferocious dragon.

Mariel slipped between two vessels and reached out with her talons. She tore loose whole strakes and slung them back at the ships, piercing the hulls and causing them to take on water. Crewmen fired desperate rounds of crossbow bolts and arrows as she passed between them. Most of their volleys went astray by a wide margin. The rest rained down on the unsuspecting crewmen who now scrambled to evade the friendly fire. The cries of injured men caught in the crossfire filled the air.

Amidst the chaos, Calidin stood with his back to the

bow of the ship, watching over their precious cargo of hostages. With arms spread wide and his glowing staff held aloft, he kept the dragons in a state of suspended animation, not quite asleep and not quite awake. They stood, half slumped over, bound in chains upon the aft deck like slaves on their way to the trade.

"Calidin!" Kell ran across the deck toward the wizard. "Are you just going to stand there or are you going to do something about that?" He pointed toward the dragon threading between their ships, wreaking havoc upon them.

The wizard shot a half-hearted glance in the direction Kell pointed. "What do you want me to do about it?" he hissed. His glance returned to the two dragons chained to the deck before him.

"You aren't immortal." Kell poked a rigid finger into the wizard's shoulder with each word. "If that dragon isn't stopped, we're all finished."

"Do you want to keep it at one dragon, or would you prefer these two join the fray? I can't keep them entranced and take care of *that* at the same time."

"Are their fetters still enchanted?"

Calidin looked at the iron bands fitted around the necks of the two dragons. The wizard closed his eyes and began to sway. He altered his operational level of consciousness to one that normal mortals could not. Feeling a subtle spell of light-headedness come over him, he opened his eyes and saw the faint green corona that surrounded the dragon's shackles.

Without resetting his conscious state of mind, Calidin leered back to Kell. Yet, his eyes were missing. A swirling green mist filled the empty sockets. Though his brain was only able to process images made primarily of shadow, the wizard saw just enough of Kell to recognize the frightened look upon his face.

"Yes, they are." Calidin's words poured not from his lips but from some ethereal place, beyond the realm of mortals. The very tone of each syllable was hollow and echoed in a place where no sound could possibly ever echo. Calidin carefully straddled the physical plane and that place from which his otherworldly powers emanated. Slowly, he pulled himself back.

Kell stared fearfully at Calidin. The chieftain backed away from him with plodding footsteps. The wizard's form phased in and out of reality like a ghostly image wavering in strength. With a sizzling crackle, his body became solid and constant.

Kell's fearful posture reverted to its haughty norm. "If these two can't set the deck on fire or break free from their bonds then I'll take my chances." His tone became pleading. "I need you more than ever, wizard. If you don't stop her, my plan will fail and everything will have been for naught."

A cautious countenance swept over Calidin. "What would you have me do?"

Kell's pleading tone grew instantly condescending. "What do you think, you moron?" He pointed toward Mariel with the scepter. "Knock that flying menace out of the sky for good."

Kell's command struck Calidin with the force of a hundred battering rams. He scanned the sky for Mariel. He watched the winged beast navigate through the air, circling about the fleet with the calculating eye of a predatory bird as she waited for the ideal moment to strike. Though she had already laid waste to Kell's fleet and dreams, and would most likely take Calidin's life before this day ended, the wizard could not find the strength to murder another dragon. He fought against the voices of reason in his mind that urged him to do his master's bidding so that he would not be returned to his torturous prison. Yet, he discovered that the thought of returning to his cell suddenly paled in comparison to the torture he knew his repaired soul would endure if he followed this command. Four hundred years of starvation. Four hundred years of restlessness. Four hundred years of being tortured by the very same means that he inflicted upon dragonkind. Calidin, whose heart was once twisted and evil, had finally found the path to absolution. The desperate hope that he might find a flaw in his master's plan finally materialized. The answer was always there, hiding under his nose. He realized that the greatest flaw in Kell's plan was indeed the greatest power he held over the dragons—Calidin himself. He made up his mind. While he could not save himself from damnation, he could ensure that he would not be the tool by which the few dragons whom remained would face their destruction.

Calidin turned slowly to Kell. "No, I don't think so." The answer poured smoothly from his lips.

Kell's eyes narrowed. He stared the wizard down with a mixed look of anger and surprise. "What did you say?" his voice rose starkly in volume and vehemence.

"No, Kell," Calidin shook his head slowly. "I refuse." He closed his eyes and stood motionless, awaiting his penance.

A blinding flash of brilliant blue burst forth from the scepter that Kell held in his hands. Averting his eyes from the light, the scepter fell from his grasp. Nevertheless, it did not fall to the ground. The scepter levitated above the deck, turning itself around until it pointed directly at Calidin. The blue light bathed the wizard, growing in intensity. With a sudden flash, the blue light vanished, and with it, Calidin. With a loud clunk the scepter fell to the deck. Within the sapphire, Calidin knelt with his hands clutched at the sides of his head, screaming in agony at the torment engulfing his body and mind.

Kell picked up the scepter. "Damn you!" he howled. Wheeling his arm back, he hurled the scepter into the air. It spun end over end before it finally plunked into the water. Sinking quickly, the powerful scepter fell to the bottom of the Baltic, taking its unfortunate passenger along for the long ride into the cold, dark depths.

24

Diving deeper and deeper, Malkolm fought against the pressure building around him to reclaim that which he had lost. The farther he went, the worse it got. Somehow between the crushing pain drilling into his eardrums and his blurred vision, Malkolm pushed himself to the brink of unconsciousness.

Through the ever-increasing darkness, his eyes could faintly discern the key chain spinning below him, just out of reach. But no matter how hard he swam, no matter how hard he kicked, it stayed just beyond his grasp. It became more difficult to keep his eyes locked on the target as he descended further. Less and less light seemed to penetrate to such depths and he was quickly running out of air. Malkolm's lungs began to burn. The arteries in his temples and neck pounded beneath his skin. He started to see small sparks of light.

Taking a risk, Malkolm pressed all the air from his lungs in one great breath. His gamble paid off for the moment as he started to sink much faster. He kicked and pressed as hard as his limbs would allow. In his head, he felt consciousness slipping away. Desperately, he reached out with his fingertips, stretching them to their fullest. He closed his eyes, clenched his teeth, and fought off the overwhelming sensation building in his head. With his lungs ready to burst from lack of oxygen, his fingertips sensed the touch of cold iron. With a renewed vigor, Malkolm pressed back the darkness threatening to take him. His eyes opened to see his fingers wrap around the key ring.

Turning right side up, Malkolm kicked wildly, propelling himself upwards toward the dim glow of the sun. Within a few meters of the surface, his lungs could no longer resist the urge to gather oxygen. Malkolm gasped, sucking in a mouthful of water that caused painful fits in his lungs. His mind and body no longer concentrated on rising to the surface, only coughing to expel the water deluging his body. And each cough brought with it another intake of water. Just when his body could no longer take the strain, he felt waves wash over him and the warmth of sunlight bathe his face. Malkolm strained his neck above the waves and breathed in a loud gasp of air. The refreshing, enlivening sensation filled him with renewed hope. Another hard cough pressed a glut of saltwater from his lungs.

Shaking the cobwebs from his mind, Malkolm found the flagship sitting just about where he left it. However, the other ships were now making violent adjustments to avoid Mariel. Not too far from where he treaded the surface, one ship crackled and hissed as its enflamed bulk sank into the sea. The crewmembers who survived clung to the flotsam and jetsam littering the surface of the water.

Out the corner of his eye, Malkolm glimpsed an immense shadow closing in on him from the left. Turning in that direction, he caught sight of a massive sailing vessel headed straight toward him; flame chewed away at the splintered, claw-rendered strakes of its hull. Malkolm thrashed his limbs toward the flagship to escape the oncoming behemoth. He passed just beyond the cutting edge of its prow before it could run him over. The vessel's forceful wake washed Malkolm toward the flagship, and he collided with a thud against the hull. The impact rattled him, making every part of him ache. Sucking up the pain, he made his way back to the breastline that dangled from the starboard side. Taking the key ring in hand, he shoved it up his arm until it stopped against his elbow and then forced it past the joint.

Taking a firm grasp of the rope, he began to scale the side of the swaying craft. His arms tugged his body from the water. Every inch of progress brought him closer to the deck. Beads of sweat mixed with the lingering seawater on his body. Every sinew of muscle of his arms and shoulders strained against the pull of gravity. Unable to climb another inch, Malkolm dangled against the hull of the ship to find that the strakes were no longer slick from algae. He had ascended beyond the waterline where only sea spray dampened the ship's bulky sides. Holding himself in place,

Malkolm rested for a few more seconds to catch his breath and pressed his calloused feet firmly against the hull. A little at a time he climbed, the deck nearly in sight. With only a short length of breastline to ascend, Malkolm felt a tremor rattle through the hull of the ship. He lost his footing but held strong to the rope. His chest, waist, and knees slapped hard against the vessel. He closed his eyes and winced in pain.

Trying to regain his footing, Malkolm felt another tremor move through the vessel. Scanning the water, Malkolm realized that one of the whales that Mariel had flown over had rammed the hull and was preparing to do so again. It bore a distinctive crescent moon-shaped mark upon its backside.

From above, crewmembers yelled and screamed at the whale. They hurled barrels and other pieces of debris down upon it. When those tactics did not dissuade the beast, other men took up crossbows and began firing bolts at it. Most of their shots either missed their mark or bounced off its thick, shiny skin. Regardless of the opposition, the whale prepared to thrust itself back into the hull of the ship.

A chorus of disjointed, alarmed voices shouted, "All hands, brace for impact!"

Fearful that the tremor might send him tumbling into the sea, Malkolm climbed with desperate speed. He finished his ascent and toppled over the gunwale just as the whale rammed the ship. The impact of its body sent Malkolm rolling into one of the aft masts. His head whacked against an iron band that wrapped around the pillar. Stars filled his sight. He grabbed at the back of his head where a dull ache radiated. Feeling that there were no cuts on the back of his head, Malkolm did his best to shake off the disorientation. It didn't take long for his eyes to focus on the two towering dragons before him, chained to the deck at the very back of the vessel. He saw that neither of them had yet to take notice of him. Their attention was on Mariel, who flew in sweeping circles above the fleet. Whoever was supposed to be guarding them had abandoned their station to attend to the immediate emergency at the other end of the ship.

Malkolm made his move.

*　*　*

Kell did the best he could to keep an eye on Mariel while she soared above them, waiting to strike. But his attention kept getting drawn back to his crew's attempts to fend off the angry whale. A sneaking suspicion plucked at him, a suspicion that something was amiss far beyond the direct assaults being brought to bear upon his fleet. He could not press from his mind the sense that this was a distraction, a decoy meant to draw his attention away from the real assault. All around the deck and in the water he searched for that which made him uneasy, but there was nothing to be found. Yet, he now felt his attention being pulled inexplicably toward the rear of the ship, to where his reptilian captives had now surely awoken from their slumber. Gazing upon them for a moment or two, Kell did not see anything worthy of the uneasiness gripping his brain. Their attention seemed not upon setting themselves free but on watching their kin assault his forces. Confident that they weren't going anywhere, Kell dismissed the worry plaguing his thoughts as paranoia and returned to the dilemma at hand.

Growing sick of the sea-borne nuisance, Kell called out to his crew to grab the grappling hooks they normally use for ship-to-ship combat and hurl their barbed ends at the whale below. Without delay, the crew loyally followed his orders. Within moments, arching volleys of rope-drawn, razor-sharp hooks filled the air. One by one they splashed down around the whale, threatening to take a bite out of it. None of them seemed to find their mark. Finally, the barbed end of one hook gashed a deep wound in its flesh. It thrashed its flippers about in the water, creating massive waves and sea spray that splashed against the flagship. Then another hook caught the whale just below the left eye. It backed away from the ship and dove down beneath the surface of the water. The crew cheered uproariously. They patted one another on the back and howled war cries of success.

Kell noticed a small speck of a shadow upon the deck that seemed to be growing exponentially. He looked up as did his crewmembers who stood in its darkening gloom. Mariel dove toward them at a frightening velocity. The crewmen didn't move. They just stood in cowered stillness, slack-jawed at the dragon barreling toward their ship.

With a desperate leap, Kell dove out of the way of her attack as she pulled out of her dive and flew across the deck. Her talons ripped through the swath of men whom stood frozen there. Screams of anguish filled the air along with a grisly spray of blood that gushed forth from the shredded bodies. The gore hit Kell straight on as his body tumbled hard against the deck of the command ship and crashed into the gunwale. His back struck square against a rail post, knocking every ounce of breath from his lungs. He choked hard in an effort to breathe. The remaining crewmembers who avoided her deadly attack seemed to snap out of their catatonic state and ran for safety, leaping haphazardly over the gunwale and into the sea.

There sat Kell, the lone man left upon the flagship. Inside, he seethed at the reality that his world was coming apart at the seams, but Kell would not show it outwardly. He pressed his body defensively against the railing and lifted himself up proudly from off the deck. With his fleet foundering at sea and his wizard having betrayed him, Kell knew his options were limited. Realizing that if he did not act quickly he would likely die at sea and his dreams with him, he drew forth from his belt pouch the invincibility potion he carried.

As he held it up to remove the cork stopper, a thunderous vibration rattled the vessel. Timbers splintered and cracked along the prow. The entire ship lurched upward against whatever it had struck. Thinking at first that it had run aground, Kell leered over the gunwale to inspect the surface of the water. He remembered that there were no sandbars or ground to run upon this far out into the Baltic. Then Kell spotted a faint shadow moving beneath the ship. Something had run into them. The whale had refocused its efforts on attacking the ship from below.

Another shudder, this time far more powerful, wracked the prow. The force of the collision threw Kell into the air along with his vial of potion, which flew from his hand and bounced along the deck and overboard. Kell crashed down upon the railing. Several of his ribs cracked from the impact. Falling back to the deck, lying on his side, he felt another shockwave. The unmistakable clatter of a massive hole being torn in the fuselage rattled through the ship. A geyser of seawater immediately erupted through the opening to the large cargo hold and rained down upon the deck; the blood that covered him washed away. His face twisted from its fearful countenance to a look of abject hatred.

Lying on his side in pain and blinking through the drops of water falling on him, Kell's attention locked on the rear of the ship, just beyond the fountain. Kell viewed his captives fully awakened and breaking free of their chains. Then he noticed another form moving about them, helping to unlock their shackles. Kell rose to his feet, a hideous frown upon his face. From the foremast, he pulled free a heavy crossbow and notched a tethered bolt into place. He tied the end of the tether securely to an iron ring bolted to the deck.

Kell moved closer to the waterspout with a deliberate gait, using the plume to mask his movements. The closer he got, the more infuriated he became. The small creature moving about the dragons was a human boy. Knowing this person may well be the traitor Magnus spoke of, Kell raised his crossbow and took aim.

25

"Thank you, Malkolm," Farimus said in a conciliatory tone. The last of his shackles dropped to the deck. "I misjudged you."

Malkolm milled about, working the key he had into the set of chains binding Fenicus to the deck. "Don't worry about it, Mr. Flint. We've got to get you two out of here before we sink into the sea."

"Dad. Give me a hand with this," Fenicus pleaded while trying to snap in two the chain that bound his wrists together.

"Malkolm, get out of the way for a second." Farimus picked up the small boy and unleashed a concentrated blast of fire upon the iron chains. The superheated iron glowed bright red. "Pull, Fenicus, pull!"

Fenicus strained hard, stretching the metal while his father continued to apply more heat to the chains. With a pop, the chain broke in two. "Give me the key, Malkolm." He reached out and took it from his friend. "Dad." Fenicus looked up at his father as he knelt down to unlock the shackles around his ankles. "Get Malkolm out of here while you still can."

"What about you?"

"Yeah, Fenicus, we're not leaving without you," Malkolm added.

The shackle around Fenicus's left ankle fell to the deck. Fenicus then pulled at the chain attached to his right ankle, drawing it through an iron loop in the deck. The shackle at the other end clanked against the loop, unable to pass through. "I'll be fine. Now get out of here."

Farimus scooped up Malkolm and leapt free of the deck, his wings flapping powerfully. A short distance above the deck, a crossbow bolt whizzed past Farimus's head, causing him to duck out of the way. When he did so, his grip on Malkolm loosened and the boy fell from his hand.

"Fenicus!" Farimus screamed.

Fumbling about with the key, Fenicus glanced up at his father and saw Malkolm falling toward him. *Uh oh!* Reaching out over the gunwale, he snatched Malkolm out of the air, turned his friend right side up, and placed him back on the deck.

"You okay?"

Malkolm's voice stammered. "I think so."

Fenicus looked skyward for his father. "What was that?"

Farimus shrugged in response.

Eager to unlock the shackle around his right ankle and escape the watery deathtrap, Fenicus realized that he no longer held the key. He leaned over the gunwale and scanned the water. Malkolm too looked over the railing.

"I must've dropped it when I caught you."

"Oh no. Not again," Malkolm whined. He slapped himself in the forehead. "Now what?"

Fenicus searched the deck for something else to jimmy the lock open, but all he found was that the ship was taking on massive amounts of water and at an accelerated rate. He felt a pang of panic and the subsequent surge of adrenaline that followed. Fenicus grabbed the chain and began wrenching at it, trying to snap off the other shackle that was jammed against the iron loop.

Malkolm dropped to his knees and added his menial strength to the dragon's efforts.

A voice shouted "Don't move!" from across the deck. It was Kell. He moved out from behind the geyser of seawater with a cocked crossbow aimed at Fenicus and Malkolm. "You're the traitor!" Kell yelled, motioning to the boy.

"Give up, Kell," Fenicus demanded. "It's over."

Farimus made a quick movement toward the command ship. In response, Kell pressed the butt of the crossbow into his shoulder and pulled the trigger just enough to make the hook that held the firing twine tremble.

"Back off, dragon, or your son dies," the chieftain warned.

"You're beaten," Mariel howled as she joined her husband hovering high over the deck of the flagship. "Your fleet's in ruins. Your ship's foundering beneath you. Let my son go!"

Kell shook his head ardently. Snapping his head back toward Fenicus and Malkolm, Kell pulled the trigger. Fenicus spun to his right, grabbing Malkolm and hurling him through the air and into Farimus's arms.

The bolt whistled through the air, rotating along its axis. It struck against the leathery membrane of Fenicus's left wing, piercing it. The prongs alongside the head of the bolt expanded upon impact, preventing it from drawing back through the tear. The damaged nerves in his wing sent jolts of pain through him. Fenicus leapt into the air and tried to fly away. The bolt bounced back and forth, widening the wound with each thrust. With a snap, his body jerked back. The chain connected to his ankle had gone taut, keeping him from breaking free.

The sensation of being a caged, tortured animal brought Fenicus to the edge of sanity. He caught sight of Kell affixing another bolt to his crossbow. The bow of the ship tipped beneath the surface of the water. With a violent, desperate jerk, Fenicus ripped the bolt free of his wing. An agonizing roar came forth from the injured dragon.

Mariel made a move to help, but Farimus grabbed her with his free arm and held her back.

Kell lifted his crossbow once more, targeting Fenicus as he thrashed against the length of chain that tied him to the sinking vessel. The young dragon then felt a great change come over him, a change he first felt days before in the bowels of the underground keep. All the events that led to this moment swirled in his mind like a tornado: Darius's brutal attack, the destruction of his homeland, the disappearance of his entire species, his battle at sea against the whalers, leading a revolt against the barbarians, and falling into Kell's hands. The child who at one time lived and breathed inside Fenicus's immature body died at that moment. Inside, that flame that sparked to life back in Berathor burned like a raging inferno inside of him. The blood in his veins pulsed and boiled to the point where Fenicus could feel nothing but complete agony. All the bony spines along his back took on a white-hot glow. The instincts screaming at Fenicus from within commanded him to draw in a lung-stretching breath like he was about to sneeze. Fenicus sensed the surge of heat in his lungs ignite the air, and he whipped his head toward Kell and set free the fury within. A billowing stream of fire poured from his lips, scorching the air as it raced toward its target.

A look of panic overcame Kell and the crossbow fell from his hands. He leapt over the gunwale and dove into the sea, abandoning his mighty ship. Kell surfaced just as the deck surrendered to the sea. Despite his obvious defeat, the chieftain managed to call forth an evil grimace as he watched Fenicus struggle against the chain about to pull him under.

Fenicus, unable to break the links with brute force, recalled his father's actions only moments before. Willing one more blast of fire forward, he unleashed an intense blast of heat upon the chain, making it glow. He pulled against his fetters, trying to snap them in two before they dragged him under. The muscles in his arms and neck strained. The chain finally snapped just as his feet met the water. Fenicus thrust upwards unexpectedly.

His father raced to his side, taking hold of him with his free arm. Fenicus, however, denied the assistance. Looking to where the flagship once sailed, all that remained was its sad master and sea of wreckage. Kell took hold of a piece of mast that floated nearby and held on tight.

"It's over!" Fenicus shouted.

Kell reached beneath his shirt and withdrew an amulet just like the one Fenicus used to make himself into a human boy. "I'll hunt you down for all eternity, until every last one of you is dead." He held the amulet tightly between his hands as if he were about to use it as the focus point of prayer. "Nothing you can do will ever stop me!" he swore loudly before whispering inaudibly to himself.

The power of the amulet lifted Kell clear out of the water with a powerful surge of magic. A burst of radiance followed, consuming him whole. It passed over him in a matter of moments, liquefying flesh and bone in the same manner that its twin affected Fenicus several times before. As his body began to stretch to accommodate the dimensions of his new form, the process of transformation brought forth blood-curdling screams. Gruesome crackling and popping sounds came from his body as the process neared its conclusion. With one final flash of light from the amulet, a new and more deadly Kell loomed before the Flint family. His newly minted body and unblemished scales shimmered in the sunlight.

Kell screamed and shot across the sky on a collision course with the Flints.

"Watch out!" Farimus bellowed.

All three of the Flints scattered, flying in opposite

directions and barely getting out of the way of Kell's ramming maneuver. Turning about abruptly, Kell unleashed a fierce yet harmless blanket of fire that swept across the sky and the Flints.

Farimus turned away from the burst of flame, using himself as a shield to protect Malkolm from harm. He then let some of the air out of his wings and glided down to the surface of the water. He set the boy down upon a floating crate.

"Stay out of trouble." Farimus winked at him. He then reached out, grabbed a length of shattered mast floating nearby, and heaved it like a spear across the sky toward Kell.

With just enough time to evade the deadly projectile, Kell stopped the motion of his wings and fell out of the way. Mariel, however, met him head on as he fell into her glide path, and she punched him in the side of the jaw. Kell retaliated by lashing out with his claws and landed a feint strike across her upper arm. The scales that covered the soft flesh beneath split wide open. Mariel clutched painfully at the wound and retreated, flying diagonally upward and away from him.

Preoccupied with Mariel's retreat, Kell did not see Fenicus catch the mast that his father threw. Like a lumberjack swinging his axe to fell a mighty tree, Fenicus came up behind Kell and brutally slammed the mast across his lower back. Kell fell through the air, back arched from the force of the impact, and splashed down into the sea.

Kell punched at the water, enraged. Taking hold of a pair of barrels floating nearby, he launched himself skyward again and took aim, hurling them at Mariel. Dodging downward to evade the first barrel, she flew directly into the path of the second barrel, which shattered upon her back. It caused her to lose her bearings and tumble seaward. At the last moment, she pulled out of her dive and snorted an angry burst of fire. Locating her target, Mariel growled viciously and rushed at Kell.

Kell beat his fists against his chest and roared. Matching her intensity and anger, he set himself on an intercepting course. The two dragons flew at speeds beyond reason. With a thunderous boom the two collided in midair. Mariel got the better of Kell. Twisting herself like a corkscrew at the final moment before impact, she added extra momentum to her flight. Mariel ploughed through him and violently jostled him off of his course. Coming around, she settled into a hover between her son and husband.

"Give up, Kell," she called to their foe. "You'll never beat all three of us."

Kell grabbed at his badly broken ribs and hissed. He rasped back, "If that's true, then I'd rather die fighting. And maybe I'll take you with me. Argggg!" Beating his wings, Kell flew toward the Flint family in a berserker rage, spewing fire everywhere and biting and clawing wildly. He moved so erratically that neither of the Flints could avoid his mania. Whenever they tried to attack him, he'd fly out of the way and direct his assault at someone else, making him nearly impossible to hit. It was like trying to catch a fly—a really big fly.

Kell ceased in his violent pursuit for a short time to catch his breath. His chest heaved. The Flints took the opportunity to regroup.

"What now?" Fenicus asked, feeling the desperation of fighting this mad man-dragon. "I can't seem to get close enough to do any damage."

"Me neither," Farimus gasped. "I'm too winded to keep up with him."

Just as Mariel was about to add her own comments to the mix, she paused and looked westward across the sea. "Look," she whispered to her men. They did as she asked. A brilliant, blinding streak of golden light moved in a sweeping arc across the water toward them. The closer it came, the more familiar it looked.

The closing object slowed and then rose up high into the air behind Kell. The streak of light was another gleaming, golden-scaled dragon apparently intent on joining the fray. The unknown dragon was much smaller than Kell. In fact, it was very similar to Fenicus. At the apex of its flight path, the new combatant set itself into a stealthy glide straight at the chieftain, picking up momentum as it flew.

With brutal force, the new dragon collided into the small of Kell's back whose body bent and flexed backward at an unnatural angle due to the power levied against him. He fought back wildly, biting and clawing at his new opponent. The two entangled dragons rose and fell, spun and whirled about in a mid-air wrestling match. The new dragon struck at Kell with all its physical weaponry and tangled its limbs up in his, greatly arresting the chieftain's movement.

Slamming his tail straight up in parallel to his own spine, Kell landed a powerful blow against his opponent. The bony spines that adorned the tip of his tail impacted against the other dragon's backside; one of the spines found its mark and pierced flesh. The smaller dragon wailed. Retracting his tail, Kell unleashed a furious barrage of successive strikes aimed at his opponent's back. The physical strength of the smaller dragon waned visibly. Its frame slumped, its limbs slackened.

Mariel sped to the aid of their fading comrade. Putting herself in harms way, she used her body as a buffer between Kell's tail and the other dragon. After taking a few direct hits, Mariel corralled his tail.

"Farimus!" she called out desperately to her husband.

Farimus launched himself at Kell. He smashed his shoulder into the chieftain's side. The tangle of dragons lurched awkwardly from the impact, and the Flints' mysterious ally slipped from the tangled knot of bodies, hitting the sea with tremendous force. Salty seawater sprayed skyward from the impact.

Fenicus, on the other hand, stood by idly, frustrated that there was so little he could do. His parents had Kell tangled up pretty well, but they lacked the leverage to land the killing strike. The other dragon, who managed to grab hold of some flotsam to keep from drowning, was in no shape to continue. The whales, who aided Mariel in destroying Kell's fleet, were busy looking over the fallen dragon. Fenicus knew that he had to find some way to bring this battle to a quick and decisive close.

His new breath weapon was of little use against other dragons, and he had no way of running Kell through with any of the floating chunks of hull or mast without putting his parents at risk. Desperate for anything that he could put to use, Fenicus scanned the wreckage below; he saw nothing but shattered timber, a few stray crates and barrels, and too many floating bodies to count. Looking back to his parents, he saw their strength beginning to wane against Kell's furious all-or-nothing fight for survival.

Just then, a dancing glint of purple light reflected off an object that floated in the water. The bizarre color caught Fenicus's attention. Examining the object from a far, he saw a small vial of purple liquid bobbing along. It was the very same vial of invincibility potion Kell dropped when the whales attacked his ship. Fenicus wondered briefly how much more difficult it would be to defeat Kell had he been able to devour the potion before he changed. Then it hit him; he was no longer a human. Kell was a dragon. And while the potion could make any human invincible, it had a much different effect on dragons.

Fenicus let gravity take control of him, sending him into a steep dive toward the floating vial. As he neared the undulating sea, Fenicus pulled out of his dive. His right hand snapped at the vial as he passed over it, snatching it out of the water like a bird of prey catching a fish. Having plucked it from the water, Fenicus sharply altered his course into an equally steep ascent in the direction of Kell and his parents.

As their son approached, Mariel and Farimus held Kell tight. Fenicus slowed to a stop and hovered just out of the human's reach, vial in hand. The human dragon fought to escape Mariel and Farimus's grasp. He snapped his jaws at Fenicus.

"To Hell with you dragon!" Kell growled. His eyes

locked on the vial of potion Fenicus held. He thrust his head toward the vial, snapping his jaws at it.

Fenicus smiled devilishly. "You want this?" he taunted Kell.

"Fool!" Kell barked in response. "Give it to me and I'll show you the true meaning of power." A line of saliva dripped in a long strand from the corner of his mouth.

Fenicus violently grabbed hold of Kell's snout and yanked his head back. He then thrust his foot into Kell's belly, forcing him to open his mouth. Flicking the cork free from the vial with his thumb, Fenicus dumped every drop into his gaping jaw. Satisfied the vial was empty, Fenicus forced his mouth shut.

With a great gulp Kell drank down the potion and closed his eyes. His face held a look of sheer ecstasy. The Flints released their hold on him and backed away.

Kell's eyes snapped open, and the look of pleasure contorted into one of abject torture. A series of furious convulsions ripped through him. The lustrous color of his golden scales faded away in a sweeping wave across his body, replaced by a jaundiced yellow-brown hue. Deep fissures and cracks formed all over him, splitting the flesh straight down to the muscle. Then a sharp scream exploded from deep within. His back arched unnaturally, the muscles surrounding his spine knotting up all at once. Each of the leathery membranes that gave his wings the power of flight turned to rotted flesh, blackening from their semi-translucent, pliable state and shrinking up until they lacked the ability to keep him aloft. He plummeted through the air and splashed into the sea.

Clawing his way back to the surface, Kell gasped desperately for air between howls of anguish and mouthfuls of salty water. But his screams stopped abruptly. His breathing ceased and a look of extreme terror came over him. A loud gurgling sound came forth from his insides, followed by a black, tar-like substance that spewed from his mouth like a fountain, pouring over the sides his face. A final convulsion wracked his body and he stiffened like a rock. His body, broken and void of all life, sank into the sea, taking the amulet around his neck with him.

Fenicus, Farimus, and Mariel flew into each other's arms. Mariel bestowed kiss after kiss upon both of her beloved men. Farimus lovingly rubbed his son's head.

When the three of them drew back from their embrace, a familiar voice leapt at Fenicus from the water below.

"Fenicus?"

Fenicus looked down to see Seamus and another whale floating below them. "Seamus!" he shouted out in surprise.

Both whales bore minor cuts and gashes from the battle, but both looked healthy enough to survive. Lying upon Seamus's back was the other fallen dragon, sprawled out and exhausted. Fenicus dropped in altitude to check on their mysterious comrade.

Drawing close, Fenicus made a startling discovery. Around this dragon's neck was another metamorphosis amulet. He wondered for a brief moment how a third amulet could exist since Balthazar told him there were only two. And then Fenicus realized it was his amulet, and the dragon lying before him was Malkolm, transformed by its magic.

Fenicus gently shook Malkolm. "Malkolm, c'mon, wake up!"

Mariel and Farimus looked to each other with the same incredulous countenance. They then rushed to their son's side.

Malkolm lifted his head. His weary eyes slowly opened. He groped about beneath him as he tried to stand, but he only got as far as his hands and knees. "Did we win?" he asked.

Mariel leaned down to place a comforting hand on him. "It's over. We're safe."

A great sigh escaped Malkolm. Trying again, he rose up on all fours and took flight. Fenicus immediately flew to his friend's side and shook his hand, their task finally complete. Fenicus then turned his attention back to Seamus.

"So who's this?" he inquired, pointing at Seamus's companion.

Seamus craned the front half of his body toward the other humpback beside him. "This is my lass. Her name's Elsa." The two moved closer together, rubbing sides. "We're off ta start a family together."

Fenicus smiled at their show of affection. "Where did you come from anyway? I thought I'd never see you again!"

"I didn't think I'd see ya again meself. But when I saw yer mum goin' at these ships wit such ardor, I figured it was a chance to settle me debt."

"Thank you, Seamus," Mariel interjected. "You helped me keep my family together."

"Yes, Seamus," Farimus added. "Thank you for putting your life on the line for us. You'll always have friends amongst the dragons."

"Well, good luck, Fenicus." Seamus waved his flipper at the dragons. "Yer a mighty good friend. Take care of yerself and yer family."

Seamus and Elsa sank back beneath the surface of the sea and swam off eastward, leaping into the air and splashing down. The dragons bid their good-byes to the whales as they swam out of view.

"Now," Farimus pondered aloud while gazing at Malkolm who hovered before him, still in the form of a dragon. "What do we do with you?"

"Farimus," Mariel suggested, "maybe we should take him with us."

"What are you talking about, 'take him with us'? I was thinking we should find a way to get him home soon. Besides, I don't know the first thing about taking care of a human. I don't even know what to feed one."

Fenicus chimed in. "Dad, Malkolm doesn't have a home. He doesn't have a family."

"That's right, Farimus," Mariel added. "He's all alone."

"I don't understand." Farimus stared at Malkolm. "There has to be someone waiting for you."

Malkolm shook his head, frowning. "They're right, Mr. Flint. I'm an orphan. I have no parents and no home. I've nowhere to go. I promise not to get in the way, Mr. Flint," the boy cajoled. "I swear I can take care of myself. I've been doing it for years."

"Please, Dad," Fenicus begged, "I've always wanted a brother. Besides, he risked his life to save us. I think we owe him. I know I owe him. If we send him back to his homeland, he'll likely die there as a traitor or worse."

"This is totally different," Farimus declared. "Malkolm, wouldn't you rather be with your own kind?"

A calculating grimace came upon Malkolm. He shook his head ever so slightly. His hand slowly moved to the amulet that still hung around his neck, granting him the power to be a dragon. He peered thoughtfully at the amulet and then back to Fenicus, Farimus, and Mariel. Pulling the silver chain up and over his head, he held it loosely in his fingers. The amulet dangled precariously over the water.

Fenicus realized exactly what Malkolm was about to do. "Malkolm, are you sure you want to do this?"

A gleaming smile formed on his face. "I've never been more certain of anything before." He then let the amulet slip from his fingers and, like Kell, it sank to the bottom of the sea.

"Well," Farimus shrugged, "I guess that settles it. Let's go home."

All four dragons gathered up their strength and flew back to Berathor. Mariel had rescued her loved ones, and Malkolm was finally part of a family.

ABOUT THE AUTHOR

C.W.J. Henderson resides in New York's Capital Region with his wife and twin sons. By day, he's an 8th grade English teacher at a suburban school district in Rensselaer County. By night, he's an author of fantasy literature. He holds both a bachelor's degree in English and a master's degree in secondary English education from the University at Albany. The greatest influences on his writing are the role-playing games he played in his youth and his over twenty years of martial arts experience. His favorite authors include J.K. Rowling, Lois Lowry, Gregory Bear, George R.R. Martin, and Jim Butcher. C.W.J. is currently finishing *Miles Away*, the first novel in his young adult time travel series, "Time and Again," and he is preparing to write the second novel in "The Blood Curse Legacy" series, *Fenicus Flint & the Dawn of Ragnarok*.

Made in the USA
Charleston, SC
02 August 2012